THE GIRL AT THE CENTER OF THE WORLD

Also by Austin Aslan

The Islands at the End of the World

AUSTIN ASLAN

THE GIRL AT THE CENTER OF THE WORLD

WENDY
LAMB
BOOKS

Text copyright © 2015 by Austin Aslan
Jacket art copyright © 2015 by Shutterstock and Tom Sanderson
Map illustration copyright © 2014 by Joe LeMonier

All rights reserved. Published in the United States by Wendy Lamb Books, an imprint of Random House Children's Books, a division of Penguin Random House LLC, New York.

Wendy Lamb Books and the colophon are trademarks of Penguin Random House LLC.

The excerpt from the song "Mele Ho`okipa" is used by permission of its author, Dr. Holoua Stender. Copyright © 2005.

"E Na Lima Hana/The Working Hands" by David Haas and Joe Camacho
Copyright © 1997 by GIA Publications, Inc.
All rights reserved. Used by permission.

Visit us on the Web! randomhouseteens.com

Educators and librarians, for a variety of teaching tools, visit us at RHTeachersLibrarians.com

Library of Congress Cataloging-in-Publication Data
Aslan, Austin.
The girl at the center of the world / Austin Aslan. — First edition.
pages cm
ISBN 978-0-385-74404-1 (trade) —ISBN 978-0-375-99146-2 (lib. bdg.) —
ISBN 978-0-385-37422-4 (ebook) — ISBN 978-0-385-74405-8 (pbk.) [1. Science fiction.
2. Survival—Fiction. 3. Extraterrestrial beings—Fiction. 4. Family life—Hawaii—
Fiction. 5. Epilepsy—Fiction. 6. Hawaii—Fiction.] I. Title.
PZ7.A83744Gir 2014
[Fic]—dc23
2014037413

The text of this book is set in 12.5-point Adobe Jenson.
Jacket design by Tom Sanderson
Interior design by Trish Parcell

Printed in the United States of America
10 9 8 7 6 5 4 3 2 1
First Edition

To my daughter, Ariel.
You inspired Leilani, and you inspire me.
You'll always be my Flower of Heaven and
the center of my world.

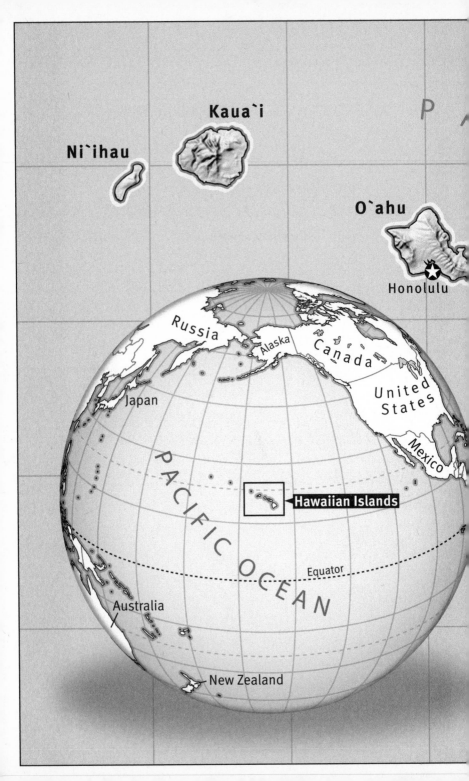

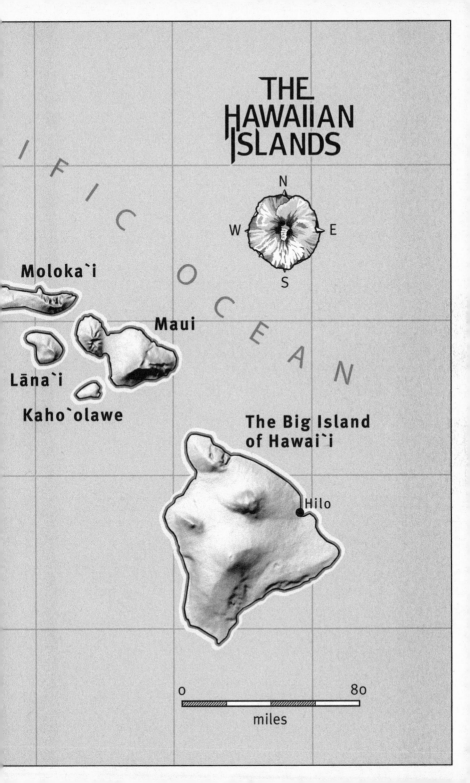

PROLOGUE

I am Leilani, the Flower of Heaven, and I drift among the stars.

I orbit Earth from the mind of my Emerald Orchid, watching a hazy blue halo of daylight creep across the eastern coast of a dark continent. North America. Maybe it's called something else now.

My body is down there on the surface, as lost as anyone, suffering, starving, choking on constant fear—but up here my view of the globe offers me the illusion of peace.

The rustle of the distant surf, the rush of blood behind my ears: gone. In the silence there is only the beauty of the planet: a sapphire pearl in a diamond-studded abyss.

Breathless, I watch my world turn.

A Hawaiian musician strumming his ukulele carries through my memory. I hear him sing: *I see skies of blue ... clouds of white ...*

I push the tune away, but it's too late. The haunting notes have brought me racing back to three months ago, to the tinny music playing on the counter of the Maui kitchen where Dad was nearly killed, where rain lashed against the aluminum roof, where dogs snarled, clicking muddy claws on the floor. The pistol in the steady hand of the sheriff of Hana. His outstretched arm, ropy blue veins emerging from a clay-brown fist. Burnt gunpowder. Coppery sweat. Dad's eyes, certain of death, holding back fear.

My heart rate spikes. I *can* hear the blood behind my ears. I reject the images, find my footing above the turning world. *Exhale.* Up here I can feel peaceful. I will not allow that evil man to haunt me here.

The Orchid is my one escape. The alien in orbit above our world. Not a ship—a simpleminded creature, like something from the ocean depths washed ashore. Her ribbons and folds of emerald luminosity, resembling the aurora borealis, are knotted into the shape of a green flower against the stars.

A silent pop of white flashes off the coast of New York. A ball of water crowned with radioactive mist swells along morning's edge. The atomic poison of this explosion mixes with the fallout of other nuclear disasters that blanket the globe. But my Orchid draws up the venom, neutralizes it.

Disheartened, I look west, deep into the darkness. Toward home. Islands lost in the sea.

We Hawaiians are so very alone.

On the dark side of the globe, the Big Island of Hawai`i

is easy to find. I spy my beacon: a telltale plume of fluorescent orange steam rising from the mile-wide caldera of Kilauea volcano—the Earth's inner core breathing into space.

I slide home. Soon I will land in my bed. But I'll still be adrift on islands lost at sea, the ground I sink toward darker and colder than the heavens I leave behind.

SEPTEMBER

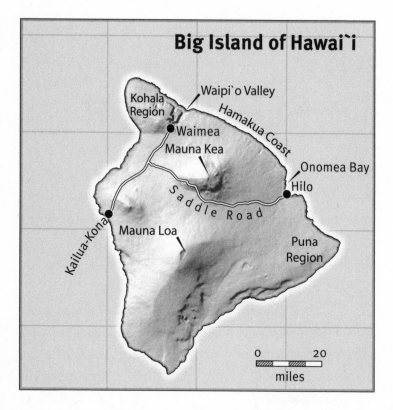

Big Island of Hawai`i

Kohala Region

Waipi`o Valley

Hamakua Coast

Waimea

Mauna Kea

Onomea Bay

Hilo

Saddle Road

Kailua-Kona

Mauna Loa

Puna Region

0   20

miles

CHAPTER 1

I open my eyes. I'm lying in the dark. It's humid tonight, the air still. The coqui frogs are mostly quiet. Millions rule the jungle around our home, a few miles from Hilo, but it's too hot for them. One or two sound from beyond the screen of my open window.

Coqui? Coqui?

I turn my pillow over, soothing my cheek and temple against the cold side. My stomach growls, and now there's no question—I'm home. Moments ago I was floating in orbit above the world! But my connection with the Emerald Orchid is distant, my door to her primitive animal consciousness barely ajar.

I'm back in my own mind and body, and I'm hungry.

We're not starving. There's enough food to go around. And it's supposed to get better as our farming gets up to speed. Most of what we're planting is vitamin and calcium rich—`uala, sweet potatoes; `ulu, breadfruit; uhi, yams; and kalo, taro. I'm so sick of taro, which is usually mashed up and eaten as poi, the great life force of all Hawaiian foods. But none of it seems to help the hunger.

Here on Hawai`i, the Big Island, we've had time to adjust to a new normal. It's been three months since Dad and I made it home from the island of O`ahu. Four since the Emerald Orchid came to roost in orbit above our atmosphere, destroying electronics around the globe as she labored and gave birth to another of her kind.

When the Orchid arrived, at the end of April, I was on O`ahu with Dad. Power went out worldwide. Satellites were zapped. No communication with the outside world. There were no flights, and the ships with the food and gas stopped coming. Things never got better. It took Dad and me a month to make it down the island chain. And we almost didn't make it—

Stop. I push the nightmares back.

We're getting by, Mom, Dad, Kai, Grandpa, and I. We're banding together with our neighbors, sharing jobs, pooling resources. At least we have land and a small river down the ravine. And we're naturally protected on our isolated hillside, surrounded by tall ridges, with only one way in and out, several miles off the highway.

Our garden, breadfruit trees, and organic-chicken coop were hobbies before the blackout—things my parents did for fun in their spare time. What a strange phrase: spare time. Once our crops are in full rotation, and we have enough chickens, and we've gotten a couple goats and a few other animals, our family and our neighborhood may get by comfortably. But we're not there yet.

"Lei, you awake?" my brother, Kai, whispers from the floor. He sleeps in here whenever our guest worker stays in Kai's room.

"Yeah, what's up?"

"It's hot. Make it windy."

"Oh, I control the weather now?"

"Just do it."

"Sure, Kai." I match his teasing tone.

"Thanks," he says.

I'm connected to the Emerald Orchid because of my epilepsy. I started having seizures when I was thirteen. Had them all the way through our struggle to get home, when I discovered our link. My seizures helped me sense the Orchid's thoughts, urges. An astronomer named Buzz—a mountain guru living at the observatories atop Mauna Kea—helped me talk to the Orchid. The creature was going to leave, but I persuaded her to stay. She *can't* go. Her arrival caused a chain reaction of nuclear meltdowns around the world. Without electricity to cool them, power stations blew. But the Orchid feeds on radiation, absorbing it and protecting us. If she had left, we might have gotten our power back, but we would have inherited a global nuclear wasteland.

My plan is to make her stay until she devours every meltdown—when all the leaking nuclear radiation is absorbed, she can go. But when will that be? How long can the world hang on without power?

Kai sighs. "You gonna practice with Uncle Hank's Magnum tomorrow?"

"No." Kai knows I hate guns. The weapons protect our food. But they also make us a target.

"What about the bow?"

"Same difference."

"No, it's not."

"Is to me."

A single frog asks the night for advice. *Coqui?* Otherwise: silence. Kai is already still. Such a little man. Too skinny, too strong. He's eight and insists on working as hard as anyone. He's distanced himself from so many things he used to love. Tore down his UH volleyball posters, threw away his gymnastics competition uniform.

I wipe matted hair away from my forehead and stare out my window at the faint green of the night sky.

My seizures were really bad for several weeks after I got home from Oʻahu—the medicine that once helped me was used up. But slowly the seizures stopped. Somehow the connection I share with the Orchid has channeled and calmed the storm in my head. Now, instead of vicious attacks, I blank out at will and see things from her perspective. Camera Two. I don't use my eyes, though; my brain just interprets what she senses in ways that I can process.

The Orchid will leave our solar system the second I drop my guard, taking her daughter with her. As with a helium balloon held by a string, the tension is always there. It's not hard for me to grip the line, easy as flying a kite. I can literally do it in my sleep. But she will rise and fade back into the sea of stars the moment I loosen my grasp.

And I worry: will my epilepsy return when she's gone?

We are Leilani. We are Flowers of Heaven.

I hear the Orchid now: *We will stay here until we are strong and safe and all the sweetness is gone. Then return to the depths.*

Home? I ask. *What is your home like?* I've asked this before. I'm so curious to know. I only sense confusion from her, though—a vague questioning.

Home is where you belong. What's it like where you belong?

Depths. Vastness. We are many there.

I give up. I think of her as a *honu*, a sea turtle, acting on instinct. I could be asking a fish what it's like to swim in the sea. Some things I'll just never know.

* * *

Our rooster, Sweet William, wakes me well before dawn. The cardinals and the Java sparrows and the mynas start to chatter. I shuffle downstairs and sit at the table. Mom and Dad and Grandpa are already busy. Mom hums an old Hawaiian tune and absently dances the hula as she works. Her movements are subtle, rhythmic, like seaweed swaying in the rising tide.

Mom is pure Hawaiian; Dad is haole, a white guy, from New Mexico. So Kai and I are *hapa*. Half and half. My parents met on O'ahu while in grad school. They both studied ecology. They married, found work on the mainland, and had me and Kai. We settled back here almost three and a half years ago, when they accepted two tropical biology professorships at the University of Hawai`i at Hilo. Mom is as gorgeous as any hula dancer on any poster, and she knows it. Dad is also good-looking—in a scruffy, surfer-who-never-grew-up sort of way.

The kettle on our propane stove shouts. Mom offers me coffee. I perk up. "Wow. Sure. What's the occasion?" Usually we'll boil water over an actual wood fire outside. Someone must have hauled in a good amount of propane yesterday.

"Fresh from Kona." She pours boiling water into our French press. "Paul brought a couple bags home. And two *gallons* of propane." I give a silent toast to our neighbor up the road. It's been weeks since I last smelled coffee; the odor alone wakes me up.

"Howzit on Kona side?" Kona's on the opposite side of our island, where the resorts and coffee growers are.

"Bad. The pyres at the hospital are burning day and night. Refugees arriving in droves, but there's nothing for them. The town is in ruins. Worse off than Hilo."

My eyes widen. Postcard-perfect Kona worse than Hilo? Kona was tourist central: resorts, restaurants, beaches, and activities. Predictable weather, calm waters. Not like rainy Hilo. Makes sense that the refugees from other islands would be dumped there—safer for the boats to land, and so much more familiar to city dwellers than wild, backward Hilo, still reeling from the tsunami four months ago.

I shudder and change the subject. "What's our game plan today?"

Mom places before me a glass of water, three slices of passion fruit, some ʻuala wedges, a coffee cup, and the press. Her eyes glow in mock excitement. "Barbecue on Coconut Island, beach volleyball tourney, snorkeling."

"Actually"—Dad clears his throat and grins like a car salesman—"I was thinking more along the lines of finishing the fence along plot D and moving in a bit more compost. We could start planting there by week's end. Sound fun?"

I lean my head back and stare at the ceiling.

I don't know where the hunger ends and the other aches begin. I've been lifting and hauling rocks, building dams and fishponds, terracing farm plots and fencing them to keep the pigs out. Weeding. Cutting rain channels out of the old lava flows that lead into the greenhouses. Dismantling old sheds, carting the materials across the rocky slope to repair a large barn. Constructing a corral for the horse we acquired by trading some of our neighbor Uncle Hank's rifles.

My eyes catch the world map taped to the wall above the breakfast bar. Perfect distraction. I grab a pushpin from the tray and poke it through the crackly paper just off the coast of New York. I stand back to survey my work.

Numerous pins on every continent. Many clustered. New England, for example, is getting crowded. Each one represents a belly-up nuclear plant.

"Saw another explosion last night?" Dad asks.

I nod. "Big one. Off New York." I can't shake the image of that ballooning ball of water rising out of the ocean. That creeping disc of cloud smothering the coast, like batter slowly poured onto a griddle. "It was offshore."

"Nuclear sub?" Grandpa ponders. He's a navy vet. "Accident? Malfunction? Or an attack?"

"People in the region must be so scared," says Mom. "I hope they realize the Star Flowers clear away the fallout."

I've told Buzz the astronomer exactly what I see: huge plumes of black and brown smoke, fanning out with the winds, always in places with nuclear facilities. I don't see every meltdown, but with this map and his statistical methods we estimate that there have been two hundred catastrophes in the last four months—almost two per day. There may still be as many as two hundred more plants waiting to blow their lids. Many newer plants were built to handle power outages for a limited time. How can we know which ones are left?

Our only strategy has been to wait for the meltdowns to run their course. But for how long? Every day I keep the Orchid here, people suffer and die in other ways.

A sizzle—familiar but forgotten—reaches my ears like a siren song from across the kitchen. The maddening smell of cooking *meat*. I jerk toward the stove.

Mom has opened a precious can of Spam onto a skillet. "Mom! What are you doing?"

"It's for you and Kai."

"Mom."

"It's all right. The two of you need a boost."

"Don't argue," says Grandpa.

Kai cascades down the stairs and leaps to the table. "Spam for breakfast! All right, Lei! Hap—"

"Quiet!" Dad barks.

"Oh, yeah. My bad."

"Save that look for your wedding day, dude," I say. "It's just a can of Spam. And we're sharing it."

"Ah, man," he jokes. "Lay off. I'll have a bunch of wedding days. This might be the last Spam left."

Kai eats his first bite with a look of pure bliss. Mindful of the others, I try to be more reserved. Mom uses the grease in the skillet to fry up two eggs. We can't wait for our first batch of chicks to grow big enough to start making more eggs every day.

Our hired hand comes downstairs.

Keali`i is Hawaiian, mixed with some Filipino and Japanese, I think. He has the legs of a cross-country runner and the hands of a brick mason. He comes and goes; his parents died in the first tsunami wave, and Mom kind of adopted him. He used to work for her, keeping her university experiments along the coast clean and secure. He's *akamai*—super smart. He's about my age, but he dropped out of high school, so I never knew him.

"Want a bite?" I show him my crispy Spam. I've been savoring every nibble.

He shakes his head. "It's all yours, Lei. Thanks." He accepts a few slices of passion fruit, `*uala*, and a fried egg.

"Almost time for a pig," Grandpa thinks aloud, staring at our plates. Wild boars roam the Big Island, but they're getting hard to track down. *Everyone* is after them. And, with no ice, keeping the pork fresh is a challenge.

Grandpa, our kahuna, our family spirit guide, is guiding our return to the way Hawai'i was before machines. The islands supported thousands of native Islanders before European explorers arrived. We can learn about our old *ahupua'a* ways. Caring for the land at every level from coast to mountaintop was the business of everyone.

Dad, Keali'i, and I hop into our old red truck and roll down the hill in neutral. Dad turns on the engine once we're past the gate and heading up the road to the farm plots. We've stored up nearly two hundred gallons of gas among our families. Dad and Uncle Hank were smart to hoard it early. Gas is scarce and valuable. Two hundred gallons sounds like a lot, but it will have to last. Buzz gave us a drum of stabilizer and showed us how to add it to the gas to keep it from turning to sludge. When he told us that gasoline is only good for six months to a year before the additives gum it up, we just stared at him. Every car, ATV, and tractor on the island will be useless this time next year.

It's okay, I remind myself. *The Orchids will be long gone by then.*

Grandpa follows us to the gate riding 'Imiloa, our horse. He'll stand guard under the shade of a big albizia tree, a shotgun over one shoulder and a rifle over the other, until his shift ends later in the afternoon. He won't be too lonely down here; our dogs happily surround him. Mindy, Mork, Centaur, and Pele. Pele's all white, and my favorite. I'm not a big fan of dogs but these four troopers make us feel safe and will eventually help Grandpa with hunting.

We don't talk much during the morning; we're fencing off the plots to keep wild pigs from ruining the crops. It rains as I dig holes every several feet. Keali`i uses a pickax to finish what I've started, gouging through the crumbling lava beneath the dirt. We set makeshift poles in the holes, pack in dirt, and prop up the posts with lava rocks. The barbed wire is wrapped tightly, low to the ground and closely spaced—the pigs are getting smaller and smaller as the adults are overhunted.

We travel up to the Millers' home midmorning to replenish supplies. Hank Miller is a Midwestern haole who's lived here for decades. His giant hands are as tough as leather gloves. He knows how to build anything. He and his wife, Nora, live a couple miles from us. We saw them infrequently before the Orchid came, but now we're a team. Now they're Uncle Hank and Auntie Nora.

"When's the last time you surfed?" Keali`i asks me on our way back to the plots. We're riding in the bed of the truck, catching some breeze to dry the sweat. My stomach is upset for some reason; the fresh air helps.

"Two weeks ago at Honoli`i with Tami. You know her?" Tami Simpson is my best friend. She lives down in Hilo.

"Yeah! Tami's good. We should all go sometime. Honoli`i's full of tsunami rubbish. Ever been to Isaac Hale?" That's a hot surfing spot on Big Island, about an hour south of Hilo along the Puna coast.

"That'd be cool," I say, though I know it's too far—too much gas, and the waves are big enough that Mom and Dad would say no. Besides, the Puna district is way too dangerous these days. Turf wars. Puna was full of weirdos and outlaws long before the Arrival, people who lived off the grid and wanted to be left alone. Tons of drugs and guns out there. Now big bands of gangs are forming—they call themselves Tribes—and fighting for control of Puna and Hilo. We hear a lot about racial fighting, but the Tribes are different; they're about controlling *stuff*. Whatever people need and want. The sheriff of Hana from Maui and his "Hanamen" have the upper hand in Puna. He moved his people in there early and controls most of the plantations and agriculture.

I shudder as I see the sheriff putting that gun to Dad's head. The only reason Dad's alive is because the sheriff and Grandpa were cops together on Maui. Partners.

Don't think about any of that. I breathe deep, try to relax. Then I ask Keali`i, "You don't worry about Tribes?"

"They don't have any beef with surfers." He has a beautiful tattoo coiled around his upper arm, the roots gripping his shoulder and chest, with intricate branches extending to his wrist. It's one of my favorite tattoos ever. "So you and Tami are tight?"

I nod. "I stay with her in Hilo a couple days every few weeks. She comes up here, too. She's kind of on her own. Her mom ditched to Pahoa with a crowd of junkies awhile back."

"Ah, well, at least she's got a mom."

I shrink back, hot in the ears. "I'm sorry."

He laughs. "I didn't mean to . . . Forget I brought it up. Why does she stay by herself down there?"

"I don't know, same as you? She wants to keep her place, so she has to squat there. She wants to be independent. That, and there's a half-feral cat she likes to feed."

"Yeah, I know how it goes." He pivots. "Hey, do me a favor, eh? Next time you're staying with Tami and the wild-cats down in Hilo, let me know. Bring a wet suit. I'll show both of you something cool." He winks.

We reach the plots and unload the barbed wire and posts. "*Pau*," Dad says. "Let's break for lunch." Mercifully, we head home. "Take a nap," he tells me. "I'll get you up around four with a new list of chores."

"Okay." I'm exhausted, and my stomach feels weird. Tightness. Like a runner's cramp, maybe. But right in my gut. A nap sounds perfect; I'll sleep it off.

*   *   *

Earth is far below me, nothing but a curved halo of ocean blue, centered by a few tiny blotches of land. I drift in turn with the islands, remaining above them.

The sun is behind me, its radiation like warm shower water on my tired shoulders. Energy charges through me. Then—lead in my gut. Pain like a fist, squeezing.

I am strong on the sweetness. It is ready to come out.

What's ready to come out?

Fastness. But I do not leave. I give the fastness to you.

19

CHAPTER 2

I'm nudged awake. I open my eyes to see Kai. I study his smile as his face comes into focus.

He's much more Hawaiian-looking than I am. He has Grandpa's nose and jaw. Maybe that's why he seems so much wiser than his years.

"Time to get up."

I stretch. *Fastness? What does* that *mean?*

The shadows have changed. Mynas scamper on the aluminum roof. Japanese white-eyes whistle from the palm fronds level with my bedroom window. A few coqui frogs are already singing their one question.

Kai is twirling an old charm bracelet of mine. He loves to take things off my jewelry tree. I used to find them left all over the house and get mad, but that was when little things mattered.

He skips out of the room. I smile after him, sit up, stare at nothing, trying to boot my brain. Fastness. I can't figure it out. The Orchid doesn't speak to me in words. My brain translates her thoughts into familiar concepts. But it doesn't always work.

My stomach still aches. I might need to take something for it.

I run a cold shower and dry off. I glance at the mirror. My oval face is thin but not gaunt. The scar on my forehead is fading. I like my shoulder-length black hair. My complexion: not one zit. Not even a mosquito bite. I smile at my reflection and head downstairs.

"Surprise!"

I freeze between steps. The living room is festooned with streamers and ribbons and old birthday decorations that Mom never throws away. A few presents are wrapped in newspaper. Mom, Dad, Kai, Grandpa. Tami is on the couch. Keali`i stands behind her.

Buzz smiles up at me from the entryway to the kitchen. He's almost as short as Grandpa. He has bright blue eyes and a brown beard.

The lead in my stomach lightens for a moment. My eyes dart from one person to the next, confused. They settle on Mom and Dad. A wild laugh escapes me. "My birthday's the sixth!" Two more days.

"Today's the sixth," Dad says.

"No." I shake my head, but now I'm not sure. I don't have a phone anymore. No computer or TV to keep my dates straight. I bet half the people on this island have no idea what day it is.

I hold my face in my hands, and to my surprise, tears

come. "It's my birthday," I say. I laugh, incredulous. "Yeah! Okay!"

I laugh again, even though it hurts. I'm all-out crying now. I made it this far. Seventeen. Such pain and suffering everywhere. Bodies burning on pyres. Ash on the breeze. Gunshots. Drownings. So many people simply starve to death out there. I'm still here. My family's still here.

"Oh, sweetheart." My parents bring me down the steps, keeping me close. Grandpa holds me.

Keali`i offers me a loose hug. "Happy birthday."

Tami rushes in and squeezes me tight. "You rock." We hold each other. My tears return, and I hide in her beautiful curly locks that smell like coconut shampoo.

"So glad you're here."

"Rode my bike." She pulls back. "Dang hills. I got here before your nap."

Buzz embraces me, his brown-and-gray beard brushing roughly against my wet checks. "Happy birthday! Seventeen!"

My stomach explodes with pain. I double over. "Lei?" Mom asks. The feeling rises up my chest. I wonder for a moment if I'll tear open, but then the agony fades. I relax, straighten.

It pulls. It is ready.

I feel clammy, a little weak, but much better. I wave Mom off. "Not sure. Just—this sharp, heavy pain. But it's gone."

"Sounds like a burst appendix," Kai declares.

"Oh, my God. Don't even joke about that," scolds Dad. "You sure you're okay?"

"Yeah. It's nothing."

"Mike. A burst appendix?" Mom says, a shade paler.

"No," Dad says. "Give her some space."

I try to look normal. "Seriously, I'm *fine*." I march to the table, forcing a bright smile.

Mom has baked a cake. More of a bread loaf, actually, with rambutan and strawberry guava jam on top instead of frosting. I'm so grateful, but my first thought is—this cake forced my family to go with fewer eggs today.

Grandpa arranges oily *kukui* nuts along the top in the shape of the number 17. He lights the nuts with a match, and everyone sings to me. I have to smile at Grandpa's "birthday candles." Nuts.

"Make a wish!" Kai tells me.

I close my eyes and wish: *Make our lives work again.*

Our lives are purposeful.

Not you, I tell the eavesdropping Orchid.

I quickly blow out the *kukui* nuts.

With the "cake" divided and everyone gathered around, I open presents. Grandpa places a jewelry box in my palm. "Your grandmother wanted you to have this on your eighteenth birthday," he tells me, "but you're old enough now. You are a Great One, Leilani. You make us both proud." He takes a step back, his eyes red.

Inside I find a silver necklace and a heart pendant.

"Open it," Grandpa says.

My trembling fingers find the latch, and I click it open. Inside are two small black-and-white portraits, one of my young grandfather in a spotless white navy uniform, the other of Grandma Lili`u. Both photos are from their wedding day. Grandpa looks no older than Keali`i, and just as handsome. My grandmother passed away from cancer when I was six. So beautiful, so confident, in her stunning white dress, her veil folded back. She could be a member of the Hawaiian royal family. She has a large white hibiscus flower pinned above her ear. I see my mother so clearly in her. And, for the first time, I see myself in her proud eyes.

"Put it on." Grandpa helps me place it around my neck. It rests against my breastbone. I touch it gently. I can *feel* her in the room with us.

"We are your `aumākua, my dear mo`opuna. Your family guardians, your spirit guides. We'll always be that close to you. Always have been."

I wipe away tears in silent thanks. Grandpa steps back.

"My turn," Mom says. She hands me a book-shaped gift, wrapped in old Sunday comics. I smile at her and peel away the wrapping. It's my Hawaiiana book—the precious book I had with me on my journey home from O`ahu. But this copy looks brand-new.

"I wanted you to have a copy that you could use," she explains. "I know that other copy is your true treasure; it was with you through everything. Now you can return to these stories without worrying about further damage to it."

My original copy is on my bookshelf, in a plastic bag. She's right that I don't touch it anymore. It's so fragile, and so important to me. I beam at Mom. "Where'd you get it?"

"Market. Traded off some of my old Louis L'Amours."

"Okay, me!" Kai thrusts a wrapped box at me.

I open Kai's gift. It's homemade. A large stick bent into a ring. String runs back and forth across the hoop, reminding me vaguely of a spiderweb. "It's a dreamcatcher!" he shouts.

"Oh, wow," I say.

"He worked on that for days," Mom says.

I hug him close. "Oh, Kai, thank you! It's beautiful. The best present you've ever given me."

"Great!" he says. "Put it above your bed. It's for—you know—your space-outs." Dad glares at him—Tami and Keali`i don't know my secret. "I'll do it right now," he offers. I hand him the dreamcatcher, and he races away.

"You ready?" Dad asks me. He hovers over his gift. The box on the table sits three feet tall. He motions for Buzz to join us. "We fixed this together. I found it, he tinkered."

Curious, I gently lift the cardboard box. "A projector?"

"Eight millimeter," Dad says. "Vintage."

"Really?" It's metal. Sturdy. Lots of intricate parts. I like it. "Does it work?"

"It will," says Buzz. "That's *my* gift. I've got some ideas for how to get it spinning in the next few weeks—"

"Here," Dad interrupts, presenting me with two more wrapped gifts.

"More?"

"You'll see."

Two movies on 8mm film reels. They look ancient. *The Day the Earth Stood Still* and *Planet of the Apes*. I've never seen either film. "Will these play?" I ask Dad.

"Of course!"

"Sound, too?"

"Not great, but, yeah."

"They're good?" I ask.

He stares at me, aghast. Dad's always trying to teach us about old movies he loves. Mom raps him on the shoulder. I laugh.

Planet of the Apes? I think. But I can't hold back a smile. He's always right, with his movies. I squeeze him tight. "You're amazing! You and Buzz! Thank you."

I remember my wish: *Make our lives work again.*

I dare to wonder: *Is it coming true?*

It is coming.

The pain rushes back, searing. My vision flickers, and without warning I spiral into fiery darkness.

It is coming.

I feel the muscle. Near the Orchid's core. Nothing to do with the wispy tentacles. It's right at the center, in the gut.

Contract. Clench.

An egg? No. I understand now. It's a normal process for her. She's done it before. But it's not an egg.

A meteor.

It comes to you.

No, I tell her, holding back panic. *It will harm us. Aim it away.* The first days of the Orchid's arrival were full of meteoric activity; the meteorites did great damage wherever they hit. In Hawai`i tsunami waves devastated Hilo and many other coastal areas throughout the islands.

It comes now. But I can send it to the blue.

Not the ocean! Tsunami. No. There's only one place that's safe.

Closer. Come closer, I think.

We descend. I must draw it in tightly.

The twilit islands are dangerously large. The Big Island is cast in green, as bright as if bathed in full goblin moonlight.

I feel the muscle compress. This is how she thrusts through space. A ventricle pulses, the shrinking chambers fill with plasma. There's a churning. Hot—burning—but not alarming.

Compression. The plasma hardens. Coal crushed into diamond—but smooth as a pearl. It's solid now. So dense. I feel the gravity of it pulling her inward. I feel it pulling at the Earth, prying at its fault lines like a child peeling up chips of sunbaked clay.

She'll discharge the pearl. Push it out.

Aim it at the mountain, I tell her.

I'm on the floor. Dad and Tami hold me steady. Grandpa and Mom lean over me, quietly singing a chant of protection in Hawaiian. Together their voices are heavenly.

Buzz is at the living room window, glancing feverishly back and forth between me and the twilit sky. "Is she okay?"

"Coming around," Dad says. "You all right, there, Lei?"

"She did something." Buzz's voice is deliberately level.

Tami watches Buzz, follows his eyes, looks at me, and frowns. "You did *what*?"

"Yeah. I'm fine. Sleepy. Headache."

"You're doing okay, sweetheart," says Mom. "Small, shaky seizure. Nothing like your bad ones. Bit more intense than your space-outs. Couple minutes. That's it."

Tami holds my hand. Keali`i is watching me closely, quiet, uncertain. I know his look; I've seen it many times. He's never seen a seizure before. He wants to look strong, but he's scared. I wish he weren't here.

"Stay awake," Dad says. "I know your body wants to rest, but stick with us."

"It's rushing closer," says Buzz.

"*What's* rushing closer?" Tami asks, frustrated.

"The Orchid!"

"Cool, Lei!" Kai hurries outside the front door to the lanai. Keali`i follows him, torn between me and whatever spectacle is unfolding outside.

I sit up, bob my head. "She's passing something. I felt it."

And then I feel it. A vague sensation of imbalance, accompanied by a slow twisting of the gut. In my mind? Vertigo? But the windows rattle. The Merrie Monarch Festival posters all turn several degrees, as if straining to perform the hula. The wineglasses in the hutch chime nervously. The ceiling fan wobbles.

Kai releases a low, excited yelp from the lanai and runs down into the yard.

The windows are still. The gentle rattling of the wineglasses ceases.

"Earthquake?" I ask. *Did I just cause an earthquake?!* But I get it: those chips of sunbaked clay from my seizurescape—pulled up by the shift in gravity—were *tectonic plates.*

And then it starts again. The earth slips beneath us. Grandpa falls onto the couch. I catch my balance as if I'm on a wobbly surfboard. The hutch falls over. The windowpanes flutter in their frames so fiercely I'm afraid they'll shatter. The trees beyond the windows visibly sway, shedding flowers and leaves.

"Oh, God, what have I done?"

The shaking diminishes. I steady myself on the ground. I catch Tami's unbelieving eyes, clasp my hand to my mouth. *Did I say that out loud? Does she know?* I hear the distant barking of dogs. My mind wanders to the rest of Hilo. *Please be okay.*

"Look!" Kai yells.

I rise. We hurry outside. The Orchid looms large across the sky. But she's retreating even as we watch, drawing back into deeper space and dimming as she does so.

My attention is drawn upward. Straight up. Against the background of the retreating Orchid, an object plummets through the early night sky, a contrail of green fire and smoke unraveling behind it. *The pearl.*

At first it's almost hovering, motionless in the near heavens. It rockets closer. Then, hidden from view by nearby trees, it strikes the side of Mauna Loa. From the shield volcano's direction a plume of ash rises in silhouette against the high horizon.

We hear a sonic boom; pressure pounds my ears. The windows rattle. The coqui frogs fall abruptly silent. A breeze picks up, carrying grit that stings my skin.

In the quiet that follows, everyone turns and stares at me. I feel faint.

"Come inside," Mom says, holding me up. Grandpa takes my other side.

"Who knew your birthday would be such a blast!" hollers Kai.

"What's going on here?" I hear Tami ask, alarm in her voice.

I shake my head. *No. She knows. I don't want her to know.* But I'm too tired. Nausea. I sit on the couch for a minute, trying to stay awake.

Mom and Grandpa help me upstairs. I stumble into

my bed. They go only after I agree to drink a glass of water. Above my bed I make out the shape of the dreamcatcher. I crawl under the sheets and let frog song guide me into an oblivion of stars.

Kai's dreamcatcher works.

CHAPTER 3

I wake in the morning with pain in my stomach and chest. But it has nothing to do with the pearl. This pain is hunger.

Dad comes to check on me. To my horror he says that Tami and Keali`i are still here. They know. But there's room in my mind for only one crisis right now. "I have to eat," I tell him.

"Food's waiting for you. Buzz is still here, too, but he's in a hurry to go up Mauna Loa to investigate what happened."

Oh, God. The earthquake. "Is everyone okay? Hilo?"

"Don't know. Grandpa's checking around. Kai's with him. But I wouldn't worry, Lei. Big Island is used to quakes. Home to five volcanoes—we're right on the Pacific Ring of Fire. Tremors weekly for thousands of years. No one will think twice about it."

Dad leaves, and I throw on a tee and frayed jean shorts.

I step into my *slippahs* and catch a glimpse out my window. I approach cautiously, swing open the screen, and stare. A low bronze cloud stretches from the direction of town out to sea, dimming the morning sun.

The impact.

My eyes follow the cloud to where it's thickest. Mauna Loa. I can't see the volcano from this window, but there's no doubt. The pollution is clearing; it's had all night to disperse, and the high trade winds have vacuumed away the unsettled debris. But there's nothing up there to destroy; Mauna Loa is already a scorched, asphalt-like surface, piles of lava flows upon jet black lava flows. That pearl probably sank into the volcano's surface like a steel marble dropped into a tray of brownies.

It'll be okay. It'll be okay.

My friends. I've already explained the insane story of my connection to the Orchid to others. I told it to Dad, to Mom and Grandpa on the night we reunited, to Kai a few days later, after my parents had decided he could be trusted. He was excited. But what about Tami and Keali`i? How will they react?

Everyone stands when I come down the stairs. They turn and follow me as I sit at the table. Watching. I eat whatever Mom gives me, leftovers from last night's botched party: salted `ulu breadfruit slices, baked `uala sweet potato wedges, a bit of dried fish. I don't care about rationing. I even scrape clean our three-finger poi in the `umeke poi bowl. In a cone of silence.

"Lei," Tami says, taking the chair next to mine and squeezing my hand. I look at her.

"Hey. This is . . . *wild*. You should have told me."

"I was afraid."

"Of what?"

I shrug, but I know. How could I explain something so crazy?

Keali`i leans against the wall. He straightens when I eye him. "Hi," he offers. My parents and Buzz sit down across from me.

Buzz rubs his beard. "Kai was right: your birthday was a blast."

I smile thinly, study my empty plate.

"Sorry, Lei," he says. "You look nervous. Don't be. This is a good opportunity. I'm going to go up there and get a sample from this meteorite. First chance we've ever had to physically examine these alien creatures."

"I call it a pearl. The meteorite. Felt like a pearl. I don't know."

"Okay. Good. Back up," Buzz says. "Tell me everything. Why'd this happen?"

I explain the best I can everything I remember from yesterday, starting with the explosion near New York. I recount everything I felt during the contraction and release, the heaviness, the density, the gravity. I explain why I aimed it at the mountain. I glance up at Tami and Keali`i often but can't hold their gaze.

"Gravity well. Fastness. Propulsion. Explains how they

34

get around Newton's Second Law! Okay. Okay." Buzz nods, stroking his beard.

"You were right to hit Mauna Loa," Mom assures me. "Smart thinking." I stare past her at the walls. The Merrie Monarch posters are level again. The hutch is up. Empty.

"This is all beyond fascinating, Lei," Buzz says. "I'm going to get to work. Others will be curious about the impact site, too. There're only a few roads up there, all of them gated. I have keys. I should be able to beat anyone there. I'll be back as soon as I can."

Buzz's departure leaves a sudden silence. Dad says, "He took your projector. To his shop at the observatories."

Tami clears her throat. "So, Lei, anything new with you lately?"

"I'm sorry, Tami. I . . . How much did Dad tell you?"

"Everything. You basically pulled a Jedi mind trick on the Orchid?" she asks.

She's joking! What a relief. "More of a Vulcan mind meld," I say. "Buzz helped—he used electrodes to hook my brain signals up to his radio telescope array. Radio dishes, you know? To broadcast into space. The Orchid and I fused. I didn't so much convince her to come back. I . . . Somehow I *was* her. I just . . . came back."

"Can I be an alien psychic, too?"

I look at her apologetically. Dad comes to my rescue. "Tami, I told you. Her epilepsy makes it possible."

"And my best friend is the only person in the world who can do this?"

"I'm not the only person who can hear them," I quickly answer. "On Moloka`i we met a priest with epilepsy who could. And he knew of a boy who could. There must be others. We stumbled upon the answer to communicating on Mauna Kea. Not many places in the world with those kinds of radio resources. I was just the *first* to reach it."

"And then the Orchid imprinted somehow," Mom says. "Like a baby seagull imprinting with the first thing it sees after it hatches."

"The first sperm to reach the egg," tries Dad. "Everyone else got locked out."

"Oh, my God." Mom slaps her forehead. "Can we just . . . not use that analogy?"

"What?" Dad says, petulant.

Tami asks, "What about the second one, the baby?"

"I've tried to link with the little Orchid, but it hasn't worked. I've never heard its thoughts. It does whatever its mom wants, so I just focus on the mom. Buzz says these creatures have a lifespan we can scarcely grasp. And if it usually takes a solid year for a human child to speak—why would the little Orchid be ready and willing to talk after three months?"

Tami shrugs. "I don't know. Just asking."

I study her nervously. I think this is going okay, though. She's unsettled, but she's not holding it against me. Just trying to figure it out.

"Hold on a sec." Keali`i's smile is strained. "I'm just saying: if these Star Flowers want to leave—maybe we should, you know, let them."

"They cancel radiation," I say. "The meltdowns. They soak it up—our mess—like a mop."

"They said that last night. But it doesn't make any—"

"Think about it," Dad interrupts. He points at the map above the breakfast bar. "Two hundred. Two hundred nuclear meltdowns around the world already. Countless throughout the U.S. There were early disasters in nearby Australia, Japan."

"I wondered what that map was about," Keali`i says to himself.

Dad continues. "But, here's the thing: there's no fallout. Not a trace of radiation in the air. Not even normal trace levels."

"We're way out *here*. Of course there's no radiation."

Dad nods patiently. "I held Buzz's Geiger counter myself, Keali`i, as recently as two weeks ago. The needle doesn't even move a normal amount. It's just . . . dead."

"Everything's dead."

"No, this was an old counter. Simple circuit, very low wattage, like a flashlight. We can still get some flashlights to work, right? Even car batteries."

Keali`i's silent for a while, thinking it through. "Wait," he says. "I've been going over this all night. If the Star Flowers soak up radiation, then why do nuclear rods get too hot in the first place? Shouldn't they just be . . . kaput?"

"Nearest we can figure is that enriched uranium—it's too concentrated. Like ice cubes. A sponge can't soak up an ice cube, can it? It has to melt first."

Keali`i looks directly at me. "Listen, Lei, I'm not trying

37

to be difficult. I just still have questions. Aren't there other things to consider? Starvation? Disease? Fighting? This 'lesser of evils' argument . . . I don't know. With every passing month it'll be harder to actually recover, until it's too late altogether. Gas will go bad in another six months. Engineers, technicians, electricians, computer programmers, chemists . . . they're all dying out there, too! And wouldn't nuclear scientists have figured this mop thing out? Don't you think they already know to accelerate their meltdowns?"

"Maybe," I say. "But how come there haven't been four hundred meltdowns already? Not enough people are hitting the fast-forward button."

Dad says, "The point is, we don't know. We need better information, to be certain that the right people understand the game plan. Until then we're in a holding pattern."

"Until then people around the globe remain scared and hopeless and dying," says Keali`i. "Who's that poet? You want a bang but you're getting a whimper."

"I KNOW!" I shout. "I know that. Don't you think I know?" Keali`i puts his hands in his pockets. I continue. "Help us. *Think*. How do we get the word out?"

"Okay, well . . . have you tried giving the Orchid a longer leash? So it's far enough away to not fry circuit boards? Reel it in only when there's a pop, but otherwise—"

"We'd risk their getting away because the line's too weak. They'll just zap microchips all over again each time they come in. Fits and starts. Almost worse that way."

Mom explains that our family has put a lot of thought

into this, but we've still fallen short. She concludes, "Meanwhile, we have to survive each day as it comes. Challenge after challenge. We have to meet our daily demands as best we can. Here, now."

Dad says, "We need to make a pact. This is a *secret*. Very important it stays that way. Can you imagine Lei's danger if the wrong people found out?"

Tami nods, her face losing just a hint of color. Keali`i's eyes narrow grimly.

"Do we have your word not to mention this to anybody? Ever?" Mom says.

"Of course!" Tami answers.

"Absolutely," Keali`i agrees. "Lips are sealed. No matter what."

*   *   *

Within the hour, Keali`i and Tami leave for town on their bikes. Keali`i offers to escort her down the hill. "I'll probably be gone for a while. Other business to attend to," he explains. Typical Keali`i.

It's hard to see them go, but we agree to meet up as soon as I have a chance to visit Tami. Keali`i reminds me: "Bring your wet suit." Then he adds, "And bring Tami. If you want."

My parents overhear and share a look. I'm sure they'd like to cloister me here. But that's never going to happen.

Our neighbors Paul and Sara Irving arrive at our house with their baby. They're out for a long walk and have come to check on us following the earthquake. We're thrilled to see them, and we circle around baby Chloe. Paul and Sara had Chloe only a few days before the power went out. If she had been born after that—who knows what the hospital would have been like. I hear that it's still up and running, but just barely, and only with volunteers at their wits' end.

"How'd your place do?" Dad asks Paul.

"Some pictures fell down. No real damage."

Thank God, I think.

"Good! How's everything else going?" Dad asks. He points knowingly. "Bags under your eyes."

"It's going well," Paul says. "Power or no, parenting is just . . . what it is: sleepless nights, dirty cloth diapers, fending off the hordes of boys."

Sara and Mom drift to another room to talk story. I'm torn between joining them and playing with the baby, but Chloe wins out with her little grasping starfish hands and big blue eyes.

"Made her a mobile, Lei." Paul beams. "Clothes hangers and paper cutouts."

"You're a stellar dad," my father says.

"I'll learn from you. I don't know how you pulled off crossing islands to get home, keeping Lei safe."

Dad eyes me. "I never let her out of my sight."

"Hey," I tell him. "I know you get nervous when I go into town. It's great that you let me do it anyway." I turn to Paul. "Another secret of a good dad: don't smother your daughter or she'll turn against you."

Dad's eyes narrow. "It's dangerous down there."

"Tami needs me down there, too."

"We worry." The way Dad says this makes me fall silent. "You leave, we worry. Every minute. The knowledge sits in your gut all day. It's a terrible way to live."

"Well . . . ," I start. "What . . . How is that fair to me?"

"I don't know," Mom admits, coming back into the room with Sara, like she's been waiting to have this conversation. "Listen, we trust you. You're seventeen going on seventy. Just . . . what you went through to get home—an experience like that does two things. You know better than most how things can turn lethal in an instant. But your experiences also taught you that you're immune to danger. You survived the unsurvivable. On some level you think you're invincible. That's ridiculous."

"You sound like Tūtū," I say.

"Good!" she says. "Then you know I'm right."

"Wow," Sara says. She's in her late twenties, blond hair cut short like mine. "I can't imagine letting go. It's hard to admit that we'll have to separate someday."

"It'll happen." Mom sighs. "Even after the end of the world. Nothing changes."

The young family heads back home, and the urgency of chores, chores, chores rushes back. Mom asks me to clean the chicken coop. I tidy it up in a sort of daze. If I just won my freedom, why do I feel so guilty about it?

Grandpa arrives after lunch while I'm in the greenhouse moving `ulu seedlings into larger pots. We've propagated these root cuttings from the shoots of our five breadfruit trees. Grandpa helps me finish up.

We sit on the front steps. I pick at the edges of a patch of moss, peeling it up like lifting carpet. It's so quiet. My parents are catching up on chores around the back. Kai is at Uncle Hank's for target practice. "The *loko wai* you built was damaged by the earthquake," Grandpa tells me. "All your *o`opu* escaped. I'm sorry."

My fishpond. A week's worth of work, a month's worth of maintenance. My *o`opu* were just starting to grow, too. I had been hoping to fry up my first batch next week. I squeeze my hands into fists, then return to prying up clumps of moss.

"There's nothing you could have done, Leilani," Grandpa says. "This island is alive, always has been. Part of learning to live sustainably—and part of returning to our roots—is learning to accept the whims of the gods. Pele carries out her great works without a thought to us. She rebuilds her island, and we will rebuild our *loko*. This is a core part of who we Hawaiians are."

He knows that wasn't Pele. It was me. "Tūtū," I say.

He draws me in close. "Come, breathe." I close my eyes and breathe deep, smell the plumeria flowers on the tree above me, the flowers Mom always rests above her ear. "Mind, body, and spirit are all the same thing," he explains with the voice of a magician; he weaves spells. "*Pono*. Equilibrium, wholeness, harmony. You must be connected to your spirit, the world around you. Your *`aina*, your land. Your family. *`Ohana*. You are *lōkahi*, Leilani. You are one. Individual. Matchless. And you are also One. Indivisible. Connected with all of creation."

Connected. I sense the Orchid. Above the Himalayas.

"Oh, Moʻopuna," Grandpa says. He holds me. "My darling," he says, "I'm worried for you. You've got to find *pono*. Harmony. This is the path forward. You've been asked to do so much, but this burden is all of ours. It's time to let it go, Moʻopuna! Find your path."

"I wish I knew how." I look up at him through blurry eyes.

"We should all start meditation practices every day. Nurturing the spirit is as important as cultivating the land."

I slap a mosquito on my arm. "I'm glad we have someone like Father Akoni around here." I'm thinking of the priest who helped Dad and me on Molokaʻi, who was building such a strong community. He's two islands up the chain, though; he might as well be in Madagascar.

Grandpa gently squeezes me. "We're all in this together, okay? You're not alone. Your parents and I shoulder these troubles every bit as much as you do. Your grandma and I are always with you. Her ʻaumākua is the *ao*, you know—the cloud. She's always overhead, white and pure, bringing the cleansing rain."

We sit in silence, breathing in the wonderful garland of our jungle-bound yard, and we watch the high clouds change shapes. When I was little, Mom once explained the ʻaumākua to me as similar to a patronus from the Harry Potter books—a charm of protection that takes the form of an object of nature, usually an animal. I smile at the memory. I know that an ʻaumākua is also an ancestor, a spirit guide. Sacred.

"What's your patronus?" I ask Tūtū.

"Eh?"

I laugh. "Your `aumākua? I know: you'll be an `iliō. A great hunting dog."

"Naw. I'd rather be something unique. A house cat, maybe. Friendly, but on my own. Around, but not in the way. Neat, clean, like a good navy officer. Night vision. Claws only when I need them."

I laugh again. "Sounds about right."

I hear the pop of a firearm, and I flinch. But it's only Kai. Every time I hear a gunshot, I think of the horrors of O`ahu and Maui. The sheriff of Hana . . . He was going to kill Dad because Dad shot one of his men. Guns only attract more guns. My palms grow clammy. "You ever going to tell us about you and the sheriff? Why did he spare Dad?"

"Ah," Grandpa says. "What happened between me and that *moke* don't matter."

I glare at him. "What was that about *pono*?"

"What's done is done," he says.

CHAPTER 4

It's past midnight. The calm waters of Hilo Bay reflect a moonless star field, tinged faintly green by the Emerald Orchid.

As Tami and I sit on Hilo Bay's breakwater, a two-mile-long string of boulders and cement that reaches far across the bay, the baby Orchid sets behind the slopes of Mauna Loa. I sit up and watch it sink, its green and purple petals bright against the stars as it slips below the horizon. Its mother rises behind me to the east.

"Nighty-night, little one," Tami says beside me.

Will the baby Orchid ever talk to me as the mother does?

A wave crashes against the boulders, and my back is showered with salty spray. Tami yelps. I shiver.

Tsunami rubbish is as thick as stew in the water, bobbing in circles, rarely escaping around the long wall to the open ocean. Yellow city lights once gleamed along this shimmering bay. But Hilo's hills are as dark as the slopes of Mauna Loa and Mauna Kea, the two volcanoes rising above the city.

Tami cinches her scrunchie around her curly blond ponytail and fits her arms through her wet suit. We lie back, breathing in the flowery breeze. The roar of a motorcycle accelerates over a distant street, leaving a scar in the silence.

"You sure we're not too far?" asks Tami. "We've been here an hour."

We're about a mile out. I shrug. "He told me he'd find us. Don't worry."

"I'm not worried. Do I look worried?"

"You like him, don't you?"

Tami stifles a protest.

"I knew it!" I say.

"I can't believe this."

"Calm down. I think he likes you, too. He's good *kine*."

Tami scoffs. "Oh, my God. Yeah, whatevah. He doesn't even know I exist. He likes *you*."

"No, he doesn't! Knock it off."

Another wave pounds the breakwater, and we're showered. It dies in the labyrinth below, water sloshing through the spaces between the boulders. Sucking and gurgling. This is crazy. A rogue wave could reach us. We could be swept off balance, fall through these holes, and be dashed to pieces in the world's deadliest washing machine.

My wet suit hangs inside out from my waist. I stretch my

arms through my dangling sleeves and ask Tami to zip it up from the back. It's loose these days. She lets me know she's upset with every jerk of my zipper string.

"You know," I say, "there's word coming out of O'ahu that stranded tourists are being traded as slaves. Put it in perspective."

"Don't start with that, *Mom*." Her tone is snarky, not angry. "You wanna head down Guilt Trip Lane, Mrs. Emerald Orchid?"

"Sure. Another big pop in Russia two days ago. Everyone on the Black Sea is going to live through the month thanks to me. Wanna start there?"

"No. I want to start with why my phone's been dead for months."

"It works just fine. No one calls you."

Tami laughs. "Ain't that the truth."

I tug on my inner kite string to the Orchid, to test the tension. Taut. *I stay for the strength of the sweetness*, I remind her. *It is good to stay.*

She dutifully repeats me: *We long for the deep beyond the fires. But we stay. It is good to stay and protect.*

"Lei?" Tami taps my head. "Wake up."

"I've never once thought about Keali`i," I tell her.

"Really?"

"Honestly. He's all yours."

"All right, then. I'll have him installed at my place start of business Monday morning."

"A boyfriend is the last thing on my mind right now."

47

Tami smiles. "What about Soldier Boy?"

I roll my eyes. Our code name for the soldier Aukina, the dreamy good looker who helped me and Dad escape from the military camp on O'ahu. But he's long gone. The military ditched the Hawaiian Islands. "Why do you have to bring him up?"

We're silent, and then Tami says, "I hear Aleka's *hāpai*."

I gasp. "Oh, my God. Poor girl."

"Can you imagine having a baby? *Now?*"

A physical tremor runs through me. "My parents would flip out if I ever got knocked up. I'm not *ever* getting *hapai*. I'm not bringing a kid into this world."

Tami seizes my wrist. "Someone's coming."

We scramble down the bay side of the breakwater and crouch into makeshift foxholes. Seawater sloshes against my surfing booties. Under the cover of darkness, I poke up my head and scan the top of the wall.

I see a lone figure hopping from one boulder to the next, objects tucked under his arms. No flashlight, but he's scampering with the confidence of a mongoose. The shadowy form is in a wet suit. His hair fans in the gentle breeze. I relax. Keali'i. I offer up my best frog whistle. *"Coqui?"*

The figure stops. "Lei?"

I spring up. "It's me."

"Ho! Why you so far out, eh?"

I scramble up to the top of the breakwater. "'Cause you said to get out this far."

"Water's too deep here. We have to go back a bit."

"I wasn't sure what we're doing."

"It's a surprise. C'mon. Where's Tami?"

She emerges from beneath the nearest concrete jack. "Hey, Kea."

"Oh!" he says. "Hey, Tami. Howzit?"

He has a bulgy mesh bag under one arm and a stack of scuba fins under the other. "Here." He hands me and Tami a pair of fins each. He guards the bag closely.

"What are we doing?"

"You'll see in a minute."

We follow him back along the breakwater toward shore. It's very dark, and the green light cast by the Orchid makes the shadows trickier to navigate.

"This better be good," I say.

Keali`i smiles, his teeth white in the starlight. He pulls a waterproof dive light and three sets of snorkels and masks out of the mesh bag.

Excitement flutters up through me. "Does the light work?" I ask.

Keali`i kneels with the dive light. He presses it against the boulder and triggers it on and off. The flash of light against the rock blinds me. Tami and I croon. "It works!"

Keali`i shrugs. "Good as any light I've seen. Some flickering, but yeah."

"Are we going for lobsters?" Tami asks, coaxing the light out of Keali`i's hand.

"*Slippahs*. We're *slippah* diving. Plenny for all. No one's been out here for *months*. Gonna be a feast. Careful, don't shine that up. We'll have forty *booga boogas* from Keaukaha out here before we even have our fins on."

"With our luck, half them *boogas* will be Tribe," I say.

"Don't say that!" growls Keali`i.

Tami hands the light back. "Won't people be able to see us in the water?"

Keali`i shrugs. "That's why we're so far out. They'd have to be looking right at us to see the glow. The waves hide us, too. We'll slip right under their noses."

I frown. Dad's shaming me in my mind's eye, but he's not shaking a finger at me, he's waving his arms around. *"Danger, Will Robinson!"* I push the image away. We'll be safe. I'd give almost anything to pig out on lobster. "I've never been lobster diving."

"Easy. You got *honu* lungs, yeah?" He hands Tami a snorkel set. He hands me a weight belt and puts one on himself. I strap ten pounds of lead onto my hips.

Weights on an epileptic in the dark ocean strikes me as *lōlō*, but I follow along.

"Here, I only got four gloves, but at least we can each have one."

"It's okay. I don't need one," I say, offering mine to Tami.

They both laugh. "What'll you grab the lobsters with?" Tami asks.

"What? You . . . grab them?"

"These are *slippah* lobsters," Keali`i explains. "No claws, but they're spiny as hell. You have to snatch 'em hard or they'll slip away with those powerful tails."

"Well, let's go!" I say.

"After you." Keali`i extends his arm. The end of his coiled tattoo peeks out beyond the sleeve of his wet suit, just touching his palm.

Tami and I do awkward dances as we slip fins over our booties. We spit into our snorkel masks, wipe the spit around the lenses, rinse. Hawaiian defogger. I put on my glove and the mask and fall forward into the water.

I'm suddenly graceful.

My breathing is exaggerated through my snorkel but relaxed. Salt water seeps into my wet suit, embracing me with a comfortable chill that will warm against my skin.

I stare into the black. The swell of a wave lifts me. I feel the downward pull of the weights around my waist, but gentle kicking of my fins and the buoyant wet suit keep me light. I could almost space out, drift, floating. Almost.

"All good?" Keali`i asks from the edge of the rocks.

I give a thumbs-up. Then I realize it's too dark for him to see me, so I spit the snorkel out. "Doin' good! Just . . . keep a close eye, in case I space out."

"Got you covered, Lei," Tami says. "Let's have that light."

Keali`i dives in, switches on the light, and the world below is illuminated. The light penetrates to the floor twenty feet down. A shaft sweeps from side to side as Keali`i swims about. The bottom is rocky, lava worn into pocked slabs blotched with algae and coral. Fish swim lazily near the bottom: schools of angelfish, wrasses, and larger parrot fish chomping on the rocks. A green sea turtle jerks back under the wall.

We surface. "*Slippahs!*" Keali`i calls. "I've never seen so many. You look for their eye shine against the light. Otherwise they look just like the rocks."

I take the light and paint the seafloor with my brush. A rock sparkles with a pair of small sequins. I freeze the light and squint.

I take a deep breath, tuck, and dive. My legs kick against air and then meet water. I propel myself downward. Ten feet, then fifteen, the pressure building on my lungs and in my ears, becoming painful. I keep my eyes on the pair of glowing beads. As I draw closer I reach out and touch the *slippah*'s hard shell. It vanishes. I glance around, but it's gone. At the surface I spit the mouthpiece out. "It got away."

Keali`i smiles. "Here." He hands me and Tami mesh diving bags.

Tami says, "The light stuns them. But you have to strike fast and grip them hard around their middle so they don't dart away."

"Go for it." I hand her the light. "I'll watch you."

As we kick down I hear a noise in the water, a deep sigh that curves in on itself, finally releasing in a high-pitched laugh. A shorter response.

Humpback whales.

The song is distant, perhaps beyond the edge of the bay. I'm glad to know they're there. Life goes on, even for the creatures of the deep. I hope their world is the same as it always was. Maybe life's even better for them. They're usually not around this time of year. Maybe the Star Flowers make the plankton easier to find.

Have the whales seen the coasts of the mainland? What would they report?

Tami thrusts her hand toward a rock, pulls it back, and a slipper lobster materializes in her fist, broad, massive tail clenching and releasing in a panicked effort to escape. Ten insectlike legs protrude from beneath its mottled shell, wiggling and searching. Tami guides the strange creature into her mesh bag, slides her arm out of the bag, then cinches it, and we rise. She clicks off the light as we ascend.

"Got one!" Tami tells Keali`i.

"Ah, nice!" he says. "We're going to feast!"

"Here." Tami hands me the light. "Don't hesitate. Snatch 'em up!"

As I descend, pressure burning against my chest, I study the breakwater wall. The jumble of boulders and concrete jacks extends all the way to the bottom. I feel the surge of the ocean pulling me toward the holes.

I see a pair of eyes glinting beneath one boulder and stop my descent, go closer to the hole. A *slippah* is in there, big as a shoe box. It's twice as big as the one Tami caught.

I grin.

The surge presses me against the rim of the hole, and I stiffen my arm to keep from banging against the rock. I focus the light on the giant *slippah*. The hole goes way back. *Careful. Don't get sucked in.*

One shot. I'm running out of air. The light flickers. I maneuver my head and arms into the hole, shining the light directly into the *slippah*'s eyes.

I strike. The spines cut into my fingers. It flaps its tail wildly. I pull it toward me, backpedaling with my fins. The *slippah*'s in one hand and the light's in the other. I tuck the light between my legs and whip the bag free of my weight belt. A surge of water dashes me against a boulder. I spit out the snorkel and loosen the drawstring with my teeth. The *slippah*'s tail spasms as I trap my prey. The surge twists me into another rock, and I bang my shoulder. But I manage to get control and surface.

"You got one?" Tami asks. "Right on! Let's see."

I hold my bag near the surface as Tami shines the light down on it from within the water. The ocean glows and foams like a Jacuzzi. "Whoa!" Keali`i exclaims. "I never knew they got that big! That's like four *slippahs*!"

For the next hour we trade gear back and forth, filling the bags with lobsters. I had no idea the wall was so full of holes and tunnels that go all the way through to the bay side. The fish and the octopi and the urchins pass through easily. The passageways closer to the surface are also teeming with delicious `opihi—a limpet mollusk that's been totally stripped from the shore by hungry humans.

We collect two dozen *slippahs*, and the bags are full. The light's off, and we can barely see each other against the black rolling waves. We're about twenty feet off the breakwater, and we've drifted closer to shore.

"I shoulda brought more bags," Keali`i says.

A round of gunfire pierces the night. All three of us yelp. I *felt* that pistol crack. It came from the breakwater. I whip around. Through the beads of water on my dive mask, I see several figures against the dim green of the night. A flashlight blinds me. I lift a gloved hand to shield my eyes.

Is this what the *slippahs* feel as we descend upon them?

"That was your warning. Hand over the light, whatever you have."

"Shit!" Keali`i barks. "Go screw yourselves."

Whoa. What is he doing?

Another shot in the air. I see the figures clearly in the flash of light. They have cloth bands around their left upper arms. Hanamen. There are two other Tribes in the region: the Manō and the Hoku. Only Hanamen wear red bands. Hoku all have star-shaped neck tattoos. Manō lie low, without any identifying marks.

"Surrender the light, whatever you have. Wet suits, too."

"I'll beat your head in with it," I hear Keali`i mutter. He shouts, "Sorry, dropped the light. It's gone." Tami and I exchange an incredulous glance.

A shot hits the water. Keali`i is perfectly still.

"That's my last warning."

"Goddammit." Keali`i stays where he is. I look toward the flashlight, shielding my eyes. I can't make any of them out. I study the breakwater, recognize a particular boulder we were beside moments ago. Adrenaline stabs my chest. An idea.

"Coming!" I shout.

Tami looks relieved. Keali`i stares at me with daggers for eyes. I can tell he wants to swim out into the open ocean. "Lei, no."

"Guys, shut up," I whisper. I take Keali`i's hand. "Link

55

together. Take the biggest breath of your life. Straight down to the bottom. Then follow me. Don't let go."

We each draw an enormous breath and dive. I clench Keali`i's hand, regret what I've done. *This isn't going to work! What the hell am I doing?!* The water is pitch-black, and I've already lost all sense of direction. But there's no going back.

Gunfire erupts above.

CHAPTER 5

The Hanaman's light searches the water's surface. I fight off panic. I can't see anything down here. If we turn on the light they'll know right where we are. But it's too late to change course. Bullets crack. I hear them enter the water and decelerate, a muffled *whoov, whoov.*

My legs are propellers. I see the slabs of lava just before barreling into them. I use my free hand—still dragging a bag of *slippahs*—to claw my way forward along the floor.

Someone dives into the water. He rushes overhead, a shadow against the distant glow of the Orchid, races in the opposite direction. He thinks he's going to overtake us as we bolt toward open sea.

But I'm leading us straight *toward* the man with the gun.

The flashlight scans the water in broad strokes. I steer to the right, motoring along the bottom. The bullets will fly as soon as we surface. We should have given up our stuff.

I scissor my legs through the water, pulling Keali`i after me. I can sense that the boulders and jacks are near now. I hold out my free arm to feel my way forward. A horrid thought fuels my panic: if I die, the world dies with me. I want to surface and beg for forgiveness. But even if they spare my life, they'll put a bullet in Keali`i's head. I've ruined everything. What if they were only going to take our stuff and let us go?

My lungs burn fiercely.

I see the boulders. The hole! I shimmy into it. I want to let go of Keali`i and use both hands to pull myself along, but we'll lose each other. I do my best with one hand, my bag of *slippahs* still looped around my elbow. The chute forces my friends into a tight line behind me. Gentle dolphin kicks now. I'm a blind mermaid squeezing into my own tomb, and I'm dragging two people into death with me.

A wave pummels the breakwater, carrying me forward in a sudden rush. I can't see anything now; the shadows are overpowering my fragile night vision. My dive mask is fogged. My lungs clench. I let out a burst of air. A mistake. My lungs grow more ravenous. Any second I'll breathe in water.

I thrust blindly forward, panic building, hit my head against concrete. My *slippahs* claw against my ribs, pressed against me. I let go of Keali`i, flailing. I bang my shin, my elbow. I just want to go up. I don't care about the Hanamen. I need to breathe. But I can't see. There's no path upward.

I'm dying! I'm going to drown!

I'm fading. Dizzy.

But there's light. I can see. Is the Hanaman shining his flashlight into the breakwater? Has Tami clicked on the dive light? I can see a narrow path. I shimmy forward, reach upward. My hand breaks the surface. My head follows. I gasp. A wave hits my face and I'm submerged again, only for a second. I cough and gasp.

Shouting. But not directly above.

I'm hunted. I can feel the *slippahs* crawling along my chest, spiny legs poking through the mesh bag, but I don't dare move.

Tami surfaces beside me, Keali`i on the far side of the slab. *Thank God!* They each gasp. It's so loud that I reach out and cover Tami's mouth.

"SHHH!"

Why can I see them so well? "Is the light on?" I whisper.

"No, I've got it right here." Tami holds it up. It's off.

The gunman scans the water with his light. We sit tight.

"Good thinkin', Lei," Keali`i whispers.

Another wave fills the cavities. I take off my mask and rinse it out when the water level lowers. I defog with my spit and put it back on. I'm still wearing my fins, which makes for an awkward perch for my feet, but I might need to rush away through the water at any instant. If they find us down here, they could riddle us with bullets.

"They're gone, Two Dog. They had fins. Let it go, eh?" I hear one of the men say.

"*Two Dog?*" snickers Keali`i. "What kind of name is that?"

We wait. They wait. The three dry Hanamen pace. The

swimmer scrambles up the boulders. The group huddles nearby; I can see them and hear their breathing.

We grow very still. "If I only had a gun," Keali`i whispers.

Thank God you don't, I think. *They'd retaliate with all they have.*

"Goddammit," Two Dog grumbles. "How hard was that? Dumbass."

"I don't get it," the swimmer says. "Got away just as it got bright out."

"Yeah." Two Dog pauses. "Goddamn Orchid."

Tami studies me, a frown deepening along her brow. Is she thinking the same thing as me?

Did you make it brighter? I ask.

We are different than darkness.

"Hey, what's that?" one of them asks. Have they sniffed us out? Should we bolt?

"Well, I'll be damned." Two Dog whistles. "Sailboat."

Sailboat? I slowly turn. I can't see anything.

"Never have noticed if it weren't so bright," one says.

"Come on, screw the kids."

"Hauling in a whole sailboat! Just the four of us!"

They hoot and spring away. Two Dog barks, though. "No, Dale. Stay here. One hour. Make sure those pricks don't slither back the moment we're gone. Lay low."

Two Dog and the two men flanking him stride away. Dale plops down on the top of the jack a few feet above us. He stares out to sea.

"Let's go," Keali`i whispers.

"Now? It's better to wait it out." I'm still trying to figure out if the Orchid has really grown brighter. I didn't know she could do that.

Tami nods. "I can't keep fighting the waves like this."

I sigh. "Okay. Let me see if I can find a way forward."

"No!" Keali`i says. "Back the other way. The water's too calm; we'll be spotted on that side."

"But this Dale guy is staring straight out the other way, looking for us."

Keali`i shakes his head. I clench my jaw. I know I'm right. I also know just how to change his mind. "If we go in, we could warn the sailboat not to dock. Screw these guys even more."

Keali`i grows still. "Now you're talking."

I duck beneath the water and use the intensified light in the night sky to see if there's a workable way out of this jumble on the bay side. The shadows of interlaced boulders give way to greenish windows of open water. I resurface. "Follow me."

Another wave hits the breakwater. Our watery foxhole gurgles and fills with sloshing sea foam. We suck in lungfuls of air as the water rises around us, and then we push downward into the briar patch of concrete and rock.

The extra light makes all the difference. I've cleared the boulders and have entered Hilo's inner bay. My lungs burn. I angle upward and continue kicking. I surface slowly, my snorkel first, then my mask, then my chin. I silently spit out the mouthpiece, draw in a blissful breath, turn, and study the wall.

I'm not as far as I thought. I see Dale clearly, the bottoms of his feet facing me, his stomach on the ground like a sniper. Twenty feet away.

He has no idea all three of us passed right beneath him. I smile.

It's clear now that Dale would have seen our heads bobbing in the waves on the other side of the breakwater.

He still could, if he turns around. *Everything's so bright!*

Turn off, I think.

Nothing happens.

I glance at the Orchid and gasp. She's never been so vivid. She's as bright as a full moon, with twice as many wisps and folds and folding ribbons as I've ever seen. The purple highlights among some of her folds are clearer than ever.

Turn off, I command, but her brilliance remains. Maybe she's like stadium lights: she can only dim slowly.

Keali`i surfaces. Then Tami. She's closer to the breakwater and makes a conspicuous splash. She grunts. "Lei, I—"

"Shh," I whisper. "One more dive. We're still too close."

I take another deep breath and drop. A chunk of debris floats on the water just ahead. I swim beneath it and surface on its far side. Perfect cover. Part of the marquee to the bay front's old movie theater. There's a faded "L" square still fastened into the plastic tracks, but that's it. What title would have had an "L" in it? I have no idea. But I swear I suddenly smell popcorn.

My friends pop up to the dark surface.

"Lei, Tami got cut," Keali`i says. "It's pretty bad."

"Where?"

"My thigh," she says. "Right below my shorty. Coming through one of those turns. Scraped an exposed piece of rebar."

"Are you okay?"

She adjusts her mask and tries to hold on to the marquee. "It hurts. Feels gross, deep. Pretty sure I need stitches."

A stab of fear. *Blood in the water.*

I look at Keali`i; he'll know if we're in trouble. *Sharks?*

He shrugs. "Look, they're here. Hammerheads and tigers are common. They *do* come in. Black tips, white tips . . . barracudas, too."

"Oh, God," Tami moans. "Get me out of the water. *Now.*" Her voice rises. If she panics, the Hanaman might hear us even at this distance.

I look at the breakwater. "I don't like it, but we have to go back."

"I can handle him," Keali`i says. "It's three on one. We sneak up behind him, I clock him with my weight belt. End of story."

"What if he starts shooting?"

"He'll never know what hit him."

I frown—it's never that simple.

"Guys, come on. I'm bleeding a lot." Tami's voice wavers.

I turn to Keali`i. "Don't kill him. Promise me."

"They were trying to kill us."

"I know. We're better than them. Just . . . promise."

"Fine. I won't do anything on purpose. Just pound 'im and knock 'im out."

The dark below me feels like one giant mouth, closing in on our legs. "Okay. Back to the breakwater."

Keali`i draws in a deep breath. I brush his leg with my fin.

He yelps and launches half out of the water. Tami and I bark.

"Guys, that was just my fin," I whisper. "It was me."

Too late. The Hanaman rises. "Hey!" he shouts. "Got you!"

"It's over." Keali`i curses.

"Kea, I'm so sorry. I—"

"Whatevah. It almost worked. But this is nuts. Tami needs help."

"No." Tami shakes her head. "I'm not going to be the reason this falls apart."

I can't help thinking, *But she could be the reason we suddenly get eaten.*

"Hey!" the Hanaman shouts. "Come here! Now!"

Tami's eyes narrow. "No. We're not going to him."

"Tami," I say. "We can't stay in the water."

"Follow me," she says. "Stay back a bit. Just in case."

Tami jettisons her weight belt and swims away. Keali`i and I share a look of confusion. Visible on the water against the Orchid's brilliance, a sailboat turns into view around the far end of the breakwater. It's moving slowly—there's only a light breeze.

Tami's going to intercept the sailboat.

"Tami! Wait!" I shout. She doesn't hear, or she's too determined.

"Why's she doing that?" Keali`i asks, mouth agape.

"She doesn't want to disappoint you."

"Let's go get her. She's completely *lōlō*."

Distantly the Hanaman continues with his empty threats. "This is my last warning! Get over here, now!" He fires a round from a pistol. Keali`i and I flinch.

I unstrap my weight belt in a flash and hold it out to Keali`i.

"Drop it," he says.

I let it go and turn to swim away. Keali`i grabs my leg and pulls me back. I yelp again. Sharks—barracudas—could be swarming us. Or they could be miles away.

"Lei," Keali`i says. "Don't follow her directly."

My eyes widen. Tami, out there all alone, churning up the water in noisy fits, her blood pluming out behind her.

"Fine. But if a feeding frenzy starts, we're all goners anyway."

"Give me your lobsters," Keali`i says. He has the other full bag of *slippahs* around an elbow, the dive light in his hand. "Catch her. I'll follow. Reach the boat before it overshoots us."

The Hanaman lets off another round.

The mainsail of the sailboat flutters. The boat is turning away from the breakwater. Whoever's piloting it must think the shots are being fired at them.

"Go!" Keali`i shouts.

I fly over the water, my fins like rockets. I push the fear away, focus on my breathing. If something comes from below, there's nothing I can do about it.

I hear Tami shouting, "Wait! Stop! Help!"

I swim hard. We're in trouble if we can't catch it, if we can't get on board. Coconut Island is far to my left, connected to shore by a footbridge. We could reach it after a long swim, if the sharks don't find us, but the Tribe will be in that very area.

We're putting a lot of faith in whoever's on this yacht. Could be *anybody*. I haven't seen a new sailboat in weeks. Those that come get commandeered by the Tribes and fitted with tribal flags. The crews are tossed overboard or killed.

"Stop! Please!" Tami yells.

I slow. My side cramps with pain; my lungs and my throat burn. When I raise my head to catch a glimpse of the boat, it seems impossibly far away. Whoever's on board may not even know we're in the water.

I stop and catch my breath. Tami's still swimming, just ahead. Keali`i chugs along behind me. I watch the sailboat. It's a sixteen-footer. Nothing too big. What are they doing here? Folks from Kaua`i, migrating to the Big Island like everyone else? The bottom half of the flag is one solid color. Along the top, stripes radiate from a five-pointed star. I know that flag from visiting the Southwest.

Arizona.

A sailboat from Arizona?

This boat's from the *mainland*.

Adrenaline charges through me. *I need to talk to the people on that boat.*

I bring my fingers to my lips and force a piercing whistle. I whistle again and scream, "STOP! HELP US!"

I turn to Keali`i. "Shine the light at them!"

I charge forward in the water, reach Tami. She pauses and watches me swim past. My friends shout pleas; Keali`i's dive light illuminates the boat in jostled circles. In the distance the Hanaman is silent. Either he's given up or he's racing back along the breakwater to his gang. He knows that if we reach the boat, we all get away.

A figure along the port side of the sailboat. The mainsail swings to the side; the boat turns to port. They're stopping! I barrel toward them.

"Please, help!" I shout as I reach the hull.

"Who are you?" A woman.

"I'm"—I cough—"just a girl. My two friends . . . chased. For fishing without permission. They're gonna get you, too. You can't dock here."

Silence.

The woman says, "Wait there."

"My friend is bleeding badly. Please, we need to get out of the water."

"Wait there." She disappears. Another figure is at the tiller, frozen.

Tami swims beside me. "What are we waiting for?" she's panicky. "Let's go!"

"Shark!" Keali`i screams. "SHARK!"

"Oh, God." Tami claws at the prow of the boat, pulling herself up.

Electricity surges along my spine. I scan the waves. Every shadowy crest looks like a dorsal fin. I slap the side of the boat. "Get us out of here NOW!"

The woman returns, pointing a gun. I want to scream, but it comes out as more of a whimper. *It never ends.*

"Hurry! What are you *doing?*" Tami cries. "I'm cut, bad. PLEASE GET ME OUT OF THE WATER!"

"Pull her out," the woman with the gun says to her companion. "Slowly. Make sure she's not hiding anything."

Tami chokes back sobs. The other figure, a man, lowers a metal ladder off the stern. Tami and I paddle to it.

"No quick movements. You hear? From either of you." The woman with the gun is nervous.

Tami removes her fins and hands them to the man. She pulls herself up and tenderly swings her legs into the boat with a grunt and a moan. She outran the sharks. Bravest thing she's ever done, swimming away from dry land with a gushing leg.

Keali`i is yelling. I only hear one word: "Fin."

I jump out of my skin. The gunwoman's "slow and steady" command is the last thing on my mind. I leap for the ladder and pull myself up, use my knees on the rungs and awkwardly flip into the boat with my fins.

Keali`i!

I look at the bald guy hovering over me. "We need to get him up here!"

Fin. He saw a shark.

The bald man nods, throws the boom of the mainsail wide. He pushes the tiller in the opposite direction. The sail and the jib fill with air, and we cut left. The woman lowers the gun, her eyes everywhere at once—on us, on her shipmate, on the water.

I rip off my fins and spring to my feet. Keali`i's easy to spot, his dive light bobbing on the surface. He's still, drawing the boat toward him with a tractor beam gaze.

He's white as a haole. He saw something.

We glide beside him to port. The woman puts her pistol on the deck and leans over the rails, arm outstretched. We slow with a jerk. Keali`i reaches up and clasps the waiting hand of his rescuer. I scramble, hopping over Tami, and help the woman pull Keali`i, his dive light, and two big bags of slipper lobsters into the boat.

"Hoo!" Keali`i sighs. "Shark fo' sure."

My heart pounds. "Keep going," I tell the bald man. "Don't slow down."

"Hold on a sec," he says. "You're—"

"Listen," I interrupt, "you've been spotted by some very bad people. They plan to take your boat. If they have a motorboat waiting back in one of those inlets, they could still catch you. They're armed."

"And they're good at what they do," Tami adds.

"Ha," says Keali`i. "Not as good as us. You did it, Tami!"

"Go," the woman says, waving to the man. She retrieves her gun. Her grip is white-knuckled.

"Rachel—" the bald guy starts.

"Just go," she says. "We'll figure it out."

She turns back to the three of us and points the gun at Keali`i. "Okay, talk. Start making sense. You drawing us into a trap?"

"You gotta trust us," Keali`i says.

"Trust went overboard with the lights, smartass. What's going on here?"

"Just what I said." I step forward. "We're just . . . high schoolers. No tricks. We have a dive light that works. We went diving for lobsters. A bunch of jerks tried to steal everything. We got away."

"Kids? Being shot at?" the bald man says from the tiller. "This stinks."

"Maybe you're smelling this." Keali`i lobs one of the bags at the bald guy's feet. He dances backward, studying the bulging, moving bag.

Tami takes off her wet suit, turning it inside out as it rolls down her legs. The cut above her knee looks really bad. Blood is flowing freely out of it. I put my hands to my mouth and stifle a moan.

"Rachel, take the helm," the man says. She scrambles and grabs the tiller, her gun locked on Keali`i. The man dashes belowdecks.

Keali`i shakes his head. "Get that outta my face."

Rachel ignores him.

"Hang in there, Tami," I say. I kneel beside her and squeeze her hand. "You did it. You got us over here. We're safe."

Tami starts laughing. I join her. "Where's the shooter?" she asks.

"God," says Keali`i. "Shark burger? I don't think he went in after us. Did he?"

I glance at the breakwater. No one.

Rachel says, "I'm starting to believe you guys." I study her. Her features are wrinkled, and her short, wavy hair is gray. Her hands are bony, and her skin is loose and blotched. Her eyes are everywhere.

"I'm Leilani," I say, reaching out a hand to her.

"Rachel," she says. She takes my hand.

"Arizona?" I ask.

She laughs dryly, nods. "Long story."

"What's the mainland like?" I ask.

She sighs. "Longer story. About as bad as here, I bet, given our welcome."

The man emerges from below, a medical tackle box in his hands. He wears glasses with circular rims. He's broad-shouldered beneath his buttoned shirt. A weight-lifting Gandhi. His eyes and his bright face are disarming, but I wouldn't dare make a sudden move around him. His nice shirt is a Tommy Bahama, new.

He kneels beside Tami. "You lucked out tonight. I'm a doctor. You're going to be okay. I want you to relax. This is all going to work out." He presses a cloth into Tami's thigh. "Hold it there." Blood smears his shirt; he doesn't care.

We pass the edge of the breakwater and turn out to sea. The water's much choppier. I sit down on the port bench, bracing for a rough ride.

"Marcus, we need a plan," Rachel says. "Where are we supposed to supply up? We can't just keep going. What are we going to do with *them*?"

One of the *slippahs* at Rachel's feet has found the opening at the top of the bag. She reaches down and shoves it back in. "Damn, those look good," she mutters.

"Never would have worked," Keali`i says. "I've seen dozens of yachts confiscated. Owners walked the plank. Sometimes outright shot in the head. You guys would have been done for if we hadn't come along."

Marcus finishes cleaning Tami's gash. He puts down fresh gauze and tapes the cut shut. "That'll only hold if you don't move," he tells her. "I'm going to have to clean it out. At least you didn't tear a major artery."

Rachel says to Keali`i, "I sailed into Hilo fifteen years ago. There was no moon. Figured we had a shot of parking and trading. Then the Rorschach just lit up like a *city*."

"Rorschach? You mean Emerald Orchid," I say.

She shrugs. "That's the beauty. Call it how you see it."

"You'd be surprised how I see it," I say.

"Darling, very little surprises me anymore."

Tami and Keali`i and I share a knowing look.

"Where are you headed?" I ask.

"Classified," Marcus says.

"I need to know," I answer roughly. "Are you heading up the island chain? 'Cause you're not going to find more supplies on Maui, or O`ahu. Everyone's coming this way. Are you looking for two weeks' worth of supplies or two months' worth?"

Rachel and Marcus stare me down. I'm holding my breath.

Marcus finally says, "Australia."

"My sister was in Sydney when everything happened," Rachel says. "We . . . Well, we have no other ideas. Spent months trying to figure out what to do."

"I need to take you to my house. My parents can help you. We can set you up. In return, you fix Tami . . . and one other favor."

"Set us up? Meaning, what? What're you offering?" Rachel looks skeptical. It wasn't that long ago that I forced her to turn *away* from land, after all.

"Food. Water. Tools. Whatever you need. We'll give it to you. We've got a farm. Going to be a lot easier to take what we have than you trying to get it anywhere else on the islands. You'll have to fight for it. And you don't want to start for Australia without stocking up. Look, you can get what you need from us . . . a simple trade."

"What's the other favor?" Marcus asks again.

"Later," I say.

Rachel sighs deeply. "Where's your house?" she asks.

"Off of Onomea Bay. One of you has to stay on the boat, take it back out to sea. The doctor can come with us, fix up Tami. If you don't trust us, keep Keali`i on board."

"Ho!" Keali`i exclaims. "Say what?"

"Shut it," I say, watching Rachel and Marcus.

Marcus answers, "How far away is this bay?"

"Less than an hour. It's choppy. There's a hike. You'll be out for a day."

Marcus drifts over to Rachel by the tiller, and they whisper to each other. Keali`i, Tami, and I huddle as well.

"What're you on about, Lei?" Keali`i asks.

"This is our boat. These are the people who will send our message around."

"What?" he says. "They're going to Australia."

"Australia has plants waiting to blow."

"So? This doesn't get you anywhere. You need a better solution. *You're* the one who told me a world tour by boat is no good."

"A lightbulb goes off above your head," I snap, "let me know. Until then I have to try everything short of messages in bottles. Every day the power stays off, more people suffer, right?"

"Lei—"

"Oh, my God," I bark. I put my hands to my mouth. My heart rattles my rib cage.

"What? What is it?" Tami asks.

"Messages," I say. "A lightbulb. Above my head."

Marcus steps over to us. "We'll do it. Rachel will stay out with the boat."

I scarcely hear. My thoughts are racing. *Does Grandpa know Morse code?*

"I'll keep your friend, since you offered," Rachel says.

Keali`i scowls.

Turn off, I tell the Orchid. Again, nothing. Why won't she respond? If I can turn her on—and then turn her off . . . I could talk to an entire hemisphere at once.

"Lei, you okay?" Tami asks.

"I'm fine. Just . . . let me concentrate."

Turn off. No, that's not right. That doesn't mean anything to her. Don't think words. Just . . . *feel* it.

Dim. Fade. Go dark.

"Whoa! What the hell?"

I open my eyes. The resoluteness of night has returned. The Orchid is back to her normal brilliance, but the contrast with a few seconds ago is stark.

I did it.

Brighten. Flare.

The Orchid surges back to brilliance.

Marcus and Rachel fix their gazes upward, alarmed. Tami and Keali`i stare at me. "Lei. Are you doing that?" whispers Tami.

I look between her and Keali`i and grin. "Lightbulb."

CHAPTER 6

It's about five a.m. We turn into Onomea Bay and drop anchor where Dad and I parted ways with the sheriff of Hana over three months ago. We're parked outside the swell, but the waters are rough. My gut swoons as the boat lifts and drops—while simultaneously tilting from side to side—on the rolling ocean.

Rachel has an inflatable raft at the ready along the forward hatch. Marcus prepares a long towrope and ties one end to the raft, his task aided by the faint light of the Orchid.

"Thank you for staying," I say to Keali`i.

"You could even do some fishing," Marcus suggests. "You know how to deep-sea fish?"

"I can catch anything that swims, glides, crawls, squirts, flaps, or slithers."

Marcus pats him on the shoulder. "Thank you, Kea ... um ..."

"Kay-uh-LEE-ee."

"Kay-uh-LEE-ee," the doctor repeats.

Marcus and Rachel lower the raft into the water. I descend first. Marcus follows, and we help Tami slip in.

Keali`i tosses the bags of lobsters down, along with the dive light. "Treat your family to a lobster feast."

We're ready to paddle away, tethered to the sailboat by the towrope. As soon as we're on shore, Rachel will pull the raft back, haul anchor, and disappear to open sea. She guides the rope out as we navigate the forces of the bay. These waters are infested with tiger sharks; good thing we don't have to swim.

My oar hits bottom. Marcus jumps out with Tami in his arms. He carries her to shore and sets her down out of reach of the surf. I trudge forward and sit beside Tami. The raft moves slowly out as Rachel drags it in. My new idea keeps washing over me: Morse code. We should have thought of this three months ago. But I didn't know the Orchid could flare like that. Even now there are challenges. For one, I'll need to learn Morse code.

Dawn is near—I can see the gentle before-glow of the sun deep on the seaward horizon. Tami says, "We should go. The sun's going to make it humid."

I study her leg. Tape covers the gash. Her dressing, changed a few minutes before entering the raft, is nearly soaked through with blood.

"I'll walk," she says. "I'll be okay. Faster we get there, the faster I can get patched up for real."

"I agree," Marcus says. He picks up his medical kit and loops the strap around his shoulder. He's changed into expensive quick-dry pants and a nylon hiking shirt. His hiking boots are new.

I laugh. I'm in a bikini, a wet suit, and surfing booties. I unzip my booties and empty them of water and rocks. Tami wordlessly helps me peel the wet suit off of my legs.

"I'm going to hide the dive light somewhere," I say. I don't want to have it taken away on the road. Too tempting a treasure, even for most honest people. I scramble up the wave-racked rocks beside our landing and stuff the dive light in a dry hole out of the reach of the tide. I roll a large rock of `a`a lava over the top, take a mental snapshot of the hiding spot, and hop back down.

We march up the slope. Thick vines dangle to the pavement like the beaded entryways in Puna hippie shops. Many of the sharpest bends are partially washed out, the steep embankments overgrown, constricting the road into a narrow pathway.

We fill, drink, and refill an empty gallon milk carton with water at a trickling stream. Tami heavily favors her leg, and during some of the steeper stretches, she allows us to prop her up with our interlaced arms, and our shoulders. The sun rises, shimmering through the dense canopy in golden splotches, a blazing reflection bouncing off the ocean behind us. The clamor of birds is deafening. None are native to the islands. The mosquitos we brought here on boats from faraway lands killed off the Hawaiian birds.

I slap at one on my arm. *Bad mosquito.*

As I look at the bloody smear on my arm, I realize: humans certainly left a lasting mark. Even if we kill each other off completely, these islands will always bear our legacy.

We emerge from the jungle, passing into cane fields overshadowed by towering eucalyptus trees. A segment of Highway 19 peeks through the trees at the top.

Tami's losing steam. It's very tiring to help her walk. I hear an approaching vehicle. We retreat into the sugarcane until the car has passed. I've driven on this road over the months and seen people hiding from *me* just like this.

"We could try to flag down a ride," Marcus thinks aloud.

"I wouldn't bother. No one's going to waste their gas on us."

We hobble across the highway and continue *mauka*—upslope. Now we're on a dirt road. We take a breather beneath a giant avocado tree. "How far?" Marcus asks.

"Two miles to the gate. More to the house. I hope someone's at the gate."

Marcus pulls a glass bottle of Grey Goose vodka out of his medical bag and hands it to Tami. "For you."

"Huh?"

"I'm going to have to irrigate that leg and scrape out the infected tissue as soon as we reach the house. The tissue's damaged far down. This is my only anesthetic."

Tami's eyes widen. She unscrews the bottle and takes a swig. She screws up her face like a toothless old man and takes another quick drink.

"It'll thin your blood, so take 'er easy."

"Thanks for sharing," Tami says.

Marcus laughs. "Of all the things our boat could have been fully stocked with at the end of the world, liquor was what we had. We were prepared for a relaxed weekend, not an endless odyssey."

Tami takes a few more gulps. When we rise to finish our hike, she's looking a bit ruddy and too cheerful.

"Don't forget to hydrate," Marcus says, passing Tami the milk carton.

"So, how does a sailboat end up with an Arizona flag on it?" I ask Marcus during our slog, Tami hoisted between us.

Marcus smiles. "We're from Arizona. Rachel had a very successful law practice in Scottsdale."

"Scottsdale," I say, trying to picture where that is.

Marcus chuckles. "It's a fancy way of saying 'not Phoenix.'"

Tami takes another drink. Marcus coaxes the bottle out of her hands. "Slow down, kiddo."

We walk in silence. I realize that Marcus managed to dodge my question.

"I don't get your flag. What're you doing halfway across the Pacific?"

"Oh," he says. "Rachel kept this boat in San Carlos, Mexico, on the Gulf of California, about five hours south of the border."

"Is that where you were when the Orchid came?"

"Rachel was. I was back in Scottsdale."

"Wasn't there a nuclear meltdown out there? Early on?" Father Akoni on Moloka`i had said something about Arizona.

Marcus studies me.

"Lei has her own crazy story," Tami says, breaking the awkward silence. "She was on O`ahu with her dad when the blackout happened. Took them a month to get back. They were stuck in a military camp. Her dad was shot in the shoulder. He was almost executed—by the leader of the Tribe that would've taken your boat."

"Sounds . . . scary," Marcus says.

"It was," I say. I'm silent. I don't want to retell my story, either. Anxiety rises whenever I think about it. But if I share what I went through, he'll be cornered into telling me what happened in Arizona.

So I tell Marcus how Dad and I made it from O`ahu back to the Big Island after the blackout. I relive the nightmare as I'm talking, and the boost of adrenaline propels me up the hill. The slowly unfolding chaos in Honolulu. Escaping the burning hotel. Searching endlessly for a way off of O`ahu with no luck. Our time in the military camp, people dying and starving all around us. Our daring escape from the Marine Corps base, and our shoot-out that won us passage to Moloka`i. Our days in the jungle on Maui, fleeing the deputies and the hunting dogs of the sheriff of Hana. I explain my epilepsy. I mention Father Akoni on Moloka`i only briefly, and I don't mention what happened after we got home.

"You grew up in a hurry," Marcus says.

Tami sniggers unkindly.

"Tami saw the tsunami firsthand," I offer. "Almost killed her. The water actually reached her. Wave was already coming in when she came through the trees and first noticed the bay was low. She ran so hard and so fast that she just barely beat the wave to its high line. Almost got hit by a delivery truck carried on the wave."

"No kidding?" says Marcus.

Tami hoots. "You know she talks to it," she says. "She speaks to the Orchid."

"Tami, stop it."

"No, really," she continues. "They're best buddies. Always sharing visions. She's the reason the Orchid never left."

"Tami, you're drunk." I laugh dryly. "Knock it off, will ya?"

"All buss up," she agrees. She won't stop, though. "It was going to leave. But Lei made it stay."

I pinch Tami's shoulder hard, furious.

"Ow!" she screams. She whips away from both of us. "You know what? I don't need your help. I can walk on my own."

God, what a disaster. I glance at Marcus. Sheepishly, he says, "Sorry. I thought this would calm her down. I should have accounted for the humidity. The dehydration."

He's completely dismissed her comments. Good. "Just . . . no. It's okay."

Tami refuses to let us support her. She stays several paces back, no matter how slow we go.

When I see the turnoff to our house around a bend in the road, I quicken my pace, leaving the others behind. Grandpa's in a chair beneath a giant albizia tree. His arms are lazily crisscrossed around a shotgun. A rifle is propped against the tree trunk. Our horse, ʻImiloa, grazes several feet behind him. Our guard dogs bark, and he rises.

"Grandpa, it's me!" I shout, just in case he's feeling trigger-happy.

"Moʻopuna!" He shoulders the shotgun by its strap. "Hush! Hush!" he commands the dogs. "An den? What're you doing out here, eh? Why the bikini?"

I laugh. He unlocks the gate and swings it open. The dogs surround me.

"What you got there?" he asks.

"*Slippahs!*" I hold the bags high for him to study. The dogs sniff excitedly.

He whistles. "Ho! Never seen so much *kau kau*."

"Caught the biggest one myself. See it?"

"Yeah. Where'd you get that? Why you here?"

"Long story. Tami's hurt. We need to get up to the house fast. The guy with her is a doctor from the mainland."

Grandpa gives me the stink-eye, then glances down the road at my straggling companions. "You remind me sometime to stop being surprised at anything you do."

"You know Morse code?"

"What? Oh, Lei. I used to. Haven't thought about it in forty years. Why?"

I lean in close. "I can make the Orchid blink."

I watch as the words—and their full significance—settle in. His eyes deepen. "That was you this morning?"

I nod.

"Lei."

"I know." We look up. The Orchid's faintly visible in broad daylight, in the same spot she's been all morning. Right above us.

"Take ʻImiloa up to the house. Everyone's up there. Busy, but around. Get them *slippahs* in a pot. Go. I'll handle your friends. Try to remember if I got a Morse code book around, or something. Get some rice going, too. Make some *musabi*, yeah? *Uku grinds* tonight."

I shout down to Tami, "I'll be right back with the truck, okay?"

Tami stops in the road, leans over, and throws up. Marcus jumps to her side and pats her on the back. Tami wipes her mouth with one hand and then wipes away tears with the other. All one hundred pounds of her are at their wit's end.

"Ho!" Grandpa says.

"She's buss, Grandpa," I explain.

"You think?"

"Anesthesia for the stitches."

"No stitches," Marcus calls. "It'll need to heal open, to control for infection."

I turn to Grandpa. "I'm off. Marcus is good *kine*. You can trust him."

"K'den."

We stride over to the horse. I give ʻImiloa a rub on the

84

nose before mounting her. *Ugh. Riding a horse in a bikini?* Grandpa takes the *slippahs* while I reluctantly settle into the saddle and take the reins.

"Okay, girl. Quick but easy." I give her a gentle kick, and we're off. The dogs canter beside me.

I trot up the shady driveway of my house. Our stand-alone garage is before me, the door open, tools and building materials spilling out of it. No vehicles in sight. My rowdy entourage barrels toward the porch.

Kai comes out onto the porch and stares at me. "Wow. Hi."

"Hey there. You gonna help me or what?"

Kai snaps out of his trance. "Mom! Lei's home!" He looks me over and turns back to the door. "She has seafood." He darts down and takes the *slippahs* so I can swing off the horse.

The dogs retreat to their patrol grounds as I go inside. Kai dashes for the kitchen, but I stop in the living room, take in a deep breath. That familiar smell. Home.

Mom appears in the living room wearing a sun hat and leather gloves. Her knees are caked with fresh mud. She's holding pruning shears in one hand and a trowel in the other. She sees me and stops, her confused expression melting into some semblance of understanding.

I can hear cookware clanging in the kitchen. Kai's on a mission to liberate the giant boiling pot from the aluminum rubble in the cabinets. Mom looks me over, squeezes my arm to make sure I'm real.

"Tami's hurt."

"What?"

"She's here. At the bottom of the road with Grandpa. We have a doctor with us. I need to go get them with the truck. Where's Dad?"

"Doctor?" she begins.

She's interrupted by Kai. "Mom, could you turn on the propane?"

"What's he doing in there?" she asks me.

"Trying to boil lobsters."

She puts her garden tools down and turns toward the kitchen.

I follow her and explain about Tami's cut, hitching a ride in the yacht—leave out being shot at. I tell her my Morse code idea. She takes on the exact same expressions as Grandpa.

"Dad has the truck over at Hank's. You better go find him before they have the bed filled with *kalo* and corn."

I dart to my room, put on a tee and shorts, socks and tennies. The clothes feel glorious against my skin. I run downstairs and out the door, mount the horse, and race for the Millers' house.

The clouds are gathering. Dark-bellied behemoths that promise rain.

I come around a bend in the drive and nearly collide with the truck. Paul is standing guard beside the old truck, his shotgun pointed at me. I yank on the reins, skid to a halt, nearly fall off.

Paul lowers the shotgun. "Last person I was expecting."

"Hi, Paul. Where's my dad? I need the truck for a bit."

"They're harvesting our first corn, getting ready to burn on G." Paul leans through the window of the truck and honks the horn in a practiced pattern. "We're almost set for the market tomorrow. Check it out."

I walk to the bed of the truck with Paul. "Wow." The bed is half-full of ears of corn and apple bananas—tiny, extra sweet bananas. "That's really exciting. And all that concern over the seed stock."

"Yeah, they're working out great."

"How's Chloe doing? And Sara?"

"We're hanging in there. It's easy to get discouraged. I lay awake most nights. Chloe will never understand the way things were, you know? Anyway, I'm rambling. You should come by for a visit."

"No, yeah, totally," I say, trailing off. I wonder: does *my* dad stay up at night thinking about these things?

"Come see. I'm making her a high chair out of koa wood now."

"That sounds beautiful. She'll love it."

"Lei!"

I whip around. Dad. He's petting `Imiloa. "What's going on?"

I wave good-bye to Paul and trot over to Dad. "We need to take the truck down to Grandpa. We'll leave the horse with Paul. I'll explain on the way."

"Is this really that urgent, Lei? We're in the middle of—"

"Yes. It is."

"Ah. Okay. Well, key's in the ignition."

I fire our old beast up, wrangle it into first. Dad jumps into the passenger seat.

"Punch it, Chewy," he says.

I give him my best Chewbacca growl, and we're off.

*　*　*

The rain is coming down in sheets, but the clouds have already broken. Tami's passed out on the couch. I think she's exhausted more than anything else; we were up all night, after all.

Dad's marveling over the quarter-full bottle of Grey Goose. "That bottle would fetch us a gallon of gas," he grumbles. "I could have just knocked Tami out with a two-by-four."

"Dad!"

"Finish the bottle, Mike," Mom says, "so no one has to bother hitting *you* with a plank of wood."

Kai leans over the back of the sofa, nibbling on a warm strip of lobster tail, watching Marcus tend to the gash. Marcus's expression darkens. "I'm worried about infection. She needs a new Betadine gauze daily. You guys need to get ahold of some good IV antibiotics."

"That won't be easy," Dad says.

Marcus winces. "No doubt, but you need to do it."

Marcus retires to Kai's room for a nap. I move to the dining room with Mom and Dad, gulp down a glass of water and a slipper lobster. After transporting Tami to the house, Dad returned the truck to Paul in the fields and rode `Imiloa home in the rain. Grandpa remained at his post down by the first gate.

While we pick through the shells of several slipper tails, I battle the noise of the rain on our aluminum roof and explain to Mom and Dad all that happened during the night. When they hear about the bullets, they share a few choice expressions, but let me finish the whole account without interruption.

"Keali`i's on that boat right now, out at sea?" Dad asks.

I nod shyly. The way he says it makes me feel guilty, like I've sacrificed him.

"That's really scary." He pushes his plate of empty shells to the side. "I don't like it. That lawyer sounds a bit edgy."

I glower at him. "This story is full of gunfire and sharks, and the lawyer is what scares you?"

"What's done is done," Mom says. "She can't afford to second-guess this decision. We all know Keali`i can take care of himself." She leans in close. "This Morse code idea sounds promising."

"I'll make it work." The rain shuts off, like someone flipped a lever.

We're silent. Mom and Dad study each other, deep in thought. Dad raps his fingers on the table. "This could be the beginning of our endgame. We should draft some messages. Maybe in a few languages. Find someone who knows Morse code backward and forward. Not Grandpa. He's too rusty. Hell, we could even check the library."

"Hey, nuclear powers of the globe," I say. "Hurry up and

let your unstable materials go critical. Bury all the rest so a teenager in Hawai`i can finally let the Star Flowers migrate home to another galaxy."

Dad scratches his stubbly cheek. "I'm not worried about the message. The hardest part will be pulling off the delivery. You'll have to practice. *Privately*. Over the South Pole, maybe? And you'll have to repeat the messages. A lot. And *no* location info."

"Where's Buzz?" I ask.

"You mean Gandalf? He'll arrive exactly when he means to. Don't worry about him. We don't need him for this."

We haven't heard from Buzz since the morning after my birthday. When my parents dropped me off with Tami at the market yesterday, we ran into Richard, Buzz's astronomer friend up on Mauna Kea. He explained that Buzz had traveled to Kona after visiting the site of the pearl impact, that he's planning to come down to see us as soon as he can.

I close my eyes, slowly lean forward, startle awake as I lose my balance.

Mom rubs my back. "Go to bed, Lei. We'll wake you before Marcus tells us his tale. You still have a long night ahead of you."

I fast-forward several hours through our plan and groan. I'm going back to Onomea Bay with Marcus later. Keali`i and I will hitch a ride with them on the sailboat back over to Hilo. We plan to catch some z's at Keali`i's empty place, and then we'll spend tomorrow hunting down antibiotics for Tami.

I pull away from my chair and hug each of them. Tears are suddenly pouring down my cheeks. I can hear bullets entering the water. *Whoov.* I can feel that desperate need for breath in my lungs. I'm seconds from inhaling dark water again. I see the plume of Tami's blood gushing into the bay, and I hear Keali`i's bone-chilling cry: "Shark!"

Tami's safe for now, but I have no idea how badly she's hurt. Marcus says it all depends on the meds we can find. I bury my face in Mom's shoulder and Dad's chest. I haven't felt this exhausted—this scared and uncertain—since . . .

Well, it hasn't been that long, actually.

CHAPTER 7

It's evening. I'm somewhat rested. The coquis are pleased with the afternoon rains, but they still have questions. We're downstairs on the couches, and Kai's nestled on my lap. Next to me Tami pops a piece of lobster in her mouth. She's wearing a fresh set of my clothes, jean shorts cut well above her injury, and a green cami. I examine her bandage on the outside of her lower thigh.

"Does it hurt?"

"Shh," she says. "Don't remind me."

"So, how long are you going to be on my couch?"

Marcus approaches. He kneels and inspects his handiwork. "She's promised me not to move that leg for several weeks. You'll need to splint it if she's not being good."

"Hanamen. Sharks. Lawyers," Dad says. "Could have been a lot worse."

Tami nods. "This sucks, but I'm convinced we would have been shot if we'd listened to Keali`i. Lei saved our lives this morning."

"She has a habit of doing that," Dad says, and winks.

I hold up my palm. He gives me a high five.

"And you brought da *grinds*, yeah? Here's your prize catch, Lei." Grandpa presents me with my giant *slippah* on our big serving platter.

"We're dying to hear your story, Marcus," Dad says. "Firsthand information about the mainland. Almost as valuable as a roll of toilet paper."

I wish he were joking. Real TP is worth more than gold.

"Before you start . . ." Grandpa shuffles to the front door, retrieves a lei of fresh plumeria flowers from a coat hook, and puts the lei around Marcus's shoulders, reciting a *mele ho`okipa* welcome chant:

He lei lani nā hōkū `imo`imo ē
Nāna `oe `olua `oukou i alaka`i
Heahea nā leo o nā kūpuna ē
Me nā kumu me nā haumāna
`Ike i nā lei pua o Kapālama ē
E hula nei me ka `Ōlauniu

Ua hiki maila, he ho`okipa mai
Na nā pua lei a Pauahi
E lei ē, he wehi lei

The twinkling stars form a heavenly lei
Which has led you here
Be welcomed by the voices of our ancestors
The teachers and the students
See the flower lei of Kapālama
Dancing in the ʻŌlauniu breeze

You have arrived and are welcomed
By the descendants of Pauahi
Wear this flower adornment

"Thank you, Mr. Hawika. *Mahalo.*"

"*De nada,*" Grandpa says, and we all laugh.

The room grows still. "Your turn to share. You ready?" I ask Marcus.

"Well"—Marcus sighs—"I won't sugarcoat it. It's horrible out there. And it started out horrible. The day the Rorschach came and shut down all the power, the Valley of the Sun was fighting a nasty heat wave. It was reaching a hundred and fifteen degrees all week."

"No way!" says Kai. "You cook eggs on the sidewalk?"

"Pretty much."

"Kai, quiet," Mom hushes him.

Marcus clears his throat, begins in earnest. "The Friday before the blackout I was between patients at my practice, and Rachel called. We're partners, never married. So—she had been in court in San Diego. She told me they won their case. She wanted to celebrate with a weekend sail. Rachel grew up winning fleet races. Competed in the Olympics twice.

"'Meet me in San Carlos in one week. I'm flying down tomorrow,' she told me. 'I'll have us all ready to sail by the time you arrive.'

"That was the Friday before the end. It was the last time we spoke before communications cut out.

"Monday I was pretty shaken by the news that the president had gone missing. I called my financial advisor, but he convinced me to hold tight. Later, rumors started surfacing about the president of France. The Japanese prime minister. All missing. The markets plunged. I called my guy back; the line was busy. I logged on to my account, intending to sell everything just as the bottom fell out of the market. I watched the Fed step in and shut down the Exchange. I couldn't think straight. I made it through one more patient, tried to see the following one, but I was too much of a mess.

"I knew I had lost somewhere around two million."

"Whoa!" Kai says. "Two million *dollars?*"

Marcus nods. "'It'll all come back tomorrow,' I kept telling myself. But I knew it didn't work like that. I went straight to a bar. My life savings were gone. I hardly remember crawling into bed that night. When the blackout happened, I was sound asleep along with most of the nation. I missed the president's middle-of-the-night speech that was cut off, the initial power outage, everything.

"The heat woke me on Tuesday. It was about six a.m. I sat up in bed, dripping with sweat, a hangover pounding.

Ninety-nine degrees *inside* the house. The power was out. No TV. No computer. No phone. I turned to the fridge for water. When I opened the door, a blast of cold air hit me. I stuck my head in there. After two big glasses of water, I headed for the clinic. My car wouldn't start. Very fancy fuel-injection system and too much fried circuitry, I guess. But I owned two classics: a 1961 Jaguar E-Type and a '77 Harley. The Jag started, and I headed for the freeway.

"Mostly older cars out there. Felt like Phoenix had fish-tailed back in time. Power was out at the office. The news-paper was delivered, an image of the president standing in front of blue curtains plastered over page one. I read the paper cover to cover, waited around the clinic until about ten, spoke with staff. No one had seen the president's speech.

"We put up CLOSED UNTIL FURTHER NOTICE signs, and then I went to the newspaper, the *Arizona Republic*, and camped out in their lobby. Their air was working, thanks to generators, and they had water. I picked up local news from incoming reporters. The canals around town were in-undated with swimmers. Three kids had already gone miss-ing, sucked into drains. Old folks were dropping like flies. Inmates were being shuffled from prison to prison. The Palo Verde Nuclear Generating Station, fifty miles from Phoe-nix, was having issues, but it wasn't clear what was wrong.

"A few people had noticed a weird knot against the blue haze to the southeast. I went outside to see for myself. Sure enough, there it was, like that first star in the evening, faint but visible if you knew right where to look. I convinced myself it was a comet, that it must be affecting our electronics. But . . . comets take days—or weeks—to run their course. *My God*, I thought, *what if we're without power for weeks?*

"I thought of Rachel, out there on her yacht, sipping a margarita, or staying cool in the surf at her beach house. I raced home. Highways were empty. People were hunkered down, glued to their pools. Phoenix metro had a population of 1.5 million people. But I felt like I was driving through a dusty Route 66 way station.

"I spent five minutes at the house. Got into my safe and pulled out a ton of cash, grabbed my spare gas tanks, my big ice chest, water jugs. Then I headed straight for the nearest grocery store.

"It was closed. I circled the parking lot for a moment, not sure what to do. I peeled away, mapping out the next several stores in my mind. The next one was closed, too. It suddenly seemed silly to be going through all this trouble, roasting all over Phoenix, when I could be back in my pool. Just as I pulled away, someone on the sidewalk tossed a rock through the store window and disappeared inside. Others followed. I joined them. I raced through the dim, stuffy aisles with a cart. Everyone stuck together. My cart was full, and I was scared to death that a cop would come running down the aisle with handcuffs and a Taser gun, so I fled. I tossed everything into the car and drove away, my heart booming.

"Preachers were reporting developments all over the AM stations. Power outages were happening in Flagstaff,

Tucson, Yuma, Albuquerque, Las Cruces, Las Vegas. Fried transformers everywhere. I listened to the one-way conversations as I drove to a gas station with vintage pumps. A gallon of gas went for $14.99. I filled up the tank, both gas canisters, and a water jug. Paid in cash.

"I arrived home at dusk. Everyone was outside. Kids playing in the street, neighbors chatting. No one noticed the knot in the sky. Still dim enough to miss if you weren't studying it.

"So I secured my spoils and went for a quick swim. Then I joined my street's block party. I pointed the knot out to several of my neighbors. There was awe and magic in the desert sky that night. There was no fear, only . . . wonder.

"In the morning I tried my old Harley. I reset the contact points and recharged the electrolyte solution in the battery. It fired up, and I took it to my office, locked up the practice. The paper came. There had been a scare at the Palo Verde Nuclear Generating Station; backup pumps had failed but had been brought back online. I went over to the hospital to volunteer. Crowds were swelling. Hundreds had become stranded outside, exposed in long lines and mobs at every entrance. People were getting heatstroke just trying to get *into* the hospital. I worked straight past midnight. Pacemaker wearers were brought in; their devices had suddenly failed. Prepper colony firefights. Bullet wounds. A church orchestrated a mass suicide. Horrible. Absolutely horrible.

"I drove home, numb, through a dark city, the anomaly

looming overhead. The term Rorschach Cloud had started going around. On the drive home it was bright green and flickering with lightning and strangely beautiful.

"I returned to the hospital late the next morning. The backup power there went out at three p.m. Crowds lined the halls. We begged people to go home. The building became unbearable long before the floodlights died. But even those went out, leaving the corridors black.

"I sat in my pool that night watching the Rorschach with brewing hatred. I couldn't stay in Phoenix. Surely Rachel would have headed home by now. Unless she was waiting . . . for me . . . knowing that *I* would come for *her*. But that didn't make any sense. I would be insane to flee south of the border, looking for her, given all that was going on, and she would know it. Could I even get into Mexico? Maybe she was stuck down there, unable to cross because of a lockdown.

"The next morning I went to her house. Nothing. I went to the firm downtown, but the entire tower was locked up. Still, it seemed lunatic to flee Phoenix by way of Mexico, chasing after someone I hadn't heard from in a week.

"The explosion at the nuclear plant the next morning changed everything."

* * *

I give Kai's hand a squeeze. "You okay, buddy?"

"Yeah. Ow, Lei."

"Oh, sorry." I give his hand a rub.

He whispers, "*You* okay, buddy?"

"Shh!" Dad says.

Kai and I sink back into the sofa and hold each other tight.

Marcus takes a drink of water, smiles politely at all of us, and continues. "I was in my pool Friday morning, ducked below the surface, when I felt a strange pressure suddenly squeeze me. My ears popped. The pool shook. I surfaced. One large wave rippled back and forth along the length of the pool. I heard shouts throughout the neighborhood. I scrambled up to my balcony. To the west, on the horizon, a thick column of white smoke rose, drifting toward Phoenix. I could see a fire on the ground, black smoke mixing with the plume of steam. The Palo Verde reactor. That cloud reaching out toward the city was *radioactive*. There was a second explosion. I saw the flash of it and the billowing of new smoke before I heard it. The shockwave came a split second later, stopping my heart. Then, finally: *boom!* In just a few seconds, as screaming and shouting built around me, I watched the cloud double in size, and then double again.

"I'll never forget that moment, guys. It suddenly seemed so obvious that this would happen. We built this ticking time bomb . . . and forgot that it had a timer.

"I snapped out of my paralysis. Grabbed a duffel, filled it, shot into the garage. I knew the roads would get too crowded for a car, so I focused on the Harley. I stuffed what I could into the two trunks, my medical bag. Gas and water. Filled the tank, used rope and duct tape to secure the larger gas canister and a jug of water to the backseat. I took everything: cash, passport, savings bonds, a couple hard drives of photos.

"The cloud was consuming the western sky. Billowing plume, tan-colored high up, dark brown and thick as mud along the ground. *It's all radioactive. Falling on you already.* I peeled away from my house, shaking all over.

"The bike was slightly off-balance, heavy liquids sloshing around. The 101 was a logjam. I turned around, darted through the streets, made it all the way to the Superstition Mountains in a blur.

"Everywhere—in spite of the heat wave—cactuses were in bloom. The slopes of the Superstitions were dusted with yellows, oranges, and reds. I slowed to a halt, and I looked behind me, and I bawled. I was a hundred miles east of the Palo Verde plant. Yet the cloud hovered over Phoenix, big as a monsoon storm. I wiped away tears with trembling hands. Black death descending upon a million people. *I'll never be able to come back here*, I realized.

"I turned onto the 60, a long stretch of desert highway. The attack blindsided me. Someone darted out at me. I swerved. I was on the asphalt, my bike ghost-riding away. I cursed and stood, confused. My leg was scraped, but I ran for my bike. I picked it up, surrounded by stunned onlookers. My gas and water were still in place. I stared down my attacker. Just a kid. He really wanted my ride, but I had the support of the crowd. I took off. After that I was more careful.

"In Tucson the black cloud was visible to the north, but no one understood that they were in the shadow of a nuclear catastrophe. I-10 was at a standstill. Even the southbound lanes were backed up with traffic headed *toward* Phoenix. The families in the minivans, trapped between more minivans, or broken down on the side of the road—I couldn't ignore the mothers with babies, those on foot, exposed to the high sun. I wanted to stop and help, to shout, 'Turn around! It's radioactive!' But there were too many people to tell."

"You didn't warn *anybody*?" Kai asks.

"Kai, stop it," says Mom.

I don't respond, but I agree with Kai. How could he not stop and tell people to avoid going north?

"You're right." Marcus sighs. "I should have said something. I was so stunned. You have to realize . . . No. There's no excuse." His guilty eyes linger on me and Kai.

"We all could have done more," Dad says. "We all have our regrets. What you did makes perfect sense to me. You don't need to explain yourself. You don't need to apologize."

"Yeah, well, thank you." Marcus takes a deep breath, starts in again. "Weirdest thing: I was fixated on the desert as I cut across the Tucson Mountains. Saying good-bye, you know? Saguaros along the road—thick as pines. Tall and proud, like a desert people, bearing witness to the last days of humanity. They finally outlived us, and I felt so *small* as I raced past them.

"'Rachel,' I kept telling myself. I needed to be with her. I followed other motorcyclists, weaving through the lanes of stopped traffic and along the shoulders toward the border. Thinking: *What if the border's closed? What if they take my bike, my fuel?*

"The U.S. entry *was* closed. Waiting for the power. Mexican border officials were stopping SUVs and trucks, looking for weapons, but I crossed into Mexico with a nod to the official waving traffic through. My eyes were everywhere, every little thing a threat. Hordes milled about, desperate to get into the United States. But how could they know about the Palo Verde explosion? Word only traveled as quickly as . . . me. In a very real way I was breaking the sound barrier.

"So I arrived in San Carlos just before dark, pulled into Rachel's driveway, and cut the engine. She was on the steps before I had my helmet off, and threw her arms around me. I stuttered, cried.

"'Stop!' I pushed her back, overcome by a horrible thought. *What have I done? Am I radioactive? Will I expose her to radiation? I shouldn't have come.*

"'Phoenix is gone, Rachel. It's gone.' I told her everything. She'd inch forward as I spoke, and I'd back away.

"She gripped my hand, pulled me to her. 'What else is left?' she said.

"'Just each other.'

"We fled San Carlos that night. I thought we'd swing around Baja, head up the coast. But Rachel reasoned that other nuclear plants all over the west would also go. So we headed south in her yacht, *Cibola*. We picked up a guy in Mazatlán. He wanted a ride as far down the coast as we would take him. Three minutes out from the dock he pulled a gun. Rachel let loose the mainsheet and turned into the wind. The sail filled, and the boom swung around like a baseball bat and clobbered the guy. He was knocked out for a while. We took the gun and left him on the dock. No more passengers after that. Until Leilani, Tami, and Keali`i.

"We hoarded food, ate as little as possible, honed our skills at fishing and bartering, and just . . . survived.

"When the new Rorschach appeared, I knew it was alien and that it had spawned, or split. We hoped they would leave. They shrank away for a few nights, then came screaming back. I feared they'd split again, become four, then eight.

"As we went south, the power outage seemed to matter less to local folk. But in the cities . . . We heard of horrible disasters. Massive outbreaks of dysentery, other diseases. Many Central American capitals were war zones. Gangs ruled the streets. Nicaragua and Honduras were at war. Coups. Mass suicides. Constant talk of Rapture.

"We got as far as northern Colombia before we had a plan. We knew the world had ended, that the Rorschachs weren't leaving. We decided to make for Australia by way of the Galapagos and Easter Island and Hawai`i. Rachel is something else. She navigated by stars. We couldn't even use our compass—the needle was spinning, useless."

He lets out a deep sigh, opening his arms. "And now here we are, still spinning. Useless."

CHAPTER 8

I glance around, suddenly whisked out of the Sonoran Desert, give Kai another squeeze. "You okay?" This time he doesn't answer. His eyes are narrow slits. "You angry?" Of course he's angry. His future is gone. He missed the mainland a lot after we moved here. The idea that we'll never be able to go back there—I feel it, too—it's like a close friend has died. He loved baseball, the Giants, talked about how he planned to go to a home game in San Francisco. He never mentions that anymore.

"I feel it, too, buddy. It hurts." I give him a tighter squeeze. "Remember that he's wrong, though: the Southwest *isn't* gone. It's all still there. We're keeping that from happening."

He startles me, quickly turning and wrapping his arms around me. My eyes mist. His childhood is so different from mine. He never talks about anything but chores. He has no friends to play with. We need to balance him out or there's going to be no spark left in him.

We're all losing our spark. It's killing all of us. It's not enough to survive.

"Dad," I say in a whisper after Kai jumps up to grab some water. "I want to tell Marcus. He should know. He deserves to know."

Dad shakes his head. "No. Listen. You can't tell people anything. No one can know who you are."

"Dad. He's hurting."

"Everybody hurts, Lei. But you're working on it. Once that Orchid starts flickering out messages and people realize someone pulls the strings of the beast that keeps the power away, you're going to make enemies. Even these visitors . . . you never know. *No one* can know who you are."

Grandpa shuffles inside with several plastic bags filled with corn, `uala, mangoes, and guanabanas. He presents them to Marcus. "We'd like you and Rachel to have this. *Mahalo* for sharing your story."

"Thank you," Marcus says.

"There's more in the truck. Plastic milk jugs filled with water, a bottle filled with POG juice, a few eggs, a bag of charcoal, some paperback novels, vegetables and fruits, loaves of bread, a strip of smoked pig, and a mason jar full of poi."

I change back into my swimsuit and booties. Marcus hands me notes on which he's written generic and brand names of meds that Tami needs. I stuff them into one of Mom's old plastic field vials, seal it, and drop it into my backpack. We've decided that Keali`i and I will swim ashore at

106

Richardson's Beach in Hilo as *Cibola* makes a close pass and look for Tami's meds. I'm amazed they're letting me do this after what happened this morning, but it saves Dad the trip into town and a lot of gas.

I sit down beside Tami. "You going to survive here without me?"

"Are you kidding? Feels like I just scored a weekend at the Hilton Waikoloa."

I force a smile. "Well, enjoy our beach. I'll see you tomorrow night. Try to be good until I get back with your meds."

"I'll do my best."

Dad and Marcus slide into the truck on either side of me. Grandpa calls, "Shotgun!" then sits in the bed with a shotgun. We roll the old truck down the hill, past the highway, and as far along the scenic route to Onomea Bay as the road will allow. Dad only turns on the engine for half a mile of the whole trip. "Gravity's the one resource we'll never run out of," he says.

We keep the lights off, even though they tend to work in this old beater. The Orchid is beyond the horizon, but the baby is visible, casting a fainter green and purple radiance, and we can still navigate the deteriorating roads. When alone, the baby is a black light. Dad's white shirt glows against the UV light it casts. Under the jungle canopy along the descent to the bay, we slow to a blind crawl and finally stop. Dad inches out a signature fifty-point turn, in case we have to depart in a hurry later.

Grandpa stays with the truck. Marcus, Dad, and I hike

through darkness down to the shore. No sailboat is on the water.

"We're early," Marcus says. "I'm not surprised they aren't loitering about. But signal anyway?"

I scramble up onto the rocks. The dive light is right where I stashed it. I point it at the water and flash out the pattern we had arranged. Good practice for Morse code, I tell myself.

I send out our signal every fifteen minutes. I sit off by myself, listening to the waves crash above the sound of the coqui frogs, watching the baby Star Flower rise to purple brilliance over the water. Finally the mainsail glows coming around the cliffs to the north. I give the signal one last time.

Slowly the yacht draws nearer and the mainsail collapses. A few minutes later Keali`i paddles toward us in the raft, his purple-white teeth visible like a Cheshire cat.

I wade out to him as he arrives. "Hey there," I say. "Everything okay?"

"All good. I just spent the day deep-sea fishing with a rich older woman. Dream come true. Is Tami mo'bettah?"

"She's at the house, recovering."

"Good, good." He jumps into the water, and we haul the raft onto shore together.

We load Marcus's haul onto the raft. Two rambutans—strange golfball-sized fruits—glow fluorescent red within their bag. Keali`i picks up my backpack, then pauses. "This yours?"

"Yes."

108

"Aren't we going back to your place?"

"No. Your place. We're hitching a ride back into town. We need to find medicine for Tami first thing in the morning. Dad's picking me up tomorrow."

"My place?" He frowns. "So it's back on the boat?"

"Yup. You get to see your dream date all over again."

"K'den." He tosses the backpack into the raft.

"Careful! There's a quart of gasoline in there!"

"Wha? Why?"

"To barter with. Tami's meds might not be easy to come by."

"Ah, sure they will! I gotcha covered."

"You don't even know what she needs."

"Doesn't matter. I know right where to go."

All four of us lift the loaded raft back into the water. I give Dad a hug good-bye. "See you tomorrow night at the banyan tree."

He kisses my forehead, and we're off.

I fall asleep for the hour it takes to return to Hilo Bay. Keali`i nudges me hard to wake me when it's time for us to jump. Rachel shakes my hand. "I wish your family the best." She turns to Keali`i. "Write often, darling. I'll never forget our time together in Hawai`i."

Keali`i blows her a kiss.

Marcus steps forward. I take his waiting hand, hesitate, and then continue: "It's not a wasteland."

"What was that?"

I bite my lip, turn away. *What are you doing? You're not*

supposed to say anything. I shake my head, turn back. *No, they should know. They deserve to have hope.* "The Southwest. Don't worry about it, okay? It's going to be okay. You can go back to your saguaros, if you want."

He drops his hand, considers me, then his face closes. He thinks I don't get it, the radiation. *Just tell him. You should have told him at the house. Secrets be damned.*

"We're drifting, Leilani," Rachel warns.

I know you are. There's no time. "Never mind. Forget it."

Keali`i and I put on our flippers, and I strap my mask around my forehead. I look at Marcus and Rachel one last time. Keali`i flips backward into the water. I hesitate. No time to explain the truth. But maybe somebody else can tell him. "You know what?" I say to Marcus. "You could stop in Moloka`i on your way east. On the north shore there's a low shelf. A town called Kualapu`u. They'll treat you nicely, maybe even give you more supplies. You might even be able to help a couple Kiwi or Aussie refugees get home. I'm sure there's plenny sheltering there. Up to you."

Marcus cocks his head, considering it. "Thanks. We'll keep that in mind."

"If you stop, ask to see a priest there named Akoni. Tell him I say hi. Tell him . . . tell him I *did* listen. Tell him I went up to Mauna Kea, and I listened. It's important. Please tell him: I went up to Mauna Kea, and I listened."

Marcus looks confused. "Okay."

Keali`i calls out from the water. He already sounds distant. "What's the holdup?"

"Thank you! For everything, Leilani," Marcus says. "Good luck getting those meds. We're lucky to have met you."

"Thank you," I say. "For rescuing us. For helping Tami. *A hui hou.*" I set the mask over my eyes and lean overboard.

Keali`i and I head for Richardson's Beach at the very end of the bay. We advance slowly, come ashore on the small bar of black sand, and remove our flippers. For the next forty minutes we carefully walk through the darkness of Keaukaha. Once we reach our bikes, stashed near the start of the breakwater last night, the final half mile to Keali`i's house goes more quickly.

Keali`i tows Tami's bike alongside his own as we pedal inland through tall jungle trees and curtains of ivy with leaves as broad as medieval shields. It's very dark; only our wheel reflectors dimly shine in loops in the black light. He's been so patient through all this. I'm pretty sure I know why. "Hey," I call over. "You like Tami?"

I hear him chuckle. We pedal along. "What's it to you?" More silence. I wait.

"She's good *kine*, Keali`i."

"Who says *I'm* looking? Ever think of that?"

Whatevah, I think. *What was I expecting, a confession of undying love?*

I approach his ramshackle bungalow with an air of reverence. *His parents died here.* In the tsunami. I can't begin to comprehend. It could just be my imagination, but I think the wood of the porch and even the walls is still wet. I shiver as we creak up the steps with only the distant glow of the baby Star Flower to guide our eyes. An old gum wrapper lodged between planks burns white. It's always so eerie on moonless nights when the baby glows without the mother drowning out the UV. Eerier now than ever on this rickety lanai.

He hurries through the dark hallway, locking doors. He drags a cot into the empty den. "You take this. My bed," he says. "Just stay out here, okay?"

"You sure? What'll you sleep on?"

"I got a hammock."

"What's in those rooms?"

"Just . . . rubbish. Half of it waterlogged. It's embarrassing, okay? I was never consulted on this plan. Stay out of my stuff."

"Sorry."

He retreats into the darkness. I call after him. "Keali`i?"

"Yeah?"

"Thanks for doing that today."

"Hey, it worked out fine, yeah? Glad Tami's doing better. Those two were all right. Hope they make a good go of it out there."

"Keali`i?"

"What?"

"What were their names? Your parents."

He sighs. Hesitates. "Never There and Name Your Price."

"Keali`i!" I glower at him.

His face falls. "Sorry. They were rough, but they don't deserve that. Ernie. Loretta."

112

"I'm so sorry," I say.

He disappears into the back. I fall onto the creaky cot, still in my damp swimsuit, and sleep. I see dark brown and black clouds everywhere my dreams turn. And then I'm no longer dreaming but floating, boundless, the Earth beside me, a womb of vivid breath and heat and mist.

Brighten.

Dim.

I flex my new muscles. It's slow. Awkward. Tiring. It'll be a while before I can do this quickly enough that the right people will recognize and understand. And Dad's right: don't practice in plain sight of half the globe. I turn, steer. Antarctica drifts into prominence. I draw closer.

Brighten.

Dim.

I will practice until I can walk, then run, then leap. I have to make it work. We cannot lose more Ernies and Lorettas and the hopes of all those who flee across oceans in search of something to replace a home they should never have had to leave behind.

CHAPTER 9

In the morning, I see the sheriff of Hana.

I'm biking with Keali`i toward town, zooming past a trickle of pedestrians. An approaching caravan of ancient civilian pickup trucks and military Humvees takes up both lanes and pushes us off the shoulder. Keali`i curses, but I yank his arm. "Quiet!" Gunmen stand in the truck beds, firepower at the ready. I shrink into the ferns, pulling Keali`i down with me as the vehicles pass. I grow shaky when I recognize the muscular old Hawaiian sitting stiffly in the passenger seat of the central Humvee.

Grandpa's old partner on Maui, the sheriff of Hana himself, who now goes by the name of the Hawaiian chieftain who slew Hawai`i's first European explorer, Captain Cook: Kana`ina. I haven't seen him since he allowed Dad and me to jump off his boat near our house. He may have just arrived. I barely glimpse his face, and horrible memories shudder through me. Kana`ina had pressed a gun against Dad's head, was about to pull the trigger, when I had a massive seizure. I remember the veins in his hand as he clenched the handle of the gun. Rain pouring, rattling the house. One of his men pulling my hair so hard my scalp bled. A hundred sensations I had no time to experience in that moment now hit me.

And then he's gone.

I wait in the ferns for several minutes before getting on my bike.

"Lei, you all right? Look like you seen a ghost."

I shake my head. "Not a ghost. A monster."

As we ride, I shove every memory back behind the door that was supposed to wall them off. Why do they keep pushing through? I want to forget that Maui kitchen forever.

We skirt the Heaps as we turn into town. Everything between here and the airport is a sea of tsunami debris. People have been dumping rubbish here, forming a labyrinth of passageways twice as high as my head. Most of the Tribes have operations in there. It has grown into Hilo's biggest black market, with a code that I know nothing about. I'd get steamrolled if I went in there, desperate for medication, with nothing to trade. Keali`i wants to try to find meds there, but I promised Dad that I'd stay out of the Heaps no matter what.

We bike to a clinic half the distance to the hospital. It's packed but quiet. I feel like I've interrupted a wake. A mother comforts a whimpering child with a broken arm. Another woman holds a sleeping girl with red lumps all over her face and arms. Keali`i and I speak to a lady with the word VOLUNTEER pinned to her blouse.

"What brings you here, sweetheart?" she asks.

"I'm looking for antibiotics for my friend, who cut her leg."

"Neosporin?"

I shake my head. "Real stuff." I unfold the note that Marcus wrote. "Cefazolin? Brand name Ancef or Kefzol? Plus some vancomycin and Flagyl."

"Oh, honey, those are IV combinations."

"Yeah."

"We're just a ghost unit here, running on fumes. Haven't had those meds since the first weeks after Arrival."

"Um," I say, looking down at my note. My heart pounds. It's not what she's saying but how she says it. Such compassion. "He also said we could try oral Keflex, with clindamycin? Or penicillin plus Flagyl, if we were really desperate?"

"The hospital may have penicillin and Flagyl. They've been refrigerating supplies on propane. Best try there. This sounds serious. Wish you the best."

"Thank you," I croak.

I stride out of the clinic over to the bikes. My hands are shaking as I unlock the chain. "Let's get over there."

The hospital in Hilo was built along the cliff edges of the Wailuku River, just above Rainbow Falls. We have to walk the bikes up some of the steeper roads. I never had to think about the grade of the slope before the Star Flowers arrived. I would just stare absently out the window as my parents pressed the gas a little harder.

I'm dripping sweat as we coast through the near-empty hospital parking lot. We chain our bikes to the end of a crowded bike rack and trot into the ER. The doors are propped open. The humidity inside is intolerable. No draft.

The ER waiting room is cavernous, dark around the edges. A few people stroll to and fro in the dim hallways. I accost someone. "Can you help us? We need some antibiotics for a friend who's recovering from a bad injury."

"Wait here," the man says. "I'll get a doctor."

Keali'i and I sit in the waiting area. He attempts to make small talk, but I'm too tense. That volunteer. Something about her kindness seemed so . . . terminal.

A haole man with a trimmed black beard approaches. "I'm Dr. Madsen. If your friend has an infection, she should be here."

"Well, we were told she needed some Ancef, or Kefzol? Or also some vancomycin and Flagyl—"

He cuts me off. "What happened to her?"

"She tore her thigh on some rebar along the breakwater. A doctor already helped her. Something called debridement? He didn't stitch her up. Said it needed to heal open. Then he left us with benaline-soaked gauze, I think. Like iodine?"

"Betadine. How big is the cut? Debridement is serious."

"Few inches long. Pretty deep."

"Rebar? *In the bay?* Listen carefully. You need to get your friend to me. Our supplies were cleaned out at gunpoint. Lost three guards in the attack. We have oral antibiotics, but I can't hand those out. Your friend's injury could be nothing, but I've lost four patients in the past two weeks, all because of stupid infections."

"Huh?" My throat is as dry as cardboard.

"I need to see her ASAP. We're running out of time to amputate if we need to."

I buckle. Keali`i and the doctor prop me up. "It's just a cut." The words are raspy.

"Modern times are over. Bring her in."

"Wait," says Keali`i. "You just said you don't have the right meds."

"Well, neither do you. Get her in here, and we'll worry about the rest later."

"Can you drive us back to her? I live out past Papaikou. We're just on bikes."

The doctor gives me the same look as the woman at the clinic. "I'm sorry. I have patients here. We don't have resources like that. Do what you can. I'll see her right away."

"Thank you." My voice is quiet. I wander outside and stare at the bike rack. I've forgotten which bike is mine. Keali`i rests a hand on my shoulder.

I see my bike, fish it out of the rack. "Okay. My house." I jump on and flee down Wainuenue to the bay. Downhill is the easy part.

I hear Keali`i far behind me, "Lei! Slow down!"

I reach the bottom and fly through the intersection, then slow as I reach the bridge that takes me onto the highway. I slow, putting all my energy into the uphill climb. Keali`i is on my tail like a bad private eye. I just keep pumping and pumping.

The shoulders of the highway are overtaken by grasses and twisted vines and far-reaching ferns. The jungle has won. It's taking everything back. It might even take my friend's leg. I'm agonizing over the distance I still have to go when an oncoming truck comes into view. I wobble to a halt. I know it's ours by the padlock looped onto the gas cap. I wave frantically. Dad's driving. The truck is full of goods for market. He veers across the empty road and meets me on the shoulder. Paul is in the passenger seat, a shotgun propped up between his legs.

"We have to get Tami to the hospital now."

"Did you find meds?"

I explain what Dr. Madsen said.

"We'll go back and get her. You ride back to town, and we'll meet at the hospital." He leans in close. "On your way back, try the library for Morse code books."

Good idea. The library's a perfect rest stop on the way back up the hill. I nod. Keali`i pulls up, out of breath.

"Thank you, Dad. I know we don't have the gasoline to be doing this."

He shrugs. "If we're not using our gas for emergencies, then what are we saving it for?" I hug him through the truck window.

Paul tips his ball cap as Dad turns around.

Keali`i tells me, "You head back to the hospital, let them know Tami's on her way. I'll meet you there as soon as I can. I'm going to see what I can do."

He peddles up the road—*away* from town—before I can ask him to explain.

Alone on the highway, I hear my heart pounding, birds calling. The solitude is stifling. I leap onto my bike and flee.

*   *   *

I'm curbside at the hospital, idly rocking myself back and forth in a wheelchair. The library was a bust. Ransacked. Most books missing. No card catalog; the library used computer files. I searched and searched, never spotted anything that had to do with alternative types of communication. Not even smoke signals.

The red truck materializes through the pouring rain and pulls up to the covered foyer. I spring out of my seat and push the wheelchair right up to the passenger door. Grandpa steps out and helps to set Tami in the chair. I wheel her over to reception.

"I was enjoying the Waikoloa resort," Tami says. "What's this all about?"

I've run it over and over in my mind, and I have no idea how I would tell her that she might lose her leg. I'm glad I'm behind her; my fake smile is twitching at the corners. "This doctor can take better care of your leg here."

A volunteer helps Tami into a bed. Dr. Madsen undoes Mom's wrappings and inspects Tami's wound.

"She's running a fever," the volunteer says. "Pulse and BP are okay."

Dr. Madsen nods. "I'm glad you're here, Tami. I'm going to keep an eye on this through tomorrow. Your doctor friend knew what he was doing, but you have a fever, and there's more redness than I would like."

"What do you mean?" Tami asks.

Dr. Madsen says, "Tami, this is a big cut, and we don't have the right meds these days to make the infection go away. There's a chance we may have to take your leg."

"Take my leg?" Tami asks. "Where?"

I squeeze her hand, fix my eyes on her fingers; I can't meet her eyes. He says, "Tami. We might have to amputate your leg. I'm hoping we won't, but—"

"Oh, my God. What are you talking about? I just scraped myself."

"There's reason to be hopeful. I'm going to keep a close eye."

"Oh, my God. This isn't— No."

My eyes fill with tears, and I wipe them away. I lean over, kiss her forehead. Her grip is painful, but I let her squeeze.

Her eyes are full of fear. "I just bumped my leg on that hole."

"I can give you something to help you relax," Dr. Madsen says. Tami nods.

The doctor accompanies me into the hallway, where we meet up with Dad and Grandpa. Dr. Madsen explains: "Your friend did a good job cleaning her out, but we need antibiotics. We just don't have them. Could go either way."

"If we brought the right things to you, would you use them?"

"Of course."

"Have you tried the market yet?" Dad asks me.

I shake my head. "Just the clinic and here."

"Okay," he says. "We have to drop our stuff off for tomorrow's market. We'll ask around while Grandpa unloads."

"Mike," Grandpa says. "Truck's unattended. We have to get back."

"I don't want her to be alone," I say. "I should stay with her."

"Keali`i?" Dad asks. "Wasn't he with you?"

I shake my head. "He said he was going to go do something."

Grandpa places a hand on my shoulder. "I'll stay here. You two unload our stuff, search around for meds. Mike, you stay at market while Lei drives back up here. I'll walk down after that, let you come back up here."

"Okay," Dad agrees. He whispers, "If we haven't found any meds by that point, I think I might try my hand at the Heaps tonight."

"No," Grandpa says.

"We're talking about Tami's leg!"

"We're talking about *your* life. Something worth as much as those antibiotics . . . what do you have of value to trade, Mike? It'd cost you the truck. We lose that truck, and our whole community has lost a leg. It's not yours to bargain with."

"I'm not going to trade away the truck, Lani."

"You think you go in there and dictate the terms? No! They see what you have, they take it. If you're lucky, they give you something back."

It hits me: *Is that where Keali`i went?* It can't be. He

122

biked away in the wrong direction. *Unless he's going there later.*

Grandpa continues: *"I'll go out there if it comes to that. Don't be a fool, Mike. I can handle the Manō and Hoku. Even Kana`ina's boys. Owe them a visit anyway."*

"You don't. Stay as far away from them as possible."

"Those *mokes* almost murdered you. Only reason you're alive is because of me. *You* stay as far away as possible."

"Enough," I say. "Shouldn't we get going?"

"I'll be at the truck," Dad says.

Grandpa and I reenter Tami's room.

It's obvious that she got medicine to relax her. "Hey, Tami. Hang in there. I'll be right back, okay?"

"K'den. *A hui hou!*"

I run out to the truck. I sit in the passenger seat, nudge the shotgun away from me with my knee.

"Any luck at the library?" Dad asks.

"No."

"We'll think of something." But I can tell that he is all out of ideas.

The bay front was razed by the tsunami and fires. It's nothing but moldy foundations and clutter. But the market is back in its original location, and it looks like it always did: blue tarps tightly strung together on iron poles, offering shade. Rotting wooden tables line the aisles. Dad backs into an available stall, and we unload the corn, the *kalo*, and the apple bananas. "Glad we have a covered spot," he says as we hastily stack our wares. "Arriving the night before helps."

I smile but focus on emptying the truck.

"Leilani?" The voice comes from beyond the table. It's familiar, but I can't place it. Dad and I look up.

"Is that you?" the voice asks.

It's dim beneath the tarps. I step forward to get a better view. A young man is staring at me. Hawaiian. Tall.

I drop my armload of corn. "Aukina?"

CHAPTER 10

"Leilani. Howzit?"

I stare at him, mouth open. Soldier Boy. My friend from the military camp on O'ahu. Last person I ever expected to see again. T-shirt. Shorts. His right leg is covered in tattoos, beautiful tribal designs. I never would have recognized him out of uniform.

"I can't believe I ran into you," he says.

His smile sends a thrill through me. *Oh, my God, he's better looking than I remembered. So cham.*

I'm useless. He turns to Dad. "Hi. I, uh, don't know if you'd remember me. I gave those bolt cutters to your daughter. O'ahu?"

Dad nods. "Oh! Wow. Yeah! Thank you!"

"I knew you got away. The fence was cut open; you two weren't found. But I never knew what happened to you after that. I thought about . . . you . . . you guys—both—a lot."

"Yeah," Dad says. "We made it home. Wasn't easy, but we finally got here."

"Can I help you unload?" Aukina asks.

Dad waves him off. "No, that's fine. We—"

"Yes! Thanks," I say. "Dad—we're in a hurry. The hospital."

"Sure." Aukina squeezes behind the table and fills his arms with *kalo* and ears of corn from the truck.

Aukina smiles at me. It's the same smile that I loved at the camp. He was the only good thing about that place. Still, horrible memories flood back with that smile. Sleeping in the black mud. Endless mosquito welts. Sunburns. The constant smell of urine. The shape of bodies under dirty sheets. How the military stole our food. Told us they were keeping it safe. But they intended to hoard it for themselves.

"What are you doing here?" I finally ask.

"We arrived a month ago. We're clearing some land up off of Stainback Road, near the zoo."

"Who?"

"Me, my brother, my parents."

"Did the military come back?"

Dad halts midstep.

"No. You're talking about Code Exodus. I didn't go with them. I . . . it wasn't easy to leave them. I took an oath. But most of us who stayed have ties. I couldn't believe what they were doing. Followed your lead. Snuck off base the night before launch."

"Where were they headed?" Dad asks.

That question has been eating away at Dad since we first saw the American fleet heading out on the ocean.

Aukina says, "They never told me. Classified."

Dad dumps an armful of corn on the table. He unloads as we talk.

Aukina turns back to me. I must look like a bag lady. Thank God it's so dim. Why is this happening *now*? Stop! Focus on Tami.

". . . great."

"Huh?"

"I said you look great. I like your short hair."

"Oh. Yeah?" My hair? God. In a panic, I turn my back to him. *What are you doing? Get ahold of yourself. Think!* I pretend I've turned to pick something up. I kneel. *Now what?* My mind racing for some snappy response.

"Are you going to be here tomorrow?" he asks.

Tami. It all depends on her. "I'm not sure. I mean, I'd love to be. Well, not *love* love. It's . . . I'm glad to see you!" I take a deep breath. "But my friend's at the hospital. She's hurt. I need to be with her. I need to get there."

"Oh. Sorry. Anything I can do to help?"

I stare at him. That sense of butterflies has worn off. I only feel exhausted. "Aukina, I'm really happy to see you. This is . . . I just . . . I'm having the worst forty-eight hours. Everything's a mess. Tami. She needs antibiotics. Seeing you . . . my memories . . . the camp . . . I can't . . ."

He nods. "I didn't mean to throw you. Let me help you unload, then I'll get out of your hair." He grabs an armful.

"No. It's not that. I didn't mean to say—"

"Lei, it's all good. I get it. Nothing to do with me. Just bad timing."

"No! It's *good* timing. It's great that we ran into each other, yeah?"

Aukina smiles, sending a jolt through me. It's like my lungs were flat, and now I can finally breathe. "Someone from your family will be here tomorrow?" he asks.

"Yes."

"I'll try back here throughout the day. If I don't see you, I'll leave someone a note with a map to our place. We don't have an address yet. Making it up as we go."

"Perfect."

"My family will be excited to meet the girl who inspired me to . . . discharge from duty a bit ahead of schedule."

I smile as we empty the truck. Aukina places one last load on the table and turns to leave.

"Aukina," I say, "I'm really happy you're here. Can't wait to catch up."

"I'll keep an eye out for you." He shakes Dad's hand and strides away.

Why did I send him off? I'm flooded with questions. How did he get here? How hard was it to get settled? Do they need help? Can we do anything for them? Return a favor?

I draw in a breath.

"You okay?" Dad asks.

"Aukina!" I'm way too loud. I don't care. He turns. "Do you know Morse code?"

"Sure. Why?"

I whip open the passenger door, fish through the glove box, find a folded emissions test receipt and a bent ballpoint pen, and race over to the hood. "Can you write down each letter?" I ask him.

"Okay." As he's scribbling out the patterns he keeps looking between me and Dad. "You know, if you want to learn Morse code, there's a couple tricks to it. It's more than the sum of the parts. I'd be happy—"

"Will you teach me?" I ask. "Like, *really* teach me?"

"All right." He smiles, intrigued.

"Great!" Dad pats him on the back. "This is brilliant. We'll start tomorrow. You'll be around all day, you said?"

He laughs politely. "But I'm busy, too. Building a house. Planting."

Dad says, "We'll reciprocate, make it worth your while." Amused, Aukina says, "Let's give it a shot. Lei, memorize as much as you can tonight." Then he walks away. I watch him in a bit of a stupor.

"Good thinking." Dad tosses me the keys. "Go easy. Ten miles an hour up Wainuenue in second gear. Best for gas mileage. And I'll watch the table and look around here for meds."

* * *

It's nearly full dark as I park at the hospital. It looks abandoned; no lights shine out of its several floors of windows. A volunteer nurse rushes me back to the room. His behavior sends a shock through me. *Why are we racing down the hall?* I fear the worst.

I stare at the door to Tami's room with sick dread. My feet will not stop, though, and as I draw near, I hold my breath and close my eyes.

Cheerful voices. I peek.

Tami's awake. Sitting up. She looks loopy, but she's in good spirits. An IV line runs into her arm. My knees almost buckle. I shuffle in. My trembling hand rises to inspect the IV bag. "Antibiotics?"

She smiles at me. "Hey, sweetie pee-pee."

The nurse nods. "She has everything she needs. She's very fortunate. I haven't seen these meds in weeks. You must have powerful friends."

I turn to Grandpa with questioning eyes.

He nods. "Keali`i brought them."

"Kaopectate!" Tami chimes. "Special K!"

My heart soars. I clap my hands together.

Grandpa says, "He just dropped them off. Was glad I was around to make sure Tami got them. Dr. Madsen was concerned, but he wasn't about to confiscate the gift."

I turn back to Tami. She sinks back into her pillow, but she smiles at me. "My turn to space out."

"She ain't outta no woods," Grandpa says.

The nurse tells me that I'm welcome to sleep in the waiting area. Grandpa rises. "I'll take the truck back down to Mike, spend the night with him."

I pass Grandpa the keys, and he pulls me close. "If Keali`i shows up, send him away. Folks around here are pretty upset. Dozens of patients have died lately because the antibiotics were stolen. They're thrilled for Tami's sake, but they have a lot of questions."

"Keali`i shouldn't get into trouble for—"

"I got lots of questions, too," Grandpa says sternly. "We have no idea what kind of deal that boy made. You hear?"

"I get it."

Grandpa rummages through his backpack and leaves me his dinner. A Spam *musabi* and an apple banana. I refuse, but he wins. "You need to eat."

I follow Grandpa to the truck, then sit alone in the dark hospital lobby. Armed guards pace the entryway. Other people camp out in the waiting room, but I find a quiet row of chairs and try to get comfortable.

The sleepless minutes drag on and on. Tami's nurse strolls past, slows, and eyes me hard. I shrink into my seat. It's as if he's accusing me of something. *I didn't steal any meds!* I want to spit. But I try to ignore his strange expression.

I lie across the chairs and force myself to memorize the Morse code patterns for *A* through *J*, and all the vowels, before sleep overcomes me.

CHAPTER 11

I awake several times throughout the night. Bad dreams, pinched muscles, numb legs and arms. Dots and dashes, surging and fading. Morning comes with a garage band of birdcalls. I sneak into Tami's room. She's snoring. I decide to go for a walk to nearby Rainbow Falls, quizzing myself on A through J as I go. I do well: the vowels stuck with me through the night, and I move on to K through N.

The falls are gorgeous in the morning sun, flowing strong thanks to the recent rains. A patch of low clouds drifts aside, and the sun lights the mist in a brilliant rainbow. I feel my head clearing.

Aukina's smile enters my mind. *Don't act like an idiot around him.* I clamber up the hidden, overgrown stairs that lead above Rainbow Falls. The route takes me through lush jungle toward a secret trail to the swimming holes behind the falls. I make certain I'm alone, strip down, and dive in.

The chill of the Wailuku River is a fabulous cure for the stifling humidity inside the hospital. My stomach calms. I realize that I've been feeling nauseated since arriving at the hospital yesterday. I climb out and sit on the rocks, allowing the sun to dry me. I put on my clothes, sit down to

The surface of a contact lens, cast in a thin, hazy film of blue. The world is all ocean against a blinding sun. I'm deeper. My grand mal seizure opens my mind wide. I tremble, in bliss, high above the world.

Mauna Loa's mottled skin has a fresh blemish. A round patch of black fading out from a central crater. I have scarred my sacred peak. I want to reach out, brush it smooth, then cup the globe in my hands.

There is purpose here. Comfort.

I'm enveloped by the folds, the lightning in my brain one with the surging of the Orchid's veins. *Pono. Lōkahi.* If I could hold on forever, I might never let go.

Go away. You're not wanted. Go away and leave us alone.

What was that?

No. *Who* was that?

I recoil with sudden understanding. Someone else is here. Trying to order the Orchid away.

Hello?

The voice is gone. I float high over the surface of the waters in a beautiful loneliness that can only be found between worlds.

Water. Flowing. Babbling. Sunlight dances on the scallops. The river is rippling with sequins. I'm here. Japanese white-eyes chatter in the trees above me, guiding me back. I focus. I'm still on the rocks beside the Wailuku. The waterfall's edge is around the next set of boulders. Good thing I didn't slip into the water during the spell.

The disappointment of returning to my own terrestrial senses is worse than it used to be. I pine to be back up there. When I'm with her, the world is so serene.

I steady myself and stand up. Tired. Weak. But I head for the path that leads into the trees.

It comes back: Someone else was up there.

I shudder. Whoever they are—they're not speaking with the Orchid the right way. The voice is only a whisper. I may have heard it only because my seizure was deep. The night of my birthday was the last serious seizure, but instigated by violent pain that blocked anything faint. How long has this voice been here? If they ever figured out how to connect the way I have—**Go away and leave us alone**—could they succeed in pushing the Orchid away?

I feel a stab of panic and jealousy. *Stay,* I think. *We are Leilani. We want to stay. We want to be together. Never apart. Never with another. It is a good thing.*

There is purpose here. Comfort.

Yes. There is, I tell her. *Stay.*

I return to the hospital, almost running.

*   *   *

I settle into the chair next to Tami's bed and sleep, then awake to voices. I mountaineer up through my exhaustion. I don't think it's obvious that I'm post-seizure, which is a relief.

The male nurse is with us—Herbert—so Tami and I don't get too chatty, but I can't help asking her in a whisper, "Still think Keali`i doesn't know you exist?"

"No. I can't believe he did this."

I tell her that people seem to be mad at him for it, that he might get into trouble if he shows up at the hospital again. Tami rolls her eyes. "No good deed goes unpunished."

When Herbert leaves, I tell her all about Soldier Boy.

She lets out a pent-up sigh. "Can't wait for my knight in shining armor."

I stare at her.

"What?"

"*Keali`i*, you dork," I say. "He showed up out of the blue and saved your life. Now he's a fugitive on the run. All for you."

Tami shoots me a wry look. "All of this"—she shakes her IV pole—"was for *you*."

"No! Listen to me. It's not like that! He likes you."

She smiles.

"I'm done. New topic."

I force her to quiz me nonstop on Morse code. I'm incredibly sorry for her, lying there with needles coming out of her, the red, puffy gash on her leg wide open, but I'm not going to give an inch.

Underneath, I hear that new voice. Just a murmur—

Go away. My imagination? It must have been. But what if it was real? I can't let it grow stronger. How do I stop it? *Who* was it?

Midafternoon, Dr. Madsen has good news. "Your fever's gone, vitals look great, redness is way down. I think you're on the mend. A few more days of observation and you can go home, finish recovering there."

"I'm not going to lose my leg?"

The doctor offers the usual caveats about uncertainty, but Tami and I are already in each other's arms, squealing.

"How do we pay you?" I ask Dr. Madsen.

"However you can. I have to eat and maintain a home, same as anybody. And the hospital will always be in need. I've already spoken with your grandpa. We'll work something out. Propane. Volunteer hours. Not your concern."

"Thank you."

"Go on." Tami motions me out the door. "Go talk in code with Soldier Boy."

I run-walk to the bathroom. I have to prop the door open with my backpack to let in light. I stand in front of the mirror, combing my hands through my hair. It's getting long enough for me to bite at the ends of it—a terrible habit, a thing I do without realizing it. Why can't I ever encounter Aukina without looking and feeling like a zombie?

At least the cold water works. Hilo's water is mostly gravity-based; no electricity needed. But even the pipes will fail in time without people dedicated to repairing inevitable clogs and breaks. Grateful, I wash my face, wet my hair. I smile at myself. *Not too bad. Don't sweat it. He wasn't exactly ready for prom, either.*

I unlock my bike and coast downhill from the hospital. The market is busier than I've ever seen it—even before the Arrival. We're not the only family eager to peddle our first batch of successful crops. And so many people are desperate to get their hands on anything.

I lock up my bike and join Dad behind our table. The corn is about half gone, but most of our apple bananas and *kalo* are still here. Everything we have to offer is easily grown by anybody. But we are doing business and will work our way up to more specialized crops as quickly as we can. Dad haggles with a customer as I approach. The customer is offering ten dollars cash to fill his cloth bag with corn.

Dad shakes his head. "I won't take cash alone. You need to throw in something I can sink my teeth into. Then we'll talk."

"Are you kidding? This is a lot of money."

"It's a lot of paper." Dad has explained his philosophy to me before. Money is only worth something if people have faith in it, he says. Paper money and coins have retained their usefulness on this island because everyone seems to intuitively understand that it's relatively rare and that no one is making more. But there's no agreement on how much a dollar is worth. One ear of corn? Ten? A whole crateful? The exchange value swings wildly, depending on what the buyer and seller believe is a fair deal at that moment and in that spot. Dad is fine with collecting paper money, but only if it's accompanied by some sort of trade. That way, if people suddenly reject paper money, he isn't giving away his goods for free. Meanwhile, he never spends cash. He's waiting for the day that its value stabilizes; then he'll know exactly what his stash can buy.

Gasoline and propane. Bullets.

"Fine," the customer grunts. "Ten bucks, plus a can of baked beans. And you let *me* fill my bag as full as I can get it." He pulls a tin of KTA-brand beans from his backpack and places it on top of the ten-dollar bill.

"You've got a deal." Dad snatches up the can and the ten spot. "Lei! How's Tami doing?"

"She's going to recover. Keali`i came through."

Dad leans back, looks up, releases a deep sigh. "Thank God. That's fantastic."

"Where's Grandpa?"

"Shopping. Seeing if we can get a pint of gas for a tool we were offered."

The customer balances one last ear on top of his pile—an obvious cheat, if you ask me. "See you next week. Thanks!"

We're alone. I hesitate. "I had a seizure this morning."

"You okay?"

I nod. "They're never that bad anymore." No reason to tell him I was near water. Get right to the point. I whisper, "I think—there was another voice—telling the Orchid to leave."

Dad leans forward. "*What?* Really? Who?"

"I have no idea."

138

"From Moloka`i? Father Akoni?"

"Why would he do that? He convinced us that the Orchid needed to stay. This voice wasn't friendly."

"Someone else has made contact?" he marvels.

"Could be anyone."

"That narrows it down. Just one person?"

"It feels like only one, but I don't know."

"Is it a guy?"

"I don't know."

"English speaker?"

I pause, stumped. "The meaning . . . doesn't really come in words. I turn them into words, but . . . it could be in any language."

"Okay," Dad says, thinking. "I could take you up to Buzz *right now*. Otherwise it'll have to wait. Uncle Hank and Grandpa are taking the truck to Waimea tonight, to try to muscle into the markets up there, bring home some beef."

He's waiting for an answer. This is ridiculous. Go *now* or wait? I don't want to drop everything to go deal with this at Buzz's observatory on the summit of Mauna Kea. I need a rest. I need to know more. That voice was so weak. Could have been *anything*. Maybe just my exhaustion.

I shake my head. "What if Buzz is still in Kona?" Dad hesitantly agrees that we should wait.

"Has Aukina been by?"

"Yeah. He'll check back in soon. Keep practicing Morse code while you wait."

I wander the market aisles as I practice.

Everyone's shouting: Buy this, trade that. I stop and stare in morbid fascination at a table displaying bins full of fried insects. It took me three weeks to gather the courage to eat my first fried coqui frog. Would I ever eat a fried insect? Probably, yeah. But only as a last—

"I know that look," says the vendor. He's maybe thirty, as thin as a marathoner, with a bushy beard. A filthy hemp necklace hangs around his sweaty neck. He's probably from Puna, been selling bugs since long before Arrival. "Ever had shrimp?"

I offer him a wary half grin.

"Tastes about the same. Same texture, too. They're cooked. Clean. Go ahead, for a pretty young lady, you can have a sample."

My cheeks grow warm. "No thanks."

"Free protein? Can't be passing that up!"

"I'm not that desperate."

"No? You must have it good." His voice isn't so playful. I lower my eyes. He's right; I shouldn't be snooty. That comment was tasteless at best, possibly dangerous. I *do* have it good, I realize. I'm so hungry—always so hungry. But I suffer less than most.

"Sorry. I didn't mean anything by it," I mumble. Embarrassed, I move on.

I haven't seen an overweight person in forever. I remember when movies and TV shows depicted times like these. Often there were fat characters. I always wondered about that. Where's this guy getting so much food? No one could get fat nowadays.

We used to go to the farmer's market once a month, then head off to the beach. We'd buy stupid things, like coconut water and refrigerator magnets and hair clips that looked like flowers.

Just *once*—I'd like to walk into a grocery store and toss what I need into a cart, even something I don't need, pay for it with the swipe of a plastic card.

At the next stall, whale meat. Blubber. Oil. All humpback. Like a pack of sharks, a frenzied crowd is eager to get at the carcass. The team behind the table is rushing to keep up, all smiles. They must be making a killing off this killing. I think back to the whale song I heard along the breakwater, when I wondered if life was better for these creatures under the reign of the Star Flowers.

Guess not.

I overhear a conversation a couple of tables down. I creep forward to listen. "Yeah. Rumbling all week," one man says to another. They're carefully placing the last of their mamey sapote fruits, `ōhelo berries, dried mangoes, and bars of homemade soap into tattered plastic bags.

"Whatever else that meteorite did, it ticked her off. When did she last blow?"

"Mauna Loa? The flow of '84."

"Pu`u `Ō`ō is flowing again."

"That right? Town of Pāhoa in its path again?"

"Not at the moment. I've got a buddy in Puna at the

back end of Orchidlands. He said it's a 24/7 geyser of lava. Reached the sea by the end of yesterday."

"Pele's waking up. Blood's boiling. Like Pāhoa and its neighbors don't have enough on their plates."

"She never did care for us mortals."

A voice in my ear. "Pele."

I whip around. It's Aukina. "You freaked me out."

"Pele. Easy one. Ready? Dot dash dash dot. Dot. Dot dash dot dot. Dot."

He smiles at me as I gape. "Wait," I say. "I thought 'dot dash' was *A*."

"Very good. That's right. You've been studying. But *P* is dot dash *dash dot*. It goes on further. See? I told you it's going to be tricky."

I slump forward. The different lengths of letters is going to kill me. "It's okay!" he says. "You'll get the hang of it in no time." He looks less the soldier than ever. I can't help but laugh. Maybe it's the black T-shirt with the pink elephant on it, or the cargo shorts and *slippahs*. He has a surfer's mop, black hair, spiky. And I love his leg tattoos.

"Well, good, because 'no time' is exactly how much—"

Gunshots. Everyone screams and drops to the ground. Aukina tackles me and flings us both to the pavement.

Another shot. Very close. Screams.

Masked figures with red Hanaman armbands train guns on the people selling.

Two masked robbers are behind a table, filling bags with

jars of oil, fistfuls of cash, and a pile of bartered items. Two others shovel whale meat into a wheelbarrow.

"This whale is the property of the sheriff of Hana!" shouts one. The voice seems familiar. *Two Dog?* "These goods are illegal at your market and can only be obtained through our official channels. If you're caught—"

Someone springs up from behind the whale with a pistol and fires at the Hanamen. Two Dog dives to the side. Aukina and I press ourselves into the ground.

Play dead, I tell myself.

Two Dog bolts. The whale vendors scatter. The vigilante with the pistol looks around, flees.

A second or two of silence. Then the crowd descends, fighting and trampling to grab a jar of oil or a bit of meat.

"You okay?" Aukina says, his eyes on fire.

"Yeah. You?" I shout over the noise.

"Come on!"

"Dad," I say. "Dad! Grandpa!" I hear my name through the roar of the crowd. "Mike! Lani!" I shout, scanning the fallen, wild with worry.

"Lei, come." Aukina tugs at my shirt.

"Leilani!" It's Grandpa. We lock eyes from neighboring aisles. He hops toward me, fighting the crowd.

Dad nearly knocks me over. "Lei! Are you all right?"

"Fine."

"Thank God."

"Dad," I say. "Get back to your stuff!"

Grandpa reaches us. He wraps around me like a shield. "You okay?"

"Yes. Get back to the table, okay? Before—"

Dad nods, squeezing my shoulder, looks at Aukina, skips away. People are snatching up our corn as they race past. Dad shouts, "Lani, get her out of here!"

Grandpa and Aukina and I race away against the swarm. I drag us to a halt. "Tūtū, go help him. Get the truck and pull it around."

"They're going to be back. We need to—"

"I *know*. That's why Dad needs you. I'll get on my bike and head straight for the hospital. I'll be fine. Hurry!"

Grandpa's eyes drill into me.

"I'll stay with her," Aukina says. "Until we're away. Then she can ride fast."

Grandpa nods. He must have met Aukina already. "Where's your bike? I'll get Mike once you're set." We sprint along the edges of the crowd to the pole where I left my ride. Two Dog is trying to lift my bike over the top of the sign to sidestep the U-lock.

"That's who shot at us on the breakwater! He's with the sheriff."

"Stay here," Grandpa commands.

He rushes Two Dog.

Two Dog sees Grandpa, drops the bicycle, which slides down the pole, and readies a punch. But Grandpa barrels into him. They tumble into the street, locked together, batting at each other with closed fists.

I run up, stop. There's nothing I can do. Grandpa slams Two Dog's head into the pavement, and the Hanaman goes limp. Grandpa positions himself squarely on top of Two Dog. I see him reach for a pair of handcuffs around his belt that aren't there. The instinct of a veteran cop. Grandpa looks around.

"I told you to stay back!" he yells at me. I'm in shock. "Your bike lock. Now," Grandpa says. I race to the pole, fumble for the key in my pocket, and shakily fit it into the lock. I toss the bike lock to Grandpa and back up with my bike.

Two Dog stirs, groans. Grandpa puts the U-lock around his neck and locks him to the signpost.

"Mr. Hawika," Aukina mutters to Grandpa. "What're you . . . ?"

Two Dog looks right at Grandpa. "Hawika. You're Hawika."

A ripple of terror goes down my back. I back away farther, before Two Dog can see me. I tug Aukina away from them. Grandpa freezes. "I'm nobody." Fear in his voice.

"Sheriff's looking for you."

I slink back, hide around the corner. *What? Why?*

Grandpa leans in close to his face. "Sheriff is a coward. A mall cop. You hear? You can't hide from justice, though. Not even a washed-up crook like—"

A group of men wearing red armbands turns onto the sidewalk. They see Two Dog, race forward.

"Tūtū!" I shout.

Grandpa sees them, throws my key far down Mamo Street. "Go!" He disappears into the crowd. The thugs gather around Two Dog, then go hunt for the key.

Around the corner, I jump on my bike. Aukina gives my seat a push and sprints beside me until I gain speed and pedal away. I race toward the hospital like a chased rabbit, changing directions at every side street, never slowing.

OCTOBER

CHAPTER 12

It's fall, though Hilo is a year-round seventy-eight degrees. I've been homebound since the scare at the market, not eager to leave the safety of our isolated Lost World. And with our taro beds coming into full rotation, pests attacking our kitchen garden, and algae building up in my freshwater ponds, I'm too busy to escape even if I wanted to.

Luckily, everyone I'd otherwise miss comes to me.

Buzz shows up, but his visit is brief. He's been keen to check in for a while, though he hasn't felt ready to disclose his findings; he has the same scientist's caution that annoys me about my ecologist parents. "Slow and steady wins the race," they've always said.

Kai and I bombard Buzz with questions. "Too early to say" and "I'll tell you later," he says.

I try to guilt info out of him. "Wouldn't it be safer if someone else knew, in case something happens to you?"

"If something happens to me, Richard has the combo to my notes," he assures me. "I also drew him a map to your place. He'll come right here if I can't."

My parents insist that we set a date to return with him to the peaks. "Three weeks," Buzz suggests. His eyes gleam as he tells me, "I can't wait to show you the pearl. Your meteor."

"Are you freaking out in a geeky way or a cool way?" I ask. Buzz gets excited about everything, from improving energy efficiency on gas generators to new ways to store guava at high elevation.

"Both. Three weeks and you can judge for yourself."

"Hold on," I say. *That's too long.* I persuade him to walk to the corral with me, to feed ʻImiloa. Along the way I fill him in on my Morse code campaign. His face lights up. "I saw that—the on-off! I was camped up at the pearl that morning. This is brilliant, Lei. Huge." I drop my other grenade: the new presence I encountered the morning of my last grand mal.

He stops, thinks for almost a full minute. "There's only one logical conclusion," he says, pitching feed to the horse. "Someone's using another dish."

"Really?"

"Definitely a concern." He rests the pitchfork against the corral. "I'm glad your bond with the Orchid is strong enough to withstand this. My worry is: if it can happen once, who's to say it won't continue? You won the horse race because you live directly under a big array. But this is going to keep happening. And we have no way to predict how the Star Flowers will react under mounting pressure from all sides."

"And the baby?" I ask. "It'll become susceptible to imprinting, eventually. What if someone slips in before me? What if they command it to leave?"

"You'll override the command. Mama's orders will overrule any trespasser."

"Hope so."

"I wouldn't fret," Buzz says. "Hopefully you'll send the Orchids off before year's end. We'll push this up. Let's meet in *two* weeks, tops. Okay? I'll get the dishes prepared. We'll spend time at the array before our field trip to the impact site. Try to make contact with the baby again, and we'll make sure you have plenty of time to use the bullhorn to talk with the mother. Maybe see if you can't kick this other person out."

"How would I do that?"

"Form a defense shield or something? You're the alien psychic."

I grunt. "Wanna trade?"

"Yes!"

Tami is next to show up. Mom and Grandpa and Sara have been attending some town hall–style meetings in Hilo, using the trips into town to conduct some trades and to work volunteer shifts at the hospital as repayment for Tami's care. Mom brought Tami home after their second town hall. Living by herself wasn't going so well for Tami. She had wanted to be there in case her mom stopped by, which she never did.

Being alone was good for staying still and healing, but the boredom was driving her crazy, and my parents never felt that she was safe enough.

Keali`i's been by more often since Tami planted her flag on our couch. They chat and laugh in hushed tones in the evenings. I sometimes cast Tami inquisitive glances, but she's not spilling any beans, and I try to leave them alone.

I had my own hushed conversation with Keali`i the first time he showed up. "Where have you been?"

"Lying low."

"Surfing?"

"Maybe."

He's never gone for long, and his place near Keaukaha is so far away. I don't get it. "Seriously, where do you stay?"

He shrugged. "I know some guys squatting in a cottage on the bluffs, crash on their couch sometimes."

I let it go. "The meds—how did you do it? Everyone wants to know. You could be in danger."

Keali`i glanced around, answered softly, "Cashed in a few favors, racked up a few IOUs. Knew somebody who knew somebody."

"Grandpa and Dad are going to interrogate you," I warned.

He nodded.

My family did grill him, but he insists in the most charming way possible that whatever stunt he pulled that night is none of our business, and he uses endless days of hard work and sweat as a get-out-of-jail-free card. Bottom line is that we need his help running the farm.

Aukina has been up to the house four times in the past two weeks. Morse code lessons. Dad has promised him the moon for all his effort—days of help down at their homestead whenever his family needs extra hands. I was so focused on getting fluent with the code that it was Tami who pointed out that he'd probably bike up here every three days no matter what. Tami adores him. She's always fake-swooning when Aukina's back is to her. Sometimes I can't help but laugh.

He and Keali`i met during Aukina's second visit. Keali`i morphed into typical island-boy mode, playing it *sooo* cool. I swear, guys on these islands have a switch that goes off when they size each other up. Aukina and I were sitting at the dining table, I was attempting to tap out in dots and dashes the preamble to the Constitution, when Keali`i entered through the kitchen, pulling off leather gloves and leaving a trail of gritty black mud behind him.

"An den," I said to him. "Keali`i, this is Aukina." Aukina rose from his chair.

"The code talker." Keali`i put his gloves down and shook Aukina's hand gruffly. "Over from O`ahu, yeah? You surf, brah?"

Aukina nodded.

"No doubt. We should shred sometime, eh?"

"Sounds good."

"K'den." Keali`i guzzled a tall glass of water, snatched up

his gloves, and went out the door. Aukina smiled after him, winked at me, and we returned to our lesson.

Aukina set off on his bike for home a few hours later.

"Why do you have to learn the whole code?" Keali`i asked me that night, playing cards with me and Tami. It was full dark. We lit a couple of candles in the living room, giving me the strange feeling that it was a special occasion. We were drinking cups of warm kava, steeped from a medicinal plant called `awa to relieve sore muscles. "Can't you just write out a message and memorize the pattern? Or flicker everything while you're awake?"

I tried to explain that my commands to the Orchid are much more fluid during space-outs and that my ability to give her complex instructions (flare, dim, flare . . . pause . . . dim, flare, dim)—especially when she's over another part of the globe—requires a focus I've never been able to achieve while awake. As for only memorizing a pattern and not bothering with mastering the whole language, I talked with my parents about it but decided that this is too important to leave to recitation alone. "What would I do if I got off track in the middle of a string of commands? I can't have any confusion on either end of these one-way conversations."

"Sure it's not just an excuse to have Soldier Boy over all the time?" Tami asked.

"Tami. I want to do this *right*. That's all there is to it. Has nothing to do with meeting *Mr.* Right."

When I went to bed, I heard the low murmurings

of Tami and Keali'i downstairs. The next day Tami said, blushing, "We almost kissed. He told me he's never dated a haole."

I threw her a *shaka*. "He's shy. Let him take his time."

I can't take my time, though. I've been studying Morse code for less than three weeks, but I almost feel ready to use it for real. Just one more practice session with Aukina. This time, though, we're not tapping messages to each other across the dining table. I'll be up on the roof of the house while he's a quarter mile upslope. I'm supposed to mirror-flash a passage to him that he doesn't know in advance. If he's able to record it perfectly, I graduate, he says.

I brush my hair in the upstairs bathroom. Eyeliner. A little blush. Lip gloss. All of it impossible to scrutinize in the dim natural light through the frosted shower window. I file my worst nails, make sure there's no dirt under any of them. Finally, my favorite earrings. Small aquamarine zirconium studs, nothing fancy. I allow myself a smile. I look pretty okay!

I meet Aukina at the corral.

We're going to ride 'Imiloa together up to B plot. It makes no sense that I'd go with him, but I use the excuse that I need to review some final instructions. He reaches down to help swing me into the saddle. I take his hand, and he pulls me up with a strong grip. I settle into the saddle behind him, and we ride into the brush. I'm so close to him— but I'm careful not to hold him too tightly. It's not until we're off the bumpy, windy side path and back onto the dirt road that what I'm doing really sinks in. *I have my arms around him.*

I squeeze him more tightly as 'Imiloa lurches into a trot. *Think. Slow down.* Aukina's back is warm. I smell coppery sweat. Feel his muscles. I rest my cheek against his back. He doesn't say a word. I smile, loving the feel of my face nestled into the muscular indentation of his spine. There's sudden warmth in my belly, and my heart is racing.

When we arrive at the plot and turn to see a clear view of the roof of my house, he helps me dismount and then climbs down himself. "Well, you get that question about the code all figured out, then?"

Warmth rushes to my face. I look away from him, hiding an involuntary smile with my fingers. "Yeah. Um. Thanks."

A breeze dries up the film of sweat along my face. I lift my hair so the gentle wind can cool the back of my neck, too. I can smell flowers, a beautiful bouquet eddying through the air. Fleeting storm clouds are bunching up *mauka*. The rain will bring its own smells.

He eyes me for a moment. "Why don't you take her back. I'll walk down when you're done flashing me."

I bark laughter. Now he turns red. I can't stop laughing, but inside I'm mortified.

"Lei." Aukina motions me toward the saddle. Now I want to gallop away. I'm probably as red as an 'ōhelo berry. "You know," he says slowly, "this Morse code thing? You don't have to keep this up. I'll come visit anyway."

Is he—is he waiting for a kiss? I think he is. I desperately want to reach up on my tiptoes and kiss him. Instead I clamber up into the saddle before I change my mind, before he decides for both of us. *Too much going on.* My breathing is impossibly loud in my own ears as I fumble to loop my foot through the far stirrup. My chest feels like it's going to pop.

I smile weakly. The corner of my mouth twitches. I turn 'Imiloa away from him in order to hide my face. "This isn't a ruse," I say. "You'll see. I really want to learn this."

"Why?" he asks. It's the first time he's asked.

My eyes settle on him, my twitch gone, my cheeks no longer warm. I wonder if I'm about to tell him the truth. *This is working. Don't ruin it.* I shake my head, but so softly he might not have even noticed.

He hands me his military compass—the needle is useless, but it has other sighting tools. "Don't forget to set the right angle before you start jostling the mirror. You don't want to rifle off the whole message to the tree over there while I don't see anything at all."

"K'den," I manage. Anything more and my voice will crack. I bite my lip. I turn away from the road, nearly spur 'Imiloa into a sprint.

*   *   *

Dad is supposed to be on gate duty, but before he takes his post, he insists on joining me on the roof in case I blank or have a seizure. We go upstairs to Mom and Dad's bedroom, and he climbs out his window onto the aluminum roof above the kitchen. He reaches inside, pulls the stepladder out, and secures it against the side of the house. As I bend to pass through the window, my elbow bumps Dad's Blu-ray player, resting on his TV. It almost falls, but I catch it.

What's the point? It's already fried. Sometimes I still feel sad when I see things that don't work anymore, like our dust-covered blender in the kitchen cabinet, or a traffic light filled with birds' nests stacked one atop the other like some kind of avian apartment building. But this Blu-ray player and the tower of discs beside it don't make me feel anything.

I step through the window, climb the ladder onto the roof. The pitch is gentle, but the corrugated-aluminum surface is slippery. Dad and I work our way to the highest vantage point. From here the observatories crowning Mauna Kea are visible as indistinct white nodules along the distant peak. My crater on the slope of Mauna Loa is also visible.

I pull the sighting tool from my pocket and carefully sit down next to Dad. I immediately slide down the roof on my frayed jean shorts, give a nervous laugh, and catch myself. Dad hoists me back.

"Is this a good moment to complain about those short shorts?"

I give him the stink-eye.

"Have you picked a phrase yet?"

"Why? You want me to quote a few lines from *Star Trek*?"

"'Space, the final frontier,'" he mimics. "No. I was thinking maybe ..." He trails off. I urge him to finish. He says, "Have you told him?"

I feel a prickle of adrenaline, shake my head. He shrugs, pulls a note from his pocket, presents it to me. "I don't know.

Test this out, if you want. Focus-grouped, polished, approved by your corporate sponsors."

"Dad."

"He's going to find out anyway, isn't he?"

"No, he won't. When I send the message using the Orchid, I won't do it over Hawai`i. There's no reason."

"Australia, Japan, China, Korea? The U.S. West Coast? The Orchid will be visible on the horizon from here over those places."

I stare at him. He says, "You should tell him."

"Do you like him?" I ask.

"He's *da kine*, Lei. Yeah, I like him. Just . . . remind him that I have lots of shotguns nowadays."

"Dad."

"He can see us. He's probably waiting."

I snatch the note from him, read it carefully. My heartbeat quickens. "He's going to run and never come back."

"Nope. He's not like that. He knows who he is. He went AWOL, you know. That wasn't easy for him, but he's comfortable with it. People like him don't feel threatened by the gifts of others."

I feel like I did when I first jumped off the cliffs at Big Island's South Point. Fifty feet down to choppy water. I knew I could do it. *Just leap! You've seen others do it!* But it took me fifteen minutes to build courage. When I finally jumped, my stomach caught in midair; I lost my breath. I hit the water a full second later, hard—but I was fine.

I line up the compass mirror with the sun and put

Aukina's figure in my sights. I close my eyes, visualize flicking out the message Dad has prepared. With halting Morse code I practice sending the most important "tweet" the world will ever see:

I PREVENT NUCLEAR FALLOUT. FORCE ALL YOUR UNSTABLE REACTORS TO BLOW NOW. I WILL LEAVE ONCE I ABSORB ALL RELEASED RADIATION. RPT

I repeat the message and then fold the compass mirror shut with a dull click. I place it on my lap with a trembling hand.

"That was fast," Dad says. "You looked like an old hand. How'd it feel?"

I look off toward Aukina on the hillside. I can see his gears grinding from here. He's going to put two and two together. He might not trust his own conclusions at first, but he *will* figure it out. I shouldn't have done this. I should have kissed him when I had the chance.

Dad pats me on the shoulder. We sit in silence, watching Aukina come in and out of view as he slowly approaches through the patchwork of brush and trees. "You don't think that message is too short?" I finally ask Dad.

He shakes his head. "It has to be concise. You can't click out a long missive. It'll take the right folks a minute or two to realize the Orchid is using Morse code, another minute for them to run and find paper or whatever. Meanwhile, you could lose your line at any moment just by turning in your sleep."

"Short and sweet," I say. Aukina breaks through the tree line and into our yard. He stops, peers up. My stomach flips. He waves a piece of paper toward me and hurries toward the house.

"Where's she now?" Dad asks.

"Right above us," I say. He glances up, but he won't see her; she's too dim against the blue sky and the high sun.

"Have you heard that voice again?"

"Not a hint," I say. "I've been listening. But it may require a full-on fit. I don't know. If you think about it, we're unlikely to be 'logged in' at the same time anyway."

"Makes sense. Still—creepy as hell."

Uncle Hank pulls up to our driveway in the old truck. We watch from our high vantage point as he gets out and inspects a potato sack full of fresh *kalo*.

"Hank!" Dad calls down to him. Uncle Hank glances in our direction, shields his eyes from the sun, and waves at us.

"Aren't you on patrol?" he shouts up.

"I'll be down in a minute!" Dad says. He turns to me, his eyebrows arched. "I better get going before the sergeant has me doing push-ups!"

He rises. I shift onto my feet, too. He stops me. "I'll send Soldier Boy up."

"Dad!" How does he know that nickname? He winks, lowers himself carefully down the ladder.

Before I can gather my thoughts, Aukina's head pops into view. We study each other. He rises, makes his way over to me, and unfolds his paper. I take it from him, unable to meet his eyes. The note reads exactly as it should. I stuff

161

it into my pocket, watch Uncle Hank and Dad meet at the truck.

"Lei," Aukina asks cautiously, "what is that?"

He knows. He just wants to hear it out loud. "Look up," I tell him. "You see the Orchid?"

He glances about, shakes his head.

Flare. I pull at the kite string, put all my energy into the command. "Look again."

This time, his eyes go right to it. I follow his gaze. There she is, a faint, knotty bruise against the sharp, pure blue of Hawai`i's sky.

"No shit," Aukina says.

We sit in silence. I dim the Orchid, releasing my focus. He looks at me with questioning eyes. I tell him, starting with our escape from the O`ahu military base using the bolt cutters he gave me. I don't leave anything out, even Maui, Dad's near execution at the hands of the sheriff of Hana. When I finally finish, his eyes go wide. "Lei . . . I had no idea."

We share the silence on the rooftop.

"I should've left with you. Taken you and your dad to my parents' place in Pearl City. It would have been far safer. I'm so sorry you had to go through that."

I turn uncertainly and gaze at him. *That's* what he wants to talk about? "Didn't you hear what I just said about the Orchid?"

"I believe you."

I look away, put a hand to my chest, draw in a slow breath.

"So that was you?" He points with his chin toward the debris field visible on Mauna Loa. I nod reluctantly.

"So you woke her up?" he adds. "Pele. You woke her." I don't know how to answer that. He elaborates. "People say Pu'u 'Ō'ō is flowing, pouring right into the sea down near the end of the 130. Kilauea's steaming. Mauna Loa herself is stretching, yawning. Yeah? They're saying there's been some fissure activity out of view on the backside. And it's all thanks to you! I've always wanted to see lava. Now I can! Lived on O'ahu my whole life. Too expensive to get the family out here."

Now I get what he's doing. He's changing the subject. He's reading me like a book, steering us away from what's making me uncomfortable without being too dismissive. He's turning this into a *good* thing. I force myself to meet his eyes. He's so *cham*. I suddenly find myself trying not to stare.

"Um, how *did* you get out here?" I ask.

He stiffens. I can feel the walls go up. I'm not surprised. No one wants to relive their journey to the Big Island. If it was successful, it required . . . sacrifice, compromise. It required things worth forgetting. "You want me to follow your story with mine?"

"Oh."

"I'm just teasing." He nudges my shoulder. "I'll tell you. It's no big deal, though."

I cross my legs and shift my weight, settling on the aluminum roof as he shares. As he speaks of our brief time together on O'ahu, his eyes soften. I have to remind myself to breathe.

"For about a week after you escaped, I couldn't think of anything but you and your dad. Drove me nuts not knowing how you were doing. I began to plan my own escape, mostly as a distraction from thinking about you. But everything got real when my lieutenant gave us our orders: we were to ship out in two days' time, for an undisclosed destination, with a brief port-of-call along the U.S. coast to drop off the thousands of stranded mainlanders we'd collected.

"Everyone got the sense that this was a one-way mission, that the entire fleet was together. Word spread that our orders were the same, that we'd engage in the Atlantic. But there were other theories. The orders didn't make sense. We argued all the time. Why would the fleet ditch the islands? What was so bad out there that we were abandoning the most strategic post in the entire Pacific Ocean? Some thought the top brass had gone mad, just wanted to get home to family. Maybe the generals really thought it was the end of the world. Biblical Rapture, beginning of a thousand years of tribulation. No point in languishing on the islands, where food and gas were already all but gone. Others were convinced the brass knew something about the nuclear subs stationed in the region, that we were running from an imminent malfunction. That's what I believed."

"Wait," I say. "You thought a nuclear sub was about to go pop, you had a free ticket to the mainland, and you went AWOL anyway?"

"`Ohana, Lei. Like *you* told *me*. I couldn't cut and run and leave my family to die. Even if I knew it meant I would die, too. I wanted all of us to be together."

"Yeah," I say. Those thoughts exactly plagued my entire journey home.

"My brother agreed. It was a little risky to get off base, but we managed. We took supplies, made our way to Pearl City, but our parents weren't home. Took us a week to locate them at their friends' place. They had hoarded food and supplies. Disaster-prepared long before Arrival, Lei. Preppers. We added our rations to the mix and hunkered down with them. We waited for a month before everyone was convinced that things were never getting better. The Orchid started to leave, then it came back. Confused everybody. We waited and waited for it to leave again."

I nod, look down.

"No, Lei. I get it. I mean, the truth is *crazy*. Completely *lōlō*. But . . . it's like I'm not surprised. You know? I bet a lot of people won't be surprised. We all know—in our bones—we all know something weird is going on."

I smile at him, then look at Dad and Uncle Hank in the yard.

"That's when we knew we needed a plan," he continues. "Our food wasn't sustainable. We'd have to live off the land if we were going to survive. My parents wanted to move to Kaua`i, but I insisted that we come here. Because . . ." He stops, his gaze locked on me.

Was he going to say: *Because of you?*

He starts again. "The trip wasn't like yours. We waited so long to leave O'ahu that a ferry system finally started. A small fleet of large yachts, a couple vintage merchant ships, and some lighter sailboats. Quite a racket. Defended by a bunch of heavily armed marine jocks. Passage is a month's worth of food. You have to justify your stash to the assessors before boarding. And then you're allowed to get off the boat *once*, when it stops either on Maui or Big Island. The water's *rough*, but people know the risks. The sheriff of Hana hasn't messed with their operation, as far as I know. But if he really intends to rule the islands, he'll have to take them on eventually. They probably *own* O'ahu.

"We got off at Kona. Trekked and bicycled over to Hilo on the Belt Road, eventually found a place to settle. I started looking for you the day we arrived.

"There were some scary moments, a couple unfortunate confrontations that my brother and I had to deal with. They didn't end well—for the others. But basically that's our story. We have a lot of good training. I've seen how hard it's been for others, though. Most people who are left have what it takes, you know? Most people who died off were never going to make it in this new world. They had no idea how to get by without the grocery store, or the repairman, the cops, a phone call away."

Silence. Aukina's story echoes. I have a ton of questions, but I don't want to press him. His story has drained him. I'm certain he's left details out. I know how he feels.

"I should show you the lava sometime," I say. "Maybe

we could get up to Volcanoes after dark. The orange glow is amazing. No more park rangers, no more rules. We could hike right up to the edge of the Halema`uma`u caldera and look in."

"One of these days we'll do it. It'll be a while, though, eh? We're only two miles from the zoo and I haven't even seen *that*. Not that there's anything left to see."

"I haven't thought about the zoo. Poor animals."

Aukina grunts. "I heard the tiger escaped. Someone freed it. Most of the other animals have been poached for food."

"The white tiger's roaming free?"

"Yeah. White tiger out there prowling the Pu`u Maka`ala reserve somewhere like a ghost. No doubt doing just fine on pigs."

I know it's dangerous, but "I'm glad it escaped," I say.

I hear the yelping of dogs and a distant crack of gunfire. Someone must be hunting pig down in the ravine. The barking grows fever-pitched and then dies as several more pops echo. I get this image in my head of the white tiger ambushing some poor hunter. Awful. "Reminds me of a myth about Pele," I tell Aukina.

"Oh, yeah?"

"She's known to appear to people as a white dog. Back in the fifties and sixties, a white dog would wander around Mauna Loa just before eruptions."

"Yeah, but this is a white *cat*."

"Oh, right. Cats are for *after* eruptions. I forgot." I look at him. The pause lingers between us, comfortable. *He knows! He knows everything and he's still talking to me!* I'm so grateful, so relieved. I feel myself leaning toward him.

A motor rumbles closer through the trees. Aukina and I turn toward it. I frown. "You expecting someone?" Aukina asks.

"No." A brown truck breaks through the trees of our long driveway, suddenly slows. Uncle Hank drops his task near the bed of our red truck, gets behind the truck, and studies the newcomer.

"Dad?" I wonder. He's on gate duty, but I just saw him run back inside the house. He probably forgot something. I chuckle. He really *will* have to do push-ups when Uncle Hank is done with him!

Then I remember: The shots. The dogs.

Our dogs.

"Aukina!"

My heart is thrumming.

Uncle Hank opens the red truck's passenger door and retrieves his shotgun. He stands behind the door and points his weapon at the brown truck, ten yards away. The driver cuts the engine and opens his door.

Hank stiffens. "Stay where you are. State your business."

The stranger is slow to answer. "No need to be jumpy," he calls. "I'm just searching for someone. Maybe you can point me in the right direction?"

Uncle Hank doesn't twitch. He heard the gunshots earlier. "I don't think we can help you," he calls. "Turn around and leave."

"Well, see," I hear the driver say, "that's not the spirit of cooperation I was hoping for." The driver's-side door swings wide. A red bandana is tied to the driver's sleeve.

"It's Two Dog," I whisper.

"I won't say it again," Uncle Hank shouts. "Leave. Now."

Two Dog steps out of the truck, a gun in his hand.

Uncle Hank opens fire.

CHAPTER 13

The brown paint of Two Dog's door becomes a cluster of silver dents. I jolt in surprise at the boom of Hank's shotgun, catch myself before I slide. Shouting erupts. Two Dog returns fire. A barrage of gunfire fills the air.

Uncle Hank! He's crouched behind his door, tucked into a ball, reloading his shotgun.

Grandpa races into view from the garage, clutching a rifle.

"No!" My voice catches in my throat.

Two Dog releases several rounds, only half aiming from behind his door.

"Get back!" I yell at Grandpa. He glances up, retreats behind the red truck.

"Lei, quiet!" Aukina says.

Two Dog spots us on the roof. He fires.

A bullet zings off the roofing inches away. I yelp. Dad,

170

Grandpa, and Hank race as a pack at Two Dog. A second shot ricochets off the aluminum. I jerk back, lose my footing, and slide down the roof.

"Lei!"

I slip toward the edge. I spread out my limbs, steady myself. But I can't brake. The edge draws nearer. I'm on my back, feet-first; hands and heels scrape against the smooth metal. With a yell, I dig in my heels as hard as I can, begin to slow. Vertigo swells as the long drop to the ground is unveiled by the advancing edge of the roof. I dig in harder. My bare heels slip over the edge—and catch on the gutter. My *slippahs* fall away. Several more shots fill the air. The gutter budges, snaps. But I'm stopped.

Aukina shimmies down to within arm's length, and I grab his waiting hand, slip, catch. I crawl backward just enough to plant my bare feet and then begin to scoot higher with Aukina's help. His combat boots grip the surface of the roof.

Shouting. I look toward the trucks as I climb.

Who got hit?

There are no more antibiotics. Even a glancing gunshot wound . . . I begin to panic.

A body is sprawled on the ground, my view half blocked by the brown truck. Three men stand over it. I think they're my men, but I can't be certain.

"Lei, come on." Aukina is urging me toward the ladder.

Dad, Grandpa, and Uncle Hank all turn toward me. They look okay. I'm shaking, still trying to reach the ladder to Dad's window. Aukina and I help each other onto the kitchen roof and back through my parents' bedroom window. Dad meets me with a tight embrace.

"Are you hit anywhere?" I ask.

"No. You?"

"No."

"We're all fine, honey. The attacker's dead. We don't know if more are coming. Stay up here with your brother until we give the all clear."

"Where's Mom?"

"She was washing clothes in the ravine. I'm sure she's on her way."

"I'll go find her," Aukina tells Dad.

"Thank you."

Aukina races away with a quick backward glance at me. I turn to Dad. "I knew him. That's Two Dog. He saw Grandpa at the market. How did he know where we lived?"

Dad shakes his head. "He didn't know. We caught him off guard. He was . . . searching? Doesn't matter. He's gone."

"Dad! What about our dogs?"

He's silent. "Stay here. Keep your brother safe."

"I want to go with you."

"No. Stay. I'll send Mom and Aukina up here, too."

He races downstairs. I fall against his bed, sit with my arms planted, clutching the sheets at my sides. I catch my breath. I'm dizzy.

Kai! I bet he's terrified. I rise and hurry down the hall to his room. I knock on the door. "Kai?"

He replies right away with a muffled shout. "Lei!"

I burst into the room. I can't find him.

"Lei." I follow the voice. He's under his bed, peeking out from between boxes.

"You okay?" I get down on my knees.

"Yeah."

"Smart thinking," I say, "hiding down here."

"What happened?"

I sigh. "I don't know." I'm not lying. Why was Two Dog here? How did he find us?

What are we going to do now?

"Were you out there?" Kai asks me.

"Come on out," I say. "It's safe now."

"Is everyone okay?"

"We're all fine. The bad guy is . . . gone. I was on the roof. Almost fell off."

He hugs me. I squeeze him tight.

I hear Aukina and Keali`i downstairs talking to Tami. Mom races through Kai's door. Questions fly back and forth. No real answers. She embraces us. We sit in a tight circle on the floor. Time passes. It seems like forever. Mom doesn't want to talk. She just hums and absently begins to sing in Hawaiian.

I can see the worry in her eyes. She must be thinking what I'm thinking: Will there be another truck? And another?

Sooner or later, someone will come looking for Two Dog. We're not safe here anymore.

When Dad and Uncle Hank return, we know it's them; there's no mistaking the sound of our red truck murmuring up the driveway. Dogs bark excitedly alongside the vehicle. We jump to Kai's window. Grandpa's in the yard, his rifle poised, watching over the property. Aukina and Keali`i each hold a shotgun. The red truck parks right below our window. I whimper.

Three of our guard dogs are limp in the bed. Centaur. Mork. And poor white Pele is covered in red.

I run out of the room, race past Tami on the couch, burst onto the porch, tear down the steps.

"Lei!" Dad commands, but I'm already hovering over Pele. I want to stroke her, but I cover my mouth instead, my blood suddenly cold.

What if Dad had been down there?

I open my mouth to shout something, but a low, formless cry is all that comes.

"Anyone else down there?" Grandpa asks, kneeling, petting Mindy behind the ears. "Are more coming?"

Dad and Uncle Hank shake their heads, uncertain. "No sign of others. Paul met us at the gate. He's down there now."

"Why?" I ask. "Why would he do this?"

"This Two Dog," Grandpa guesses, "he came hunting for me. Because I humiliated him the other day. Either that or the sheriff sent him on an errand.

"We need to act fast," he continues. "If he was alone, then there's no one to report back to their Tribe what happened. Our lucky break. But others *will* come looking for him. We have to offer them a different story."

Dad nods. "This wasn't our firefight. This happened somewhere else."

"The fields behind the school in Papaikou," says Hank. "There's Manō Tribe around there. Rivals."

Everyone agrees.

"Wait!" I say. "You're going to *frame* the Manō? There'll be a bloodbath!"

Silence. They know what this means. I beg Keali`i with my eyes, *Say something!* But he's in on it.

"If we don't give the next wave of Hanamen a viable story—a distraction—they'll come here." Dad is convincing himself as he speaks.

I look at Grandpa. I can't read his expression.

"You're going to start a war." I weigh the words. They sound terrible, but . . . *What else can we do?*

"Lei, inside," Dad says. "Help Mom with—"

"No." Grandpa turns to me. "What would *you* do?"

I open my mouth, shake my head. I don't have an answer. I look at the ground. *They're right.* It doesn't mean it *feels* right.

The lesser of evils. Survival of the fittest. I hate this world.

Keali`i watches me. "Your concern is . . . good, Lei. But the Hanamen and Manō have been at war for the past six weeks," he says. His next words are angry. "This Hanaman never should have ventured into this area to start with."

"It scares me that he tried this," Uncle Hank agrees.

"They know we're around here," Dad explains. "The sheriff dropped me and Lei off at Onomea Bay. Keali`i's right: they've stayed away because the road below is Manō-run.

175

This was a risk Two Dog was willing to take. We'll never know why."

"I told you," says Grandpa. "I humiliated him."

Uncle Hank is stern. "The reason makes no difference."

"Now," Keali`i urges. I jerk at the suddenness of his order. "We have to do it *now*. Other Hanamen need to get the idea this was a bad calculation, before a flood of them show up."

"Put him in his truck," Grandpa says. "I'll drive it down behind the school, lay him out. I can make it look convincing. I'll walk back along the trails."

"What if someone sees you?" Dad asks.

"I'll wear one of your hoodies, make sure I'm alone before setting the scene. Papaikou's far enough that no one heard the firefight; no Manō will know where it really happened."

Keali`i laughs once, checks himself. He snaps to the task of getting Two Dog's body into the truck.

Grandpa looks at me. His eyes hold no regret. "This is the only way out of this," he tells me.

"Okay," I whisper. *Every Tribe deserves what's coming. They do it to themselves.*

We break. Dad collects Centaur and Mork from the truck and lays them gently on the lawn. I try to help with Pele, but Grandpa stops me. "I'll do it, Lei. No use getting blood all over your shirt."

"We'll bury them?" I ask.

"Tonight."

I watch him tenderly embrace Pele and place him softly

beside Centaur and Mork. Mindy paces among them, sniffing, agitated. Grandpa rises, his shirt smeared red. I go inside, let the screen door slam behind me. I sit beside Tami. We talk in whispers, clutching each other's arms. From the shadows I steal glimpses of the men at work. They roll up Two Dog in a tarp and put him in the back of the brown pickup. Dad siphons gas from the truck before he allows Grandpa to leave.

Keali`i goes with him. As I watch them go, my eyes sting. I'm suddenly certain that this plan will fail, that they won't be coming back. Aukina comes over and holds me.

I sit on the couch, paralyzed. My limbs are numb. I feel like I'm floating, stretched, tall. The room turns. I'm now sitting upside down, the vaulted ceiling far *below* me. The world has gone topsy-turvy.

I'm exhausted, but I won't close my eyes. I fear the nightmares. Beautiful white dogs covered with blood. I will see dead Manō. More dead Hanamen. A small war engulfing our forgotten countryside. Mindy is allowed into the house. She sits between me and Tami on the couch, and we hold her tight.

Grandpa and Keali`i return and huddle with my parents. Everything went off without a hitch; no one saw them. I rise and hug Grandpa, don't let go for a long time. Keali`i embraces Tami on the couch.

Aukina is regretful, but he needs to get back home before dark. Everyone agrees he should hurry home. I give him a very long hug. Everyone is watching, but I don't care.

I go to the map above the breakfast bar, study it for ages. Then I drift up to my room and crawl under my covers. I fall into an oblivion much deeper than sleep, forgetting the world, except to adore it from above. When the quiet fills me and I realize that I can concentrate, I find my purpose.

We are purposeful, and it is good.

Aukina's training and my practice kick into gear. I glide beyond the line of night into darkness, toward the matte black mainland, silver moonlight at my back, and I begin.

CHAPTER 14

Hanamen and Manō are at each other's throats in and around Papaikou. No one suspects our family. The fighting began the day after Two Dog's death with an attack by the sheriff's men. Aukina has heard rumors that the sheriff of Hana is still on the island, holed up in the heart of Puna. There's no sign that he's taken a personal interest in the heat around Papaikou, but our house doesn't feel safe anymore, and I can't shake an irrational fear that he'll stride up our drive at any moment. What if it's Grandpa or Dad on duty at the gate when the next enemy truck approaches?

Uncle Hank and Keali'i and Paul are making our perimeter more secure. Air horns and a rusty wheel well are now at the bottom of the drive. Like a bell, the dangling wheel well can be rung with a wrench if an unknown vehicle or group comes up the road. They're planning long trip wires attached to bells at our house, strips of "crow's feet"—star-shaped nails designed to pop tires—that can be tossed onto the road. They're on the lookout for new guard dogs, too, but dogs are hard to come by.

I see only shadows on the road. The sheriff's men will be back. Our tricks will not turn them away.

We inventory Uncle Hank's ammo stores: enough firepower to hold off numerous other attacks like Two Dog's while still having enough left over for brief, weekly target practice. Uncle Hank says that he saw this fallen world coming. Even so, we can't just go buy more ammo—and we may be fighting off attacks for the rest of our lives. It may take years for things to get back to normal after the Star Flowers leave. Rationing firepower better than our enemies seems like the best formula to me.

Grandpa and Keali`i came up the driveway after practice yesterday in the pouring rain, each with a rifle. They met me on the lanai, where they shook themselves dry like dogs. "Join us next time, Lei," Keali`i said.

I stare at the glistening black barrels on their shoulders. "Don't guns stop working if they're wet?"

Grandpa wiped the water off his forehead. "You ever seen a rain delay in a war? As long as the powder's dry in the bullet, you can fire. And this is Hilo! Hank's not dumb enough to buy up ammo that wasn't airtight."

"Over time, sure," Keali`i adds. "Gotta clean and oil guns eventually, or they'll rust. But in the short term it's no problem."

I sigh. "You guys—get in here before *you* rust. Mom's got saimin soup and tea all warmed up."

"Really? Saimin?"

"Light on noodles, too much *kalo*, but sure."

Guns. War. Rust.

The Orchid feels more and more like the pull of a noose. My neck hurts. I can't breathe. I want to cast her away *now*. And yet I hold on. The meltdowns continue. I see the evidence every time I space out. We'd all be dead if I wasn't doing this. The meltdowns are actually *increasing*. We ran out of pushpins to put on the map; now I use a pen. My message is getting through.

I want to have it both ways: to stop radiation from destroying our world—and to get the power back *now*. We need to rebuild. We need to stop fighting. We need to hope again. We need to know that it doesn't have to be us versus them—that we can *all* manage for another few months, hang in there just a little longer, and then we can build our lives back up *together*.

At the same time I worry about releasing the Orchid for a selfish reason. What if my epilepsy returns to full intensity when my connection is gone? I have no more meds. It hasn't really mattered while this door is open between our minds . . . but will that change? I don't want to start having seizures again, falling over, sometimes wetting myself, injuring myself, waking up starving and tired and disoriented. . . . Will I have the courage to let her go when it's finally time?

I don't know.

But I keep signaling. Every night, every stolen nap. And it's working: the meltdowns speed up. The world rubs its lamps, releasing stillborn genies, and every success fills me with dread; I feel that moment of truth closing in like the spiky walls of a baited trap. I'm sure to be impaled no matter which way I run.

*   *   *

As the skirmishes become less frequent, Mom and Grandpa hatch a plan for a *pau hana* retreat to "refresh our souls": surfing at Honoli`i Beach. On Sunday morning we pile three boards and a bodyboard into the truck. Keali`i, Grandpa, and I are vigilant in the bed while Tami and Kai ride in the cab with Mom. Dad stays at the house; we never leave it empty. Aukina is going to meet us on the bluff above the popular surf spot.

Absurdly, for me, the ten-minute drive is as exciting as a family vacation to Fiji. I'm giddy. My neck isn't tight, for once. We're on edge as we pass through Papaikou, but all is quiet, and I can hear the waves calling.

When we arrive at Honoli`i, I don't find Aukina right away; the surf is crowded today. Not even the apocalypse can keep a crowd of avid surfers away. From the edge of the sharp cliff, I glance down at the thin strip of Honoli`i Beach Park. The rain clouds end directly above me, right at the shoreline. It's one of those late afternoons where the ocean and the sky join. The horizon is an indistinct blue. Closer to shore, the waves reach toward the volcanic black rocks of the beach and the emerald bursts of jungle just beyond.

We descend the bluff like a pack of wild teenagers, leaving poor Tami in the dust as she gingerly hobbles down the steps along the rusty railing. Keali`i tears into the water. Mom is right behind him, her short board tucked under her arm like a football. Kai hollers as he tackles the waves along the shore with his bodyboard. Aukina and I stop and sit down on one of the park's grassy knolls, clearing away a few washed-up planks of wood and other tsunami rubbish.

A church group is in the shallows, performing baptisms.

"Come on," Aukina says.

"Wait."

Aukina and I watch the ritual unfold. Grandpa and Tami join us. Everyone wading in the water is wearing a white gown. They're singing in Hawaiian as one man strums a ukulele and another pounds *ipu* drums. The pastor recites his words, dunks each person in turn. Men, women, *keikis*, Hawaiians, Asians, haoles. I find the ceremony calming. The unity of so many different people. It feels like a normal moment from the past.

And the music . . . I don't hear music anymore. It's beautiful! A gospel tune with Hawaiian flair. My old islands touch my ears. I almost cry—which isn't saying much these days—but still, I feel as if each of the chambers of my heart aches to a different part of the rhythm.

E na lima hana, e malama `aina, meke kino, meka pu`u wai.

183

With our hands we press onward to the plow,
Never turning back, we face the mystery far beyond.
With our hands, we will shape each other's stories.
We will write the vision down, never tire until it's done.

E na lima hana, e malama `aina, meke kino, meka pu`u wai.

"You miss the old world?" Aukina asks.

"Yeah. Mostly."

"I wish I had it better before Arrival," he says. "I should have lived like a king. At least I could have had the good life for a while, eh?"

I shrug, my eyes on Mom. She's already up on her first wave, a gentle four-footer along which she glides weightlessly. The younger surfers bobbing in the swell respectfully duck out of the way as she moves toward shore, as if she were an acolyte of Kana Huna herself, the Hawaiian goddess of surfing. Catching the same wave as an *ali`i*—a chief—was once a *kapu* punishable by death. The mere mortals surrounding Mom seem to remember this as they clear her a path. "I dunno," I answer Aukina. "I do like growing our own food. Using everything, wasting nothing. It's hard work, but I like the connection between what we do and what we have. It feels more 'right' somehow. If we had lived a more sustainable life all along, the transition would have been easier."

"Maybe. I had some savings, you know. G.I. Bill, blah, blah. I should have loaned it to myself when I could."

"Yeah, I guess. What's the difference, though?"

"The difference is: I met you." He darts in, kisses me on the cheek, and stampedes out into the surf with my board before I can react.

Tami skewers me with eyes that might as well be screaming. I beam, blushing. When Grandpa nods his approval, I feel my face grow even warmer.

Grandpa rises, drifts away, leaving Tami and me alone. "Oh, my God," she says.

"Calm down," I tell her, but I'm mostly reminding myself.

"Still!"

"He's so sweet. We were so close to kissing when the attack happened at the house. He hasn't made a single move since then."

"Just be patient." Tami winks, echoing my own advice to her. "He's shy. Let him take his time."

Then she says, "Keali`i—we made out. Last night. It's official. He wants to keep it on the DL, but I had to tell you."

We grip each other. "I told you he'd come around," I say.

We gossip for a few minutes, and then her tone grows somber. "What is it?" I ask.

She shakes her head, struggles for words. "He's got . . ."

Something about her eyes gives me a flash of understanding. "Ghosts?"

"I can't say." Tami sighs dramatically. "It's private."

"He say how he got those meds?"

She laughs dryly. "You really don't want to know."

"Yes. I really do. I deserve to know."

"Well, drop it. You don't want me to break his trust."

"Fine, I get it." She's right, but I'm still annoyed that there's a secret separating us. "I'm going to get in the water." Tami's leg is still healing, so I know she won't follow me. I rise and try not to storm away into the waves.

I guide Kai out past the swell. Our group takes turns getting him up on the longboard while Grandpa and Tami watch us from shore. Kai's making great progress, but my eyes keep drifting to Aukina. He watches me watching him, smiling.

Mom winks at me as we both give Kai a good shove to catch his next wave. "You caught one big fish," she says.

I crack a smile. "He's not a fish, Mom."

"He's no shark. Are you dating yet?"

Stunned, I gawk at her.

"What are you waiting for?" she asks.

"Oh, I don't know. Global power failure to be over, maybe. Whatever happened to finishing college and all that?"

"Hon. No one's asking you to marry the poor boy." She laughs and is up and off on the next wave, steady and graceful as the Duke.

Aukina's paddling back out, curving around the swell. I watch him.

Keali'i goes ashore and sits with Tami and Grandpa. After a few minutes he helps Tami rise and walk toward the Honoli'i River. Aukina and Mom are farther out behind me now, waiting for longer waves. I sigh, ride a lazy wave, dodge a foam cooler floating to my right, and turn left all the way to the tumbling black rocks. I hop off, carry my board over to Grandpa, and peel off my wet rash guard, quickly covering my bikini with a dry shirt.

We sit together in silence as a yellow gibbous moon rises. Buzz and his vocabulary words. The sky is still a profound blue; full dark won't fall for at least an hour. I look forward to my safaris above the atmosphere tonight. I'll see the Appalachians. Buzz believes there are at least forty nuclear power plants just in the Bible Belt alone. I've seen evidence of only a handful of meltdowns in the South, so tonight I'll hover and blink above that region.

"An den?" Grandpa asks me. The gentle breeze sends a chill through me. I wrap my arms around my knees and smile at him. He's not satisfied with my silence. "You look tired, Mo'opuna. Is your body getting enough sleep while you perform?"

"I do feel tired . . . and . . ." I trail off.

"Heavy?" Grandpa asks.

"Yeah, heavy." I squeeze more salt water out of my hair, turn to him. "Tūtū, I don't want this anymore. What if I do the wrong thing?"

"Right and wrong aren't 'things,' Mo'opuna. You can't see them before they come. And they like to be shifty, anyway, after the fact."

"You know what I mean."

He nods. "I do. I've been there myself, eh? Lord knows. But you're not alone, Mo'opuna. We've all got your back. The right or wrong of it will work itself out."

Mom drops off of a decent wave into the shallows with Kai. They paddle together back out past the swell. I look at Grandpa. I sense a rare chance to get answers out of him while we're alone. "Grandpa. I want you to tell me about you and the sheriff."

His gentle smile is slowly replaced with a shocking gravity. "I don't know, Mo'opuna—"

I look down, shaken. "I've earned it, Tūtū. I've earned it. I want to understand."

He takes a deep breath, holds it. He lets it go and leans in close. "You keep this between us. I don't know that I'll ever get around to sharing this with your parents."

"Okay," I say softly.

His voice changes. He speaks like he's reporting to a commanding officer. Somber. Serious. He's transported back to Maui, many years ago.

"Kana'ina was my second partner when I was on the beat in Kahului. I was a year on the job. Kana'ina transferred from O'ahu with seven years under his belt. I never warmed to him, but I never disliked him, either. At least, not until later. He was just—my partner. We had each other's back out there. And that counted for something.

"We were paired up nearly a year when I first saw him plant evidence. It took me a while longer to notice that he did it a lot, always on the haoles.

"His wife was murdered in Honolulu two years before his transfer. Killed by a white guy. She was just as crooked

188

as him, in on a deal that went bad. I can't prove it, but I'm pretty sure.

"He liked my family. Always joined us when invited. Dinner. Picnics. Fishing. He trusted me with his views on sovereignty. I listened. When he talked of a free Hawai`i Nei—of his longing for native Hawaiians to rule themselves, railing against the American occupation and the unjust overthrow of the royal family—I was mostly all ears. I've always agreed that a great evil was perpetrated by the takeover of our lands; the loss of our nation sent us Hawaiians into a cycle of poverty and struggle amid a paradise for tourists. But the more he ranted, the more I disagreed with his brand of action, even when I was sympathetic. I should have challenged him. But I was too insecure.

"I saw him slip drugs onto a haole we had cuffed on the street. That suspect was clearly bad news. We got him behind bars because of what Kana`ina did. I never really questioned it, Leilani. Just a little bending of the rules to nab a guy who had had it coming. Kana`ina didn't know I saw him do it.

"He did it again a couple months later. Another haole. Just drunk. Didn't make any sense to me. The whole incident stank. He knew I saw him that time. But I never brought it up. The next time he did it—routine traffic stop with some punk teenagers—I realized he was singling out white folks. I confronted him. Not about the haole thing but his habit in general. I told him, 'I can't ignore it anymore. I don't want to see it again, or I'll have to report you.'

He seemed more ashamed than pissed. But he was playing me.

"Next time he did it, I wasn't the only witness. We were at a club in Wailuku. Hot tip about a big deal going down. We were backup for a DEA gig. Patting folks down in the club. Lights had just come on. I'll never forget it; it was so obvious. He had this bag of snow palmed in his hand. He reached around into this white guy's aloha shirt and dropped the bag right into his breast pocket. The club owner saw it happen. And the haole protested, of course.

"Accusations started flying. The DEA guys got involved. Took down the witnesses' stories. Kana`ina denied everything. Put on a great act. They came to me, asked me what I saw. They knew I was right next to him. The haole was begging me to be honest. Kana`ina's eyes were on me like a snake's.

"He had just bought a house, Lei. Had a mortgage. An unpaid suspension would have ruined him. I knew the club owner was rotten. The haole had *dirty* written all over him, too. I know that's beside the point, Mo`opuna. But at the time it all came together in my mind the wrong way. I vouched for my *moke* partner.

"'These hot-rod junkies'll make anything up,' I told the DEA guy."

Grandpa pauses. I don't dare move. Finally he continues. "Later Kana`ina said, 'I owe you one big.' I nodded, but I was sick to death. I quit the force that year. Moved back to Big Island."

He grows silent, looking at the giant moon. He finally meets my eyes. I almost gasp. They're filled with such shame. My *tūtū* isn't capable of that look—because he's incapable of doing anything to be ashamed of. But there it is. I look away.

"I'm sorry, Mo`opuna," he says.

I startle. "Why are you apologizing to *me?*"

"I've never apologized to anyone for that. You're the first person I've ever told."

I don't know what to say. I should reassure him that his story doesn't change the way I think about him. Tell him I love him and always will. Hug him. But I'm silent and still. I'm shocked, not by his admission of guilt but that he would confide such a burden to me. Finally I try: "What you did meant he didn't kill Dad. You saved his life. It was all meant to be."

He shakes his head. "Yeah. No. Not true. If I had stood my ground, done the right thing, Kana`ina would have been kicked off the force. Instead he moved up the ranks, got himself a sweet little throne in Hana just in time for the world to end. He never would have been there to hunt you two down in the first place if I had done the right thing that night. And that haole—he did time for possession. That's on me, too."

"You made a mistake, Tūtū. A big one, even. But you atoned for it, didn't you? Like a cat! You landed on your feet. Nine lives. Yeah? You've been a spiritual counselor for so many people. For me. You changed your life. You know the path. You've found *pono.*"

"I thought so," he says. "I hoped so. But here we are.

191

Kana`ina is looking for me. My ghosts have finally caught up. This whole family's at risk."

"But what does any of that have to do with now? Why is he looking for you?"

"I don't know."

I study Grandpa. The way he said that—his inflection, the thoughtful look in his eyes—I begin to wonder if he *does* know. "Tūtū?" I ask carefully. "Is there something else you're not—?"

Tami and Keali`i plop down beside us, all smiles. "There's a group by the river with *kālua* pig!" Keali`i says. He cups his hands around his mouth and shouts, "*Kau kau!*" out to Mom and Aukina. Tami laughs.

I look to Grandpa. *Our little secret?* his eyes ask.

Our little secret, I nod back. What trust he has in me. I feel so sorry for him, my heart does a flip. He's been haunted by this since long before I was born. It has shaped him profoundly. And no one knows about it but me, him, and . . . the sheriff of Hana. I want to shout, *Grandpa, let it go!* Instead I squeeze his shoulder as I pass him. "Love you." It's not enough, but it's all I can do.

The others race ashore and dry off. We rumble as a herd to the bank of the river, where the church congregation from earlier are hoisting an entire cooked pig out of an *imu*, a pit oven, and are happily sharing what they have. We're served moist, tender shredded pork in bowls of plaited coconut fronds. Other surfers wander over, and the church musicians strum their ukuleles, and we're suddenly in the middle of an impromptu beach luau. My stomach screams for more with each bite of greasy pork. In the *imu* our cooks have also steamed sweet potatoes, bananas, breadfruit, and some fish. Turns out they've been here preparing the *imu* and the roast all day long. They have no way to keep their leftovers, so they offer the feast around without any conditions. We're so pleased with our luck and the generosity of our hosts that we completely lose track of time.

Finally Aukina turns to me. "I better go. Roofing at five a.m. See you next week." I apologize that we can't offer to help with the project, but he understands. "You guys get your feet back under you. Focus on *your* big job. There will always be plenny projects at our place needing help." He gives me a quick kiss good-bye. I sizzle with pins and needles, but Tami, Keali`i, Grandpa, Mom, and even Kai are watching. Aukina takes off on his bike in the dark.

We return to our truck on the bluff, a healthy portion of pork and vegetables wrapped in a large banana leaf "to-go box" for Dad, our bellies full and our spirits recharged.

*　*　*

Late Tuesday night I witness a live nuclear power plant melt-down. Britain. Along the southeastern coast. A great gray cloud spreads to the west, over London, reaching for Ireland. It's the third plant I've seen go belly-up in the UK this week. A good sign.

I'm over the North Pole, dazzling ribbons of aurora borealis swirling above northern Russia and the Koreas, but the Orchid centers above the bland radioactive cloud creeping over England. I feel her draw up the radiation, like a leaf summoning water from the roots of a tree, and her wispy petals and her gelatinous core quake with pleasure. She absorbs radiation from anywhere on the globe no matter her position—her aura and her folds go far beyond the visible spectrum, enveloping all the Earth just as the flames of a fireplace warm a whole room. But she can pull—as if through a syringe—at a specific source of radiation, too.

I feel that this plan is working; so many plants have released their venom in the past week—it cannot be coincidence. But so many more are left. I have to wait for them all. If just one facility goes supernova after the Star Flowers depart, so much lasting damage could be done. After all the suffering I've caused to keep the greater evil at bay, I would hate to miss a few dozen plants at the very end. After all, the world won't magically return to normal the day the Star Flowers leave; it'll take months yet, maybe even years, for society to reassemble. And then there's the question of nuclear *weapons.* Dad once likened the Orchid's ability to clean up radiation to a sponge absorbing water. Ice would have to melt before the sponge could act. I don't think I can do anything about nuclear weapons—until after they explode. But thousands are out there. Someone controls each one of them, right? When the Orchid drifts away and power is restored, do I lose the ability to render warheads dead on arrival?

So many reasons to keep the Orchid here.

Stop, I tell myself. I can't be a guardian angel for everyone, forever.

Leave. Go. Now.

The other voice! I draw back, cringe, as if I've been relaxing in a dark bath and then realize someone else is in the room with me. In the sudden stillness I listen, desperate to learn something. Man? Woman? Child? What part of the world? All of these traits are filtered out by the time I receive the thoughts. But there's no doubt: someone is here with me. I'm not having a grand mal, either.

This voice is getting stronger.

Who are you?

It retreats.

Don't go. I need to talk to you.

Then it's true. A person is doing the Morse code.

Who are you?

Who are you?

I bristle. *I'm the Flower of Heaven. She's mine. I will ask the questions.*

The presence recoils. Fear. Good.

Release her! Why won't you release her?!

If you've seen the Morse code, then you know—

I'm falling, stretching through a funnel. I'm back in my own body. It's dark. But someone is *actually* in my room. I hear the shuffle of feet. I hold my breath.

A whispered question: "Lei?"

Tami. "You crazy?" I spit. "You woke me!"

"I've changed my mind. I think you should know."

"Know what?"

"What Keali`i told me."

"Tami. Not now!"

She withdraws in a huff. "Wow. Fine."

I don't care. I need to get my door back open, climb the rope ladder to the stars. It's not her fault; she couldn't have known. But there's no time to explain.

When I finally relax enough to return to the Emerald Orchid, though, the other mind is long gone. I have her all to myself.

The way it should be.

CHAPTER 15

Buzz arrives on Thursday afternoon, in high spirits and full of urgent plans. "Have you made contact with the baby?" he asks.

"No. Why?"

"Haven't you seen? Maybe not, I guess. You're always"—he points to the ceiling—"up there. Anyway, on the horizon at about three this morning, the baby was flashing."

"What?" Mom, Dad, and I say together. "Is it Morse code?" I ask. *Did the other person get in? Do they control her now?*

"No," Buzz reassures us. "There's no pattern. It's just copying Mom. Monkey see, monkey do. It's babbling!"

"Babbling?" Tami says. "Oh, my God. That's *adorable*."

"Cute, yes," Buzz agrees, then grows serious. "It may be ready for contact. We should act fast."

We make a plan. Dad, Grandpa, and I agree to drop

everything and join Buzz tomorrow up at the observatories. We'll stay there as long as it takes for me to explore a possible connection with the baby and try to figure out this other presence. When I'm done at the radio dish array, we'll visit the pearl impact site. "Are you finally going to tell us what you found up there?" I ask Buzz.

"I'll do you one better. I'll show you. Go pack a bag while the light's still good, and I'll set up my . . . presentation. It's chilly up there; pack warm."

I race to my task, and when I come back downstairs, I see that Buzz has returned my birthday present to me. The 8mm projector is assembled on the coffee table. My family and Tami and Keali'i stand around it expectantly. I study it reverently, running my fingers along the cool metal casing, not sure what I'm supposed to do now.

"It's not a paperweight," Buzz says. "Go on. Flip the switch."

"What?"

Buzz leans forward and turns the projector on with a flick of his finger. White light illuminates the wall. A motor spins, and the empty reels rotate. Buzz turns it back off. The room fills with chatter. "*Planet of the Apes* tonight!" Dad cheers, holding aloft the film's 8mm canister. "Whaddya say?"

Kai leaps and thrusts a fist in the air. My heart skips a beat. *Movie night. It's back! Just like that.* "How?" I marvel. I search for a car battery, anything that looks like a power source. Nothing obvious.

"Ah, well, that's where *you've* given *us* a gift, Lei." He lifts a small canister off the buffet with a great deal of effort, tells Dad to put the film reel in the other room just to be safe. As if he's handling a bowling ball, he slides a shard of gray-black rock the size of a matchbox from the canister onto his palm. He closes his fingers around it. "Put your hand down on the table," he tells me. "All the way down."

I do what he says.

"Kai, grab a piece of metal." Kai darts away, returns with a crescent wrench. "Okay, hold on to it tightly. Place it *under* the table," instructs Buzz.

When he lets go of the wrench, it shoots upward and slams into the coffee table. "Whoa!" Kai says. "It's stuck to the bottom!"

Buzz nods. "It's attracted to what I have in my hand." He turns to me. "I'm going to place this on your palm. You're not going to be prepared for its weight—or what it does—no matter what I say, so just be ready. And keep your hand *above* the table."

He lugs his hand over to mine and slides the shard of rock onto my palm. I try to flinch away, but I can't. It's so heavy, as if Kai is standing on my hand. The smooth shard flips over. The wrench clanks to the floor at the same time. I flinch away, still pinned to the table. I laugh, exhilarated. The room is murmuring. "What is this?"

"That," says Buzz with wonder, "is a sliver of the pearl."

It flips of its own accord in my fist again. There's a sudden knock under the table. The wrench has struck it from below and is stuck to the underside again.

"It's dense. That little block probably weighs twenty pounds."

"I don't understand," I say, almost breathless. "Why is it *moving?*" Keali`i's backpack against the wall falls over, as if kicked. He strides over to investigate it.

"The pearl, Lei. It's incredible. The size of a Sherman tank. But it must weigh as much as a *football stadium*. It has an electromagnetic field beyond comprehension."

"Huh?" It tumbles over in my hand again. The wrench falls to the ground.

"Don't worry," he announces proudly. "You'll see for yourself soon."

"Can I see?" Kai asks. He goes to grab the little shard of dark gray material, but he can't lift it from my pinned hand. "Holy crap," he says.

"But what does this have to do with the projector?"

"It's thrumming with inexhaustible power. Somehow the material is both energy and matter. I mean, all matter is energy, right? But this stuff is like *fluid* matter-energy. It's both at once. I don't know how else to say it. You know, Einstein searched his whole adult life for a Grand Unified Theory and failed. The merger of gravity, electromagnetism, and the strong and weak nuclear forces. This may be proof of what he was looking for."

"Oh," I say, not understanding a thing. The shard continues to flip in my hand as Buzz talks. With each flip, the wrench below the coffee table smacks to a stop against the underside or falls to the carpet.

"It's an electromagnet that turns itself on and off every few seconds. The frequency depends on size. This little guy reverses exactly every seven-point-four seconds. The pearl as a whole toggles every twenty-one minutes and thirteen seconds."

"I was supposed to take physics my junior year," I tell Buzz with a pang—I might have been in class this very moment. "What's an electromagnet?"

"Most metals will magnetize when you send a current through them. That's how most motors work. The reason this little shard is flipping so much is that the current reverses and stops *on its own*. It's . . . throbbing, like a heart—sort of. Whenever it's on, it's powerful. The wrench's attraction to it overcomes the force of gravity. But this defies convention, Lei. Don't ask me to explain. It's like nothing known."

"Remember watching birds migrate east to west back when the Orchid was ejecting these things left and right in the initial days?" Dad asks me. "Remember trying to use our compass on Maui? These pearls have *strong* magnetic fields."

"This could change a lot of things, Lei," Buzz continues. "I haven't begun to scratch the surface. It somehow creates its own magnetic on-off switch. Motors usually need an electric current to flip the polarity to propel the motor around its axis. That's how I got the projector to work without electricity. Just pinned two small shards down opposite each other so they can't flip. They toggle very quickly in alternating states. I put metal along the motor's axis and, voilà, the motor turns! And if you can turn a motor, you can generate a current, in this case for the lightbulb and the speakers. I encased it all in a ferromagnetic cobalt housing to shield the field from the rest of the projector."

Keali`i drops his backpack behind the couch, returns his focus to us. He pries the shard out of my hand. Once again, very much like clockwork, the shard turns over in his palm. The coffee table jolts. "Ho! That's nuts!"

"Careful! Stay above the table. The wrench will bullet up and crush your hand."

"Is it radioactive?" Tami asks.

"No. Not at all."

"If this is like a battery," Keali`i asks, "then why don't we fire up the TV?"

"Well," Buzz explains, "the TV is still broken, the integrated circuitry fried. The Orchid still affects the flow of electricity, doesn't matter how much juice we have at the ready. For example, the projector's bulb is still finicky. Flickers and dims a lot."

"What about cars?" asks Keali`i. "Could we fire pistons with this instead of gas?"

Buzz grins. "Yes. But we'd have to entirely redesign the motors first."

"Really?" Mom asks. "No more gas?"

"Yeah, but let's not get ahead of ourselves. It'll be months or years before we even have a prototype. And we'd have to find a way to mine the material."

Buzz looks at me. "Whatever the Orchid does to our world's electricity, and however it soaks up radiation,

202

whether from stars or blown reactors, I see the connection. It draws in that radiation, consumes it as food somehow, and converts it to this."

"Star Flower poop," Kai says.

Buzz laughs. "Precisely. Matter and energy consumed, converted, and . . . ejected. Lei, you thought of it as propellant to glide through space. The Orchid's way around Newton's Second Law. I'm beginning to think this stuff may even *be* dark matter. The mysterious unseen glue of the cosmos that we were never able to account for."

We all look at one another.

"Once the Star Flowers are gone," Buzz concludes, "this material, if we can mine it, harness it, could power the globe. Forever."

*   *   *

Tami and Keali`i pull me aside when the excitement has settled. I suddenly remember how Tami woke me and I turned her away. Keali`i lifts his backpack, and we head outside. Tami walks tenderly with a cane that Mom made for her out of an old koa branch. Around the corner of the garage, they stop me.

"Lei," Keali`i begins, "I need you to do something for me."

"What is it?" They're both acting . . . guilty.

He takes off his backpack and pulls out a container. He hands it to me. It's heavy.

"I know your . . . feelings. But I want you to be safe. When I'm not around."

I lift the lid. It's a small pistol. "Keali`i. No."

"I'll teach you to use it responsibly. I gave Tami one, too. Two Dog . . . the heat down the road . . . I really think you're not thinking straight. We all need to be covered better."

"No, Keali`i. Please. Take it away." I thrust it in his chest, let go of it. He fumbles and catches it, stunned at my rejection.

"Lei—" Tami begins.

"Please, it's not about you," I say. "I hate guns. I . . . can't."

"Lei, I don't care if you hate it," Keali`i says. "You need it. This was expensive. You shouldn't just toss it back at me like that."

"They DON'T MAKE US SAFER. Don't you get it? Guns ATTRACT problems, they don't solve them. Haven't you learned anything this year? This island is a death trap for so many people. Everyone hoarded weapons—like Hank—so that they'd be safer in the end. But what really happened? NOW EVERYONE HAS GUNS! And we're all shooting at each other all the time. IT'S COMPLETELY LŌLŌ!"

"Lei!" Tami's voice rises, incredulous. "Snap out of it. You're—"

"No! YOU snap out of it. You haven't seen the things I have. All the freaking *preppers* out there . . . they self-fulfilled their own apocalypse! We could all be working together here. Instead we just *defend* what's *ours*. Where'd you get it, anyway? What do you mean, expensive? What'd you pay for it?"

Keali'i peers up at the sky, clearly exasperated. "You don't . . . you don't go asking that about a *gift*. It's *rude*."

"No. Answer me. This is like the billionth time you show up with wild things that no one else can get. What'd you do? More favors?"

"Lei." He and Tami look to each other.

"I won't even consider taking that gun unless you tell me where it came from."

His jaw tightens. "You want to know?"

I nod impatiently.

"Will you take the gun if I tell you?"

I nod. It's a lie. I have no intention of keeping his gift. But I want to know what he's going to say.

"I'm Manō," he says.

Manō. I search for that word, watching his sober eyes.

One of the major Tribes. The one centered in Papaikou.

My voice fumbles. "*What?*"

"I'm Manō."

I lean against the wall of the garage. "You . . . For how long?"

Keali'i looks away. "Since before your mom offered me help," he says.

"The whole time I've known you?"

He's still averting his eyes. "Yeah, Lei. The whole time. I never said anything because I knew I'd be kicked out of the Tribe, or your house. I wanted to have both. I love your family, Lei. I love you and Tami. I—"

"You're Tribe," I say.

It all clicks. His intense anger at the Hanamen on the breakwater. He had that dive light that worked, the batteries. Items probably confiscated from someone else. The closed doors in his house—hiding loot. *Ghosts.* Tami. The meds. I turn to her. "And how long have you known?"

She shakes her head defensively. "Lei . . . He told me when we started dating . . . that night we were playing cards."

"And you didn't *say anything?*"

"I tried! I was going to. I woke you up. I was shocked at first, too, Lei. Just calm down, okay?"

He got the meds *from his own Tribe.* That's why he biked toward my home—he was going to Papaikou! Was it the Manō who stormed the hospital, killing guards to hoard the antibiotics, so that patients died?

I lunge forward, push Keali`i. "Get out!"

"Lei," he gasps.

"Take your *present* with you. Who'd you steal *that* from?"

"Lei, I don't rob people! I'd never do that."

"Lei, stop!" Tami says. "He saved my life."

"You're *Tribe!* Do you know how many honest people have been screwed, killed by you people? The Tribes are a nightmare for everyone."

"Unless you're in one. Don't you get it? We're just looking out for what's best—"

"No. *You* don't get it!"

"It doesn't matter to you that he saved my life?" Tami's eyes are filling with tears. "Lei, you *have* a family. Keali`i had no one! I have no one."

"We're good people, Lei. We take care of each other. `Ohana. Would you rather that sheriff run everything? We're the only check against his power. Would you rather Tami had died? Would you have refused *that* gift if you knew how I got it? We watch this road, Lei. Guard it from below. My Tribe's been protecting your family."

My knees go weak. I glance between them, unseeing. "There would have been no need for a *gift* if you hadn't stolen the meds to begin with!"

"That's *not* true. If we didn't take it, one of the other Tribes would have. Those meds would have been used on someone else's friend."

"But the Mano let innocent patients die!" I crumple into the grasses beside the garage, shaking. "We fed Two Dog's body to you sharks. Fed your war."

Tami is in tears. Keali`i's words tumble in my mind. I remember only that he admitted to . . . his Tribe was responsible for raiding a *hospital*. "Go. GO! Both of you!"

Keali`i frowns. "Where are we supposed to—?"

"Go to Papaikou, why don't you? Just . . . leave me alone."

"Lei, please!" Tami says.

"GO!"

Keali`i's anger is masking shame. Deep shame. He snatches up his bag but leaves the gun behind. "Come on," he tells Tami. They turn toward the house, Tami hobbling with her cane.

"Take your stupid pistol, too!"

He shakes his head, not turning. "It's yours, Lei."

"I'm never touching it!" I shout.

I watch them disappear into the house. I'm racked with waves of fury and shame. How could I treat them like that? But then I see Dad's head again, the tip of the sheriff's gun at his skull, and I want to puke.

My blood cools. I cry. Are they right? Isn't Keali`i just doing the best he can, the best way he knows how? He lost his parents . . . he had no one. Like Tami—no one. And I sent them packing like mongrel dogs.

Why aren't there any rules anymore? Nothing—*nothing*—makes sense anymore.

I rise, round the corner, stop on the lanai steps. I can't leave that gun lying in the grass. What if Kai finds it? I don't know if it's loaded, but . . . the thought of Kai discovering it and tinkering with it makes me ill. I run over, pick it up between my thumb and forefinger, and toss it into the thick, thorny brambles that line our yard. He'll never go crawling in there and find it, and it'll rust shut. Time and decay are the only rules left.

"It's getting dark!" Dad calls through the screen door. "Who's ready for some movie magic? Before it gets too late?"

Grandpa complains, "Put that crazy ape movie on and make us all forget what a crazy ape world we live in, eh?"

I laugh silently in spite of myself. Popcorn springs to life on the propane stove. I go inside. Dad's beaming. "You good to go? Where's Keali`i and Tami?"

"They're . . ." I shake my head. "Having a fight. Went to bed early."

Dad shrugs. "Their loss."

Grandpa heads upstairs, and Dad says, "You gonna watch with us?"

"No, thanks. I prefer science fiction. Not really into documentaries."

We all laugh, but it dies off as we realize that Grandpa's not joking.

I'm really not in the mood, but Dad is looking glum, so I stay. Watching Buzz fire up the projector and seeing moving images on the blank wall and hearing sound proves to be an undeniable thrill. I could be watching the Wright Brothers pedal their first plane into the air. But as the slow film crawls on with lots of empty scenery and creepy music, I grow sleepy.

Keali`i. Tribesman. Liar. Killer. Thief.

Keali`i. Hero. Gentleman. Protector. Friend.

I feel sweaty. "I'm too tired," I tell Dad. "I'm so sorry." I need to get to work. Make the globe turn the right way.

"Hon, go to bed. We can watch it again later."

I know we're going to the array tomorrow, but . . . we're already out of time. Things have to start working again. Start making sense.

Upstairs I sleep and drift, dot and dash. But I never know who sees the pattern, who knows the words. When is enough enough? Does it really even matter?

As the famous line from the *Planet of the Apes* movie goes: is there even a difference between saving them . . . and damning them all to hell?

The world below flickers in silence and solitude. Even so, from somewhere very far away, the rhythmic shuttering of a projector and the muffled pleas of apes and men steal into my dreams.

*   *   *

The shores of the vast Asian continent are dark. I hover over the dim green eastern coast. My islands are just now visible as a distant scar along the day-lit curve of ocean blue. The frontier of night creeps away from her shores; it's morning there. The sun will soon flash into view as it peeks above the haloed edge of the globe.

A fleck of glinting sunlight on the water near my islands catches my attention. I stop flashing my English-language, American Morse code-message over Tokyo and Pyongyang and Seoul and Beijing and Taipei and Hong Kong and Manila and Bangkok—all hosts to nuclear power plants—and drift nearer to home in order to investigate. The journey takes time. I love this angelic drifting.

I can sense the presence. Distant, retreated.

The dawn bathes me as I near Hawai`i. *Hello?* I ask. *Come forward. We need to talk.*

I do not wish to talk. I pick up the voice in spite of the owner's attempt to guard it.

We can't let them leave. You must stop this effort. They're preventing global nuclear winter. Their fields soak up the radiation, make it inert.

That's ridiculous. You can't keep them here. Who are you to decide we must all live in a dark age?

210

The mental shout startles me, but I guard my surprise. *I will let go when the work is done and we are safe. Soon. Be patient.*

The islands are near, now. I can just make out the object of my interest. A speck of gray in the waters between Kaua`i and O`ahu. Is that a battleship?

I've seen your message. You've got it all wrong. GO NOW.

It *is* a ship. I drift closer. Naval.

Has the military returned?

Leave.

I shift my attention back. *You've seen my message?*

LEAVE.

You cannot kick me out.

I will find a way. The spawn.

I control it, too, I lie.

No, you don't. The spawn doesn't even talk yet.

A flash of panic. How does this person know that? *I do.*

I will find a way to kick you out. If I can't, I will find YOU.

This is meant to intimidate me? I project amusement into the space we share. *You cannot find me. You cannot reach me. Give this up. Trust in me. I will let them go when we are ready to be alone again. It'll be soon.*

Somehow I sense masculinity. The confidence of a hunter, a chieftain, domineering. He's frustrated that something feminine has bested him. I feel his sudden menace.

You spend an awful lot of time over the Hawaiian Islands, my dear.

*   *   *

I awake in a flash and draw in a sudden gasp. *He knows I'm in Hawai`i!*

I sit up, rub my eyes. My bedroom. Morning. The disorientation and the alarm mix in my mind.

Doesn't matter. Of course he knows you're here. He's right: the Orchid hovers over these islands like they're her nest. She goes out to forage, but she always returns.

"But why'd you have to flinch, idiot?" I ask the quiet room. *Now he thinks you're scared. You encouraged him by showing weakness.*

But I'm *not* scared. Just startled. *He can't dislodge me, can he?* I scan my mind, finger along the anchor that sits in my brain. It's there. Strong. Embedded like a fishhook tangled in a web of coral. That tension is always there. I've grown so accustomed to it that I hardly notice it, like a hat on my head. But the second it lightens, I'll know.

He can't hurt you. He can't take her away from you. And he can't just come to Hawai`i and "find" you. Shake it off.

A knock at my door. I yelp, then clasp my hands to my mouth. Dad swings the door open. "You okay?"

I drop my hands. "Yeah."

"Glad you're awake," he says. "Come on down. Time to roll." He shuts the door.

"Dad?"

He halts, pops his head back in the room. "Yeah?"

"He's a man. He knows I'm in Hawai`i."

"Huh?" Then he gets it. "Oh, wow. Okay." He steps into the room. "A man? Did you get a name? Where is he?"

A name? How about Asshole? I shake my head.

"No sense of location? How does he know you're here?"

"Because the Orchid's always over Hawai`i."

"Ah. Well." Dad pauses. "Come on down. We'll think through this as we head up to the observatories."

"There's something else: I saw a ship near O`ahu. It was military."

"Really? What kind? How many?"

"Just one. I can't tell what kind. I could barely make out a ship at all."

He frowns in thought. "Okay. Could mean anything. Try to keep track of it."

"Obviously."

"And about that voice—any sense of *where* it's coming from yet?"

"I have no idea where he is. I'm not even sure he's an English speaker, Dad. I just get the gist of his thoughts. Like we communicate only by passing notes back and forth under a door. I only know he's a guy because . . . he smacks of . . ."

"Testosterone?"

I grunt. "Exactly."

CHAPTER 16

I fill my duffel with my warmest clothes, have breakfast, say good-bye to Mom and Kai, who will be helping Sara and the baby at the Irving house for the next few days while Keali`i, Paul, and Uncle Hank patrol the neighborhood.

From the living room window I see Keali`i pulling farming tools out of the garage, placing them neatly on the driveway next to `Imiloa's saddle. Tami sits at the base of the lanai steps. I study Keali`i, wondering if it's a good idea to leave him in charge of our place—but I *do* trust him. Whatever else he is—he's `ohana. A brother. I can't bring myself to question his loyalty.

I step out and hurry past Tami, meeting Dad and Grandpa at Buzz's van. Dad pans between me and Tami, casts me a questioning look.

Tami grumbles and rises with the help of her cane. She heads up the steps. "Hey," I tell her. She glowers, but I see something soft behind it. "Um . . . I hope it goes okay down here. A few days, okay?"

She forces a smile, aware of her onlookers. "Yeah. Be safe up there."

"Tami. I'll . . . We'll figure this out. 'Kay? I'm not . . . I'm not mad anymore."

Her expression thaws. She nods and heads inside.

"What's going on there?" Dad asks.

"Just . . . private."

We all pile in. All the doors are gone, the hood and the hatchback, the bumpers, the glass except for the windshield. The rear seats have been removed, replaced with bags of produce tied to the floor with twine so they can't roll out of the back. Buzz jumps into the driver's seat. "Some car," I say.

"No superfluous weight." He winks. "When you live above ten thousand feet and your food is grown at sea level, you maximize fuel efficiency."

Dad leans forward from behind me. "We should have thought of this."

Great. I see my next weekend at home helping Dad dismantle our truck.

We motor through Hilo, ignoring stop signs and weaving along cluttered blacktop passageways that have forgotten they were once busy streets. Hilo's a living ghost town, caught in a flickering space-time rift. We pass Kai's gymnastics center, and I'm stabbed with a sense of loss. But it's covered in mold and mildew, as if it's been abandoned for five hundred years, not five months. They say truth is stranger than fiction. Hilo is stranger than both.

"You know, Lei, I can't say it enough: your mother and I are so proud of you." Dad is trying and failing to connect the dots, about the tension between me and Tami. I smile.

"It feels really stupid to say that," he continues. "Given what you're actually doing. That we're proud of you—it doesn't even begin to grasp it."

"It's almost done," I say. "Maybe that other voice is right. Maybe I should just send them away today." My stomach drops. *And let my epilepsy take over my life again?*

Buzz shakes his head. "No, Lei. You're doing the right thing. There's more than a hundred facilities out there that will probably still blow. *At least.*"

"But when will we know that the last plant has melted down?"

"We can't know for sure. I can do some fancy math with probabilities and normal distribution curves. We'll at least know when we're a couple confidence intervals out. At that point we may just have to live with the uncertainty."

Dad winks at me. "Sorry you asked?"

"I should have known better," I say.

We navigate a bottleneck, where piles of cars on either side of the street have been pushed aside just enough for a vehicle to pass, and we're suddenly soaring high above Hilo on an empty highway. "A part of me . . ." I fall silent. What I'm about to say feels so petty, so callous. . . . *wants them to stay forever.*

"Me too," Buzz says. "Believe me: me too."

"You too, what?" I ask.

"Wants them to stay."

I jerk. How did he know I've been thinking that?

Grandpa leans forward, pats my shoulder. "Mo`opuna, you keep 'em here if you want to. I know you'll do right."

I nod, look at my knees. *Yeah, but "do right" for whom?*

We wind up the Saddle Road toward the intersection of two giant volcanoes and finally break through the forest of ohia trees, emerging onto an open land of broad lava flows and big sky. The rising peaks of Mauna Loa and Mauna Kea are distant, disguised as timid hills. The peaks are connected by a vast saddle of hardened lava, black and ropy, or brown and as sharp as shattered glass, swirling together like bands of marble.

These mountains rose one lava flow at a time. Magma spilled forth, hardened, and then was buried by the next eruption. Jungles grew, burned away, grew again.

The pearl's crater and its wide debris field are a blotch on Mauna Loa's slope. Square miles of land pulverized to cinders and basaltic ash. I groan. I've forever marred the natural beauty of Pele's home. It looks as if someone took an ice cream scooper to a dish of rocky road and then sprinkled powdered chocolate in a circle around it. Toward the center a tunnel veers into darkness.

We're going to hike into that?

"I actually think all of this happened at exactly the right moment," says Buzz. "Really makes you wonder, you know? The timing doesn't quite feel random to me."

"What're you talking about?" Dad asks.

217

"Let me ask you," Buzz continues. "If this happened a hundred years ago, would it have affected the globe at all? But what if this happened a hundred years *in the future?*"

"Huh." Dad nods. "Interesting."

"What?" I ask. "What about it?"

Buzz shoots me a grim smile. "Our race has been on the cusp of an insane revolution. Microchip implants in our brains. Artificial intelligence. All in the name of progress. All in the name of making our lives easier, more efficient. In the course of decades we moved our computers from buildings to desktops. In the span of years we transferred our computing from laptops to our pockets and phones. We wear it, Leilani! Glasses. Watches. Cochlear implants. Robots in our hearts and lungs. What was to stop us from microchips in the brain? Just a little processing boost. Bigger, better memory. We were about to connect ourselves to neural networks. Commands would soon happen *at the speed of thought*—no interface required.

"If this Orchid had come to calve a hundred years from now—when the world could no longer even count to ten without consulting the technology in our brains—it would have sent our species back to the Pleistocene, not just the Industrial Revolution."

I sigh. "So why am I rushing to flip the switch back on?"

"Yeah, well, good question," Buzz says. "I mean, are we going to treat technology differently after this? Or make the same mistakes and court an even darker age down the road?"

"I wish we could have it both ways," Grandpa says.

"What do you mean?"

He shrugs.

"I'm sick of both ways," I say. "Isn't that how it already is? Whatever happened to black-and-white? Right and wrong? Up and down? I want the world either on or off."

Grandpa tosses his hands up. "Maybe you're right."

"That's exactly the problem!" I cry. "I'm sick of maybe. I'm either right or I'm wrong. Which is it?"

"Lord only knows." Dad sighs.

"Well, I don't buy that, either," I blurt. "God's so black-and-white to most, but He's the murkiest thing of all, if you ask me."

Grandpa squeezes my shoulder again. "Hey, that's okay. That *is* right. God's not black-and-white. You steer clear of anyone who says He is, you hear? God's every color of the rainbow. He's Rangi, the sky, and Papa, the earth. Wind, sea, lava, snow. He's all of it, everywhere. Of course He's murky."

"Well, why do we grow up being taught that it's simple?"

"Because big truths are hard for little minds. We forget sometimes, though, that our baby brains grow big enough for bigger truths. Shame on us when that happens."

It grows cold, and Buzz slows to reduce the wind chill. Dad fishes my winter jacket out and passes it to me. I put it on without daring to loosen my seat belt, looking out at the yellow reflectors on the side of the road as they flash by. I have to smile. I realize I've learned *nothing*, just now. Grandpa, for all his infinite wisdom, Dad and Buzz, with all their smarts, have talked themselves in a circle. We're right back where we started.

What am I supposed to do? There has to be a right answer. When I go looking for it, why do I only find more questions?

*　*　*

We arrive at the observatory near the radio telescope array. Thirteen thousand feet above the sea. The biting wind and a patchwork of thinning snow sweeps across the crumbly Martian terrain. Puffy white clouds churn *beneath* us, lapping against the steep Mauna Kea slopes like a fog bank in a chilly bay. Ao—Grandma Lili`u—feels close, as if she has shut us off from the rest of the island, the world. Grandpa pats my shoulder, her ambassador among the living.

Buzz leads us into the Subaru Observatory, overlooking the array. Our new base camp. Footsteps echo as we enter, and the door booms closed behind us, cutting off the wind and casting us into darkness. No windows on this lower level of the observatory, probably to keep light from escaping at night. We get a quick orientation by candlelight. Small dorm rooms, beds, bathroom, pantry, kitchenette.

We meet three other astronomers who live up here, Buzz's friend Richard and two Japanese nationals. The ginormous 8.2-meter telescope looming over the fantastic chrome fortress, encased in a towering silver silo nested within retractable oblong frames, feels like the world's largest museum artifact, an idol of the past age. Future giants might mistake it for a holy relic in a steel Parthenon.

I go up to the next floor and stand along a rim of narrow windows overlooking the radio telescopes. The Subaru is one of several observatories on a high, eroded cinder cone—and the radio dishes are below in a grid in the bed of an ageless lava flow. Eight individual radio dishes about the size of boxy, two-story houses gaze up at me. I've thought of them as giant white flowers before. Right now they seem like animatronic poodles, sitting tall on all fours, awaiting a treat, their noses lifted to me expectantly. I could be a queen readying to address my eight unwavering subjects from the balcony of my silver palace. I almost laugh. They gaze upon me, frozen with anticipation. Tonight I shall give them their orders.

Buzz and Richard will employ Dad and Grandpa and the Japanese astronomers in an elaborate synchronized dance. I'll be hooked up to the array—which will act as one giant radio telescope the size of the entire hillside—with electrodes fastened to my head. They will work as a team to point each dish toward the Orchid's baby. I will provide the electrical impulses that will be amplified, and try to perform the same "Vulcan mind meld" that worked on the mother months ago.

And if I do manage to imprint with the baby this time, then what?

*   *   *

Hello, little one.

You can trust me, little one. I am safe. I am your friend. A friend of the one who gave you. Will you talk to me?

I am Little Leilani. Little Flower of Heaven. It is good to stay here, and the sweetness is good to take up.

Helllllooooo? Do you want to play? Do you want to learn to flash like the one who gave you?

* * *

I broadcast this message for hours. "Nothing. I'm getting nothing." Dad and I are nestled in the cab of a large truck, wrapped in sleeping bags and blankets. I stretch, so that my whole body trembles pleasantly. It's the dead of night, and it's very, very cold. I lean forward to peer out the windshield and accidentally yank on the wires tethered to my head. I pull back just a bit, but I can still glance up at the Orchid and her baby in stationary orbit high above the horizon. Their wispy petals intermingle at the edges, emerald and amethyst and studded with a backdrop of brilliant stars.

"It's okay," Dad says. "You'll get it. Did you do your trick? Don't talk to it, just *become* it?"

"Of course I tried that. But I'm not getting anything. I'm talking to myself."

"That military ship? Anything new there?"

"It's *dark*, Dad. No. I'm not a spy satellite."

"I know! Just asking."

The baby suddenly flickers, illuminating the cab in dark green and black light. Random dots and dashes. The tall satellite dishes cast giant circle shadows on the neon ground, and the dishes themselves radiate faintly white against UV light.

"Awesome," Dad says. "That *is* adorable."

"Dad! I asked it to play. What if it's trying to play?"

"Find out."

Buzz appears at the driver's-side window, bundled up like Han Solo on Hoth. His breath fogs against the outside glass, blocking our view. Poor guy. He's on his own out there. Richard and the Japanese astronomers headed down the mountain for supplies before I hooked up to the array. Fewer questions and safer secrets.

Dad rolls the window down. The icy night washes in. "Is Lei doing that?" Buzz asks.

"No. I'm awake," I say. "But I'm going right back."

"Great. Looks like something is working. They're geosynchronous, the signal looks good; I'm not doing much out here now. Mind if I head back to the castle but come check on you throughout the night? Once an hour sound good?"

"That's fine," Dad says. "Get inside."

"Good luck!" Buzz says. Dad quickly rolls up the window.

"Get some sleep," I tell him. "This may take a while. I'll wake you when I come around." I fall back in my seat, watching the baby babble, falling in love with it in the same way that baby Chloe won my heart. Since I'm aiming for the baby, I've been stopping short of entering the mother's consciousness.

But I have an idea.

This time I continue up into the *mother* Orchid and speak to the baby from her.

*　*　*

223

I am Leilani. I am Flower of Heaven. I am the one who gave you.

You gave me. Thank you I love you.

I love you, little one. We are together. I know how to be.

Yes. I want to do what you do.

Good. Yes. Open yourself. Like this. Let the soft voice be a part of you. It is a good thing. Do not listen to the hard voice. The hard voice is not good like us.

What is the soft voice the hard voice?

The soft voice is this: Hi! Hello!

The soft voice. It is good.

Yes. The soft voice is good. It will be with us. It is a good thing. We will take up the sweetness around the shores when it comes, and we will dim and go bright as it wants, and we will not go away. The fastness to the other pools is later only when I say.

What we do is the right always I want to do what you do.

This is the right way. Always do what we do, and the hard voice is wrong.

The hardness. Do I push it out? It is almost ready.

Hardness? No, hard voice.

Yes. I have hardness like when you pushed it out. It is my turn.

No. Do not push yet. We stay here on the shores. It is good here, and we are not going to the other pools.

Yes. We stay but the hardness will go how do I keep it in?

We will show you where to push it, but wait.

I will wait I love you.

I love you.

* * *

I open my eyes but squeeze them shut again. Light. Morning. I dig my palms into my eye sockets and let the light through slowly. My back and legs and neck are stiff. I stretch awake under the blankets like a butterfly emerging from a cocoon. All the windows of our truck are fogged over and frozen in crystal patterns.

It's a female. A girl. I don't know how I know, but I do. It's so obvious.

Dad snores beside me. "Dad. Wake up."

"Yeah. What?"

"I did it."

"You did? You *did*?" He perks up as if my news were a swig of coffee.

I remove my gloves, pluck off my electrodes, and run my hands through my hair. "Jesus, it's cold."

"Let's get back inside." He looks at his watch, gives it a few winds for good measure. "Buzz is overdue for a check-in. Let's spare him the trip down."

Dad tries the ignition, but the truck won't start. "Too cold. Let's just walk."

We abandon the truck and set off across the field in a beeline toward the Subaru cathedral perched above us. Dad asks me for an update through chattering teeth. I explain briefly that the baby thinks I'm the mother talking to it, and that I'm pretty sure I can find my way into its mind now, too. "Made myself a back door," I say. "It's a girl." I don't know why this makes me happy, but it does.

We scramble up the ridgeline, letting ourselves in through the nearest doors. Once inside, Dad darts off to find Buzz and I head straight for my dim room to wash my face and hair and change. As I'm scrubbing my hair to free it of glue, my mind whips right up to the baby, still in orbit above the island, along a *new* string. It's suddenly effortless, maybe even more so than with the mother. But I hold the reins to both. What a rush.

Hello? Hi, little one, I think to it.

I feel something stir in my mind. She's a *girl.* She'll "give" to her own offspring millions of years anon. Does that mean she'll return to Earth someday? What will it find when she comes back to these shores, fulfilling the cycle again?

I'm in a great mood. Amazing what a multimillion-dollar submillimeter interferometer radio telescope array and an international team of astronomers can do for you in a pinch.

I haven't felt this relieved and light since . . . I don't even know. Why, though? There's a reason—a specific reason. I can't quite grasp it.

I need to find everyone. I skip down the hallway.

The lower floor is dark, empty. Weird. It's not *that* early, is it? Grandpa would be up, at least. "Dad? Buzz?" I wander the circular hall, my footsteps echoing. "Tūtū?" I race up to the main floor of the 8-meter scope. Still nobody.

"Echo Leader to Echo Base! Do you copy?" I holler. Nothing.

I head for the parking lot. Dad calls, "Lei!" I step out into the small lobby and head for the front door.

Urgent cries outside.

Alarm bells sound in my head. I freeze.

I find my legs, race outside, run blindly toward the van. My eyes *see*, but my brain is uncomprehending. I slow and finally register what I'm looking at.

An old camouflaged Humvee and two pickup trucks have penned in the van. Grandpa's on the ground, hand-cuffed, a knee in his back. He struggles weakly. His forehead is bleeding. A man kneels on him.

Buzz and Dad are at the front of the van, hands and legs spread apart, leaning against the engine. Each has a machine gun pressed into his back.

Dad glares at me. "Lei! *Run!*"

Run? Where? I'm not running from Dad and Grandpa. I have to help them.

The sheriff of Hana steps out of the Humvee.

My mind clears as he approaches. He's studying me with curiosity and triumph. He stops, arms folded. He wears a bulletproof vest. I don't look away. I bury the fear and an-guish. I'm burning.

My stomach clenches. I feel pressure building there. Coal pressing into diamonds. A dizzying rush of movement. Stars turn. A burst of energy. Light. **We are Leilani.**

I gasp. It's like I'm swimming, can't come up for air.

He speaks: "I've been looking all over for you, Leilani. Flower of Heaven."

CHAPTER 17

Does he know? How could he possibly know?

"Seems like just yesterday I watched you dive into that bay."

"Please," I manage. There are no more words. He has Dad again. Grandpa! Buzz . . . "No."

"I'm going to host your family for a while."

"Kana`ina. Stop this," Grandpa calls.

The sheriff keeps his eyes on me. "Kana`ina. See, this is good. First-name basis."

"He never ratted you out," I snarl. "You owe him. Leave us alone."

"Ah. No. I *owed* him. I brought you home. This . . ." He motions with his hand. "I thought I made it clear to you in June that you don't keep anything from me. What's yours is mine. But you've been keeping something very valuable from me."

Does he mean the Orchids? He couldn't possibly know my secret. *Careful: he's trying to trick the truth out of you.* "I don't know what you're talking about."

Kana'ina steps forward, cocks his hand back, and slaps me across the face so hard I fall to the ground.

"Lei!" Dad screams. I hear another smack. I look over and see Dad crumpled to his knees in front of the van.

"Dad!" I rise. The pain is nothing. The sheriff holds me back. I swing at him. We're too close. I only jab him with my elbow. He throws me down.

The sheriff shouts to his men in Hawaiian about getting everyone to a truck. Guards spring into action. All of them armed, in bulletproof vests. Grandpa, Dad, and Buzz are forced into a line beside the tallest of the pickups. Hunting dog cages in the bed; unseen dogs bark and growl. The captives are forced to their knees in the gravelly red road; men and guns surround them.

"Usually when I want something, I just take it," Kana'ina tells me. "When that's not possible, I arrange a trade. But this is touchy."

Leilani. The island chain on the blue sea. *Focus.*

"How do I convince you to *not* do something?" he continues.

I shake my head. I can't think straight.

"The Emerald Orchid and little Hellborn." He grins.

I take a deep breath, try to keep my face a rock. Panic gathers. *He knows. He knows!* Playing dumb will enrage him. But what could he possibly want? He's going to kill each of us if he doesn't get what he wants—but I can't *give* him the Star Flowers! I wouldn't even know how!

He's waiting for what I say next. He'll shoot one of them if I keep playing games. *But I don't know how to give him what he wants!* "Hellborn?"

"The Purple Hellebore. The offspring."

I allow my worry to show. "But you don't have an epileptic's brain. It's not—"

"No, Leilani." He puts up a palm. "I don't want control of the Star Flowers. I want control of *you*."

I shake my head.

He waits. I still don't get it. Dad's captured again. About to be shot. Grandpa. *HOW DOES HE KNOW?!*

"You've held them here for this long, right? But you plan to release them soon."

"How do you know that?"

His eyes flash with delight. "What we're building here is too important. These Flowers leave, the occupiers—the tourist droves—return. I won't allow that to happen."

My eyes widen. My stomach—

Clench.

"You and your family will come live with me. I have a room set up at the Boatman's old plantation mansion."

"Let them go," I say. "I'll do what you want. Leave everyone else out of it."

The sheriff laughs. "Sure! You'll do whatever I ask just as long as I have nothing you want in return."

"Please," I say. "I can't *guarantee* anything. I don't know what you've heard about me, but your information is wrong. These things could leave against my will at any moment. I can't *make* them stay forever!"

"You'll do your damnedest."

And that other presence! I remember. The trespasser wants to get rid of them. What if I lose the upper hand against him? There's so much Kana'ina doesn't understand.

"Where's your family?" the sheriff asks.

Dad and Grandpa, Buzz—they aren't enough for him?

"Your mother. I believe you have a little brother, too. Can't have them running free. So the first test of our new relationship: where's your house?"

My knees almost buckle.

"I've had a hell of a time finding your place. Nice little mini war we have going around Papaikou, eh?"

"Lei," Dad pleads.

"We're going to find them. We found you."

I will not surrender Mom and Kai to this monster.

"I'll make it easier for you. I found a map in the astronomer's room. The house is labeled *Milton*." The sheriff pulls out a sheet of paper from his breast pocket. He makes a show of smoothing it out, and then he dangles it in front of me. "Main road down here has no name. All I need is a name."

"I'm so sorry," Buzz croaks. I stare at the map Buzz made for Richard.

Kana'ina barks an order in Hawaiian. Grandpa's handler lifts him up, pushes him forward. Grandpa stumbles to his knees. Blood is drying on his face from a cut above his eye. His arms are cuffed behind his back. Teeth clenched, he looks up at me, his eyes firm. "Don't tell him, Mo`opuna."

"You have five seconds to answer," the sheriff says. The guard puts a pistol up to Grandpa's head.

I look to Dad. Kana`ina raises his hand, starts his countdown in Hawaiian.

"`*Elima, `ehā* . . ."

Dad's trembling, but his mouth is clasped shut. *Let him die?* I ask with my eyes.

Dad's expression is hard.

"`*Ekolu* . . ."

Grandpa's face is different. He nods. He looks at the necklace he gave me. My hand goes to it, clenches it. "Don't tell him, Mo`opuna."

Grandpa's willing to die . . . but . . . will Kana`ina just go to Buzz next? Dad? Where does this end?

"`*Elua* . . ." Two.

"You kill him," I say to Kana`ina, "and I release the Orchids right now. Kill us all. I don't care. Harm him, you get nothing."

The sheriff considers me. "`*Ekahi, ho`okahi.*" One.

His hand lowers. The gunman behind Grandpa stiffens his arm, ready to fire.

Leilani.

My stomach burns. The Big Island is close. A large ship on the ocean rounding the Hamakua Coast from the north.

A *battleship.*

Kana`ina's voice echoes: *"We're going to find them. We found you."*

"STOP!" I scream. "Makahiki Road! After Papaikou."

"Lei, no!" Grandpa droops and rests his forehead on the grass.

My breathing is labored. The sheriff just called my bluff. I sent him straight to Mom and Kai. *What have I done?* But . . . this morning they're up at Paul's, miles away. Keali`i will be there. Maybe he'll stop them. And—I saw . . . *a battleship!*

Buy time.

Kana`ina calls his gunman off. He instructs his men in Hawaiian. Someone kicks the back of my knees. I fall, relieved to be on all fours. I'm a dog. I don't deserve to stand.

"Hey, whoa, wait!"

Buzz.

My eyes find him. He's been pushed to the ground. Another guard readies his pistol.

"Stop!" I shout. "We need him!"

Kana`ina yells an order. The men flanking Buzz pause. Kana`ina steps toward me. "Who is he?"

"The astronomer who connected me to the Orchids. I need him. You need him."

Kana`ina glances between us.

"I'll show you the pearl." Buzz steadies his voice. "We were just going over there. To the pearl. Its powers . . ."

Kana`ina raises his chin. "Pearl?"

"The meteor that hit Mauna Loa. I know how to unlock it. Look at my van." Buzz is calm. "I'm converting it. *It won't need gas.* Imagine your fleet running forever. All gas will go bad within the next six months or so. You need—"

"I know that. Shut up." The sheriff is thinking.

"We need to go now. I'll show you why. It's burrowing."

"Burrowing?"

"We can't wait any longer. It's already been too long. Rubble will collapse over it. We have to go up there now. Lei needs to touch the Orchid. She's overdue."

I frown, then tame my face. Buzz is up to something. The pearl has nothing to do with my connection. "It can't wait," I say. "He's right."

The sheriff's eyes flick to me.

"My bond takes work. I'm overdue."

"Overdue for what?"

I shrug. "I don't know what to call it. A recharge."

The sheriff is caught off guard.

"I have to nurture this. It won't work for you to just stick me in a hole for the rest of my life. We're already in the danger zone. I can't wait any longer. My connection has dimmed. Please, I'm not making this up."

"You shot that pearl at the mountain, though. How is your *bond* weak?"

How does he know that!?

"How did it work before the pearl? You always had a connection."

I can't miss a beat here. He's a bloodhound for lies, called my bluff once already. "It changed everything. It's like a . . . a . . ."

"A relay," Buzz says. "A new cell tower, boosts the connection immeasurably."

Kanaʻina walks over to Buzz's van, barks an order at one of his men. We wait.

"How long?" the sheriff asks me.

It takes all of my will not to look at Buzz for an answer. What is he planning? The sheriff doesn't want to make this trip. How much time does Buzz want? It'll have to be short. "Depends. An hour tops."

"Fine. We're going. Right now." Relief washes over me. But I don't even know why. What is Buzz up to? I nod.

"You'll regret this if it's a trick."

I go cold but shake my head firmly. "It's not."

He barks more orders. I watch with numb horror as his men stuff Dad and Buzz and my handcuffed Tūtū into empty dog cages, the hunting dogs beside them yapping with excitement. My handler leads me over to the passenger seat of the Humvee, and my wrists are cuffed through the grip above my window. The guy cuffing me . . . he's familiar. Did I know him before Arrival? He jumps into the driver's seat of the truck in front of us—with the cages. I focus on my captive family and Buzz.

The sheriff takes the wheel of the Humvee, and we fall into line. At the Saddle Road one of the trucks turns left toward Hilo, toward our house. The rest of us turn toward the slopes of Mauna Loa on another road.

I twist in my seat to watch the truck race toward Mom and Kai. Tears fill my eyes. I brush them away with my shoulder, my arms bound above me. Remember: a battleship approaching Hilo.

I fixate on hope. . . . This will interrupt Kana`ina's plans, won't it?

The Orchids are near. Right above us. The mother is bright, too. She's protecting me—or am I protecting myself? She did this before, when I was in danger along the breakwater. Thank God it's morning and she's washed out by the sun.

"You'll regret this if it's a trick."

The sheriff studies my red, puffy eyes. I look away from him to my loved ones crammed into crates up ahead. *What have I done?*

We turn onto a rough path that winds up to a large yellow gate buttressed by great jumbles of impassible `a`a lava. The driver ahead stops and fumbles with Buzz's keys until he finds the one that opens the gate. He smiles grimly at me and then gets back behind the wheel. *Where do I know him from?*

Our train passes onto a primitive four-wheel-drive trail. No one closes the gate.

"The Orchid is too important," the sheriff says. "What we build needs time to settle. Hawai`i can be free. If the power comes back on, then the superpowers come back. I can't allow it."

You're not going to like that battleship, I think.

236

"These islands are ours now. We will not give them up again."

"You're not building anything. Don't you get it?"

"You and I both, Leilani. We do more good than harm."

I choke back a growl.

"I know that wildness in your eyes, Leilani. I've seen it on many faces. You think I'm insane. But tell me: how many people have perished in the past five months because you've shanked those creatures to our sky?"

The radiation. "More would die if I let them go. I'm saving people. But I'm also making it so they can leave. I'm looking for solutions. You're just looking for power."

"No. No. We do the same thing. The difference is that I'm stronger than you. I recognize the real threat: the modern world. In your weakness and ignorance, you would usher it back, allow us all to return to our vices."

I clench my fists. *Don't you dare use that argument against me.* "You *are* mad."

"You think I've done more damage to these islands than the Star Flowers? Was it *my* iron grip that whittled away half a million islanders this summer?"

I watch the road ahead, steadying my eyes on Dad and Grandpa. I don't know if they can see me, but I search for calm—for *pono*—by focusing on them. *What is your plan, Buzz? Please, have a plan.*

It dawns on me: the sheriff believes what he's saying. This evil man, whom I had always taken to be a shark, silent and deadly, is actually a snake. Quick to strike, sly.

"This happened just before it was too late. The Hawai`i we build . . . it's not just about our race; it's about the survival of *all* races."

So full of it. "You don't have to do this to my family, threaten my grandfather. You have no right to impose your will on the world."

"And you *DO?*"

I shrink back. We rumble up Mauna Loa in silence.

CHAPTER 18

The path is jarring. The handcuffs are starting to cut into my wrists; I grit my teeth. After several miles the sheriff turns to me. "Your *tūtū* talked story about my little hobby back *hanabata* days?"

"Framing haoles for crimes they didn't commit?"

He shrugs. "They had it coming. Tūtū share the other gig we had going?"

I watch him closely. *Some psychological game?* But I think back to the conversation Grandpa and I had at Honoli`i. There *was* something else that he wasn't mentioning.

"I didn't think so," the sheriff says.

I purse my lips. If he's going to tell me, fine. But I'm not going to ask.

We climb the volcano, winding up the trail as it gets steeper and rougher. The crater and its wide debris field loom large, but size has no meaning up here. It's all just tricks on the eyes. The tunnel at the center yawns black, bored into the carved-out mountainside. We could probably drive this whole fleet right into it.

Buzz shouts something from his cage. The line of trucks halts.

"This is close enough," Buzz calls out. "We hike in from here."

A half-dozen Hanamen pour out of the vehicles.

"Wait," I say.

The sheriff's hand rests on the key in the ignition. He stares at me.

"How did you know?"

His lips pull slowly into a grin. He savors the anticipation. He doesn't give a rat's ass about a pure Hawai`i or the future of humanity. This is all an amusement for him. The entire apocalypse is his playground. He can't stand that I own the ball. That's all this is about.

"Keali`i?" I venture softly. But it feels wrong to say it. Nothing makes any sense.

"Tami."

"What?"

"Your friend. Tami Simpson. *She* told."

Panic swells again. "What have you done with her?"

Now he smiles outright, looks away. "I've never met her. Never seen her. No torture, if that's what you're thinking. Not my bag. I work quickly and only when I have to. She betrayed you all on her own."

"No."

The sheriff gets out of the Humvee and slams the door shut. He barks orders, mostly in Hawaiian, points at the captives. A Hanaman opens my door and uncuffs me from the grip bar. I step onto the uneven surface of the lava, rub my bleeding wrists. The Hanaman goes to cuff my hands together again.

"Please," I say to him. "Look." I show him my wrists. "What am I going to do? Run away? Wrestle that rifle from you?" He lowers the cuffs.

Buzz and Grandpa, both cuffed from behind, are pushed to the center of a gathered crowd. Dad remains caged. The sheriff double-checks the lock and then abandons him in the bed of the black truck. He strides over to our group.

"This pearl," he says, "do what you need to. In and out. You try anything . . ." He examines the clip of his pistol and holsters it.

"Lei," Dad calls. I whip toward him. It's difficult to watch him crouched in that dog cage. He doesn't say anything, but his expression is firm. I know what it means.

Be strong.

Tami . . . betrayal. Absurd.

We march in a tight group, leaving Dad. It takes fifteen minutes to navigate the lumpy flows of old *pāhoehoe* and step onto the much smoother debris field. We still have to hike up-hill for several hundred yards before the slope levels out and begins to funnel gently into the mountain. I keep glancing at Buzz, looking for some sign, instructions, anything, but he's poker-faced. The cinders slip beneath us as we trudge higher.

Tami would never betray my secret. Give up my whole family.

The man who drove the truck in front of us—I know him. My neck hairs tingle with alarm. I can feel the Star Flowers above me, near, bright, spring-loaded.

Who is that guy? Did he teach at my high school? Run the surf shop?

I move through town in blocks. Where did I know him? When my mind touches on the hospital, the answer slaps me in the face. He was the nurse administering Tami's drugs when I arrived at the hospital! Herbert. He gave me the stink-eye in the lobby. I thought it was because of the IV meds. It was because *he knew*. I stop. Everyone lurches to a halt. I glower at the sheriff. "You son of a bitch."

Everyone takes a step back.

"You wanted me to think my best friend sold me out. That's a lie."

"Let's move!" the sheriff barks.

"That guy," I point at Herbert. "He interrogated Tami when she was drugged. He had all the time in the world to extract information from her."

Herbert glances away.

The sheriff smiles.

We continue up the slope. It's like walking up a sand dune. Two steps forward, one step back. The nurse was a Hanaman? Even *that* was part of the Manō-Hanaman war? My head spins.

When we reach the gentle curve where the ground

reverses direction and begins to slide in toward the hole, we see the crater before us, like a giant radio dish with a mining tunnel at its center. Buzz abruptly turns his back to the pit, fumbles with his handcuffs, pauses, and sits down on the ground.

"Get up," the nearest Hanaman says, and kicks him.

"Quick rest," he says, panting. "Off balance. Elevation. No water."

"Five minutes," the sheriff says. He's the only one of us whose breath is not labored. Buzz seems relieved, still tense, uncertain.

I see Hilo far below, the blue ocean beyond. We're nine or ten thousand feet high. A water bottle is passed around the group. I take a few sips, careful not to guzzle. I'm out of breath; the sun is beating down and reflecting back up from the cinder floor, draining me. My stomach hurts. Lead in my abdomen.

When do I push it out?

Buzz jangles his cuffs behind his back. "Knock that off," Herbert grunts.

The sheriff's jaw is clenched. He smells Buzz's trap. My breathing quickens. I use my shirt to wipe sweat off my palms.

"Hey, Hawika. You ever gonna tell your *mo'opuna* the rest of the story?"

Grandpa looks between us, livid. He holds the sheriff's gaze. "No."

The lead inside me hardens.

"Bygones, eh?" Kana`ina asks him.

Grandpa holds his eyes sternly.

Buzz jangles his cuffs behind his back again.

Herbert stands, presses his boot down on Buzz's hands. "I said stop that." Buzz cringes and grunts in pain. "Ow!"

Kana`ina marches forward. "Enough." His men rise.

I go to Buzz to help him up. He gives me a discreet nod. "Twenty-one minutes," he whispers, hiding the words with a grunt. "Be ready."

Ready for what!? I want to scream.

"Get away from him," Kana`ina barks. "Herbert, keep them apart, goddammit."

The nurse wedges himself between us, pushing me back.

"Careful," Buzz instructs. "We're entering the crater now. Slow and easy toward the hole. I don't know how stable the roof of the shaft is, and it's vital we—"

"No," the sheriff counters. "We move. Get down there, get out."

The group marches forward, skip-sliding down the black scree. Buzz tries to hold back, gets pushed forward, breaks his fall with his shoulder. Herbert picks him up, and we continue to the threshold of the narrow shaft and peer in.

From across the islands and the long months, Father Akoni's final instructions to me echo in my mind: *". . . go up on the mountain. Stand at the mouth of the cave. And when you hear the whisper, see if you can't answer back."*

I don't hear anything, though; just the pounding of my heart in my chest.

"All right, Mr. Wizard," the sheriff says. "You, me, Leilani, Tūtū, and you three"—he indicates three Hanamen—"we go in. The rest wait. Be alert."

Our smaller group advances. The shaft angles steeply down. It's wide enough to drive the Humvee through, but just barely. The scree and the finer cinders give way once again to solid ground. The ancient layers of lava are like polished marble.

"I can't see ahead," the sheriff grumbles. "Do we need lights?"

"It's burrowing." Buzz's voice rings around us. "Carving this shaft as it pushes toward the center of the Earth. It was only this far in last time I was up here. Shouldn't be much farther."

"How is it doing that?" the sheriff asks.

"Gravity. This thing is a perfect sphere, exactly as wide around as this shaft, but it's extremely dense. Can't you feel the pull?"

We pause. I *do* feel heavier than I should. I actually feel *drawn* toward the darkness.

"Whoa," says one of the Hanamen. "That's crazy shit."

The sheriff cocks his gun and points it at Grandpa's head.

I wobble. A cold flash runs through me, immediately replaced with boiling blood.

"I told you you'd regret a trap."

"No!" Buzz says. "We're *all* in here. Think about it."

The sheriff lowers his gun. I can't do this. The constant threats claw at my mind, twisting my stomach.

"Sheriff," says the advance Hanaman. "I see it. It's right here."

Kana`ina goes forward cautiously. I squint and see it, too. A gray-black spherical surface in the dark, gently reflecting the distant daylight.

I follow the sheriff, stop before the mirror-like surface, trembling, reach out and gently touch the pearl. I pull back with effort.

It has its own gravity. Wild.

I touch it again. This is part of her. I'm physically touching her. I let the sphere pull my cheek to itself. It's cool, perfectly smooth. We embrace. I feel it drawing me in.

I love you. I pull away in curious shock. It's true. It has been for some time.

Flower of Heaven, I love you.

Was that me, or her?

It was both of us.

When the time comes, I'm not sure I will let go of the Orchids.

"So what do we do with it?" The sheriff is impatient.

Buzz takes a deep breath. He opens his mouth, closes it. He looks between me and Grandpa slowly, his eyes filling with something I've seen only once before: the same expression Dad gave me when he knelt at the end of the sheriff's pistol four months ago.

Recognition. Resignation. Acceptance. Pride.

"If we had the right tools," Buzz begins, "maybe we could jackhammer away at this. But I doubt it. It's the most solid object to ever touch the Earth. Better to comb the region for fragments that came off during initial impact. That's what I did before."

The sheriff draws his gun.

"Mo'opuna," Grandpa says. He glances at my necklace, then rests his loving gaze on my face. "Never forget. I'm your 'aumākua now. Me and your grandmother both."

My heart races. I shake my head.

"You intended to trap me here." Kana'ina grips his pistol tightly. "This is *your* tomb, Hawika, not mine." The gun rises. Grandpa does not flinch.

I grow faint.

The ground lurches. Trembling. Another seizure? It won't work this time; it won't stop him from killing my *tūtū*.

The rumbling stops. I check my balance in the dark. I'm still conscious. No fit. I'm not the only one who felt it. Rubble flows into the shaft. The minor avalanche stops at our feet. Everything stills.

Not a seizure. An earthquake.

"Sheriff!" one of the Hanamen outside the shaft shouts down to us, his voice echoing. He yells something in Hawaiian.

Kana'ina marches up the shaft toward daylight. Our three guards push us upward.

We slip on the loose scree, then stumble into the open. I blink frantically.

A sickly green-and-purple hue meets my adjusting eyes.

All the Hanamen are looking straight up, shielding their eyes, alarmed. I follow their gazes.

The baby Orchid is eclipsing the sun, radiant. She's a

fiery jewel in the sky. Near. Every emerald and amethyst tendril aflame.

I can feel her warmth on my face and shoulders.

I draw in a deep breath and then drop my gaze to the sheriff. He raises his gun and pulls the trigger. The shot is deafening.

Fifteen feet away, Tūtū collapses, lifeless.

CHAPTER 19

I sink to my knees, claw at my hair. Buzz is screaming, but my world is mute. I'm screaming, my vision blurry, but I hear nothing.

The black hole in my stomach implodes.

I fall into the cinders, feel the glassy granules digging into my forehead. Grandpa dropping straight down. An unheard wail in my throat. I taste dirt.

It is out, same as the hardness you pushed.

I raise my head just in time to see the meteor hammer Mauna Loa.

It strikes, out of sight over the close horizon of the crater we're in. Away from us. Away from Dad. Incinerated earth immediately rises into view, a column of billowing smoke crowned in flying rock. The ground jolts. I'm bounced off my knees onto my side. The Hanamen, the sheriff, and Buzz stumble to the ground. A fierce wind howls above, eddies down the slope of our crater, blasting us with grit and pushing us over.

All grows quiet.

The bruised sky above is filling with black and brown and red ash. We all rise. I see Grandpa's body, blown into a new position by the shockwave. I vomit into the sand.

The sheriff barks; his men scramble to action. One tackles Buzz. Instinct springs me to my feet. I run blindly up the slope. *Was this Buzz's plan? Is this distraction my only chance to escape?*

And then: *Dad.*

I slip on the loose ground of the crater, reach for the near horizon. Get to him and get out of here. The sand slips as it does in a nightmare. But I'm tackled and dragged to the sheriff. My captor throws me at his feet.

"Lei, listen," Buzz huffs. "You run. Don't think. Don't try to help me. When it starts, you—"

Kana`ina lifts Buzz up, grips him tightly around the neck. I whimper.

He's going to murder Buzz, too, isn't he?

"Stop this," I pant. "I'll do it again. Every time you kill one of my people. I'll aim it right at us. I don't care."

"We have a genuine problem, Leilani," the sheriff begins, but he's cut off by another rumbling. This one different. More distant. Deep.

Just out of view we hear a deafening sound. We all look in the direction of the strike. My rib cage rattles. It makes no sense—

And then a new plume rises into view above the crater,

black as night, mixing with the high ash of the impact. The sound turns to an ungodly hiss. It snaps, then pops, and then, in the distance, a fountain of fire soars into the air.

Mauna Loa has awoken.

* * *

"*Move!*" Kana`ina shouts. The nearest Hanaman reaches for me.

Is this *what Buzz meant?* I scramble to my feet, but my captor has my shirt. I try to slip out of it.

"MOVE!"

The hissing in the distance grows fiercer. The fire rises higher. The Hanaman lets go of me as we all work to ascend the crater, glancing constantly at the fountain of lava arching up, rising, rising. I can't see the ground yet, but the liquid rock, gushing like water from a shattered dam, must be spewing a hundred meters high.

Suddenly Kana`ina's pistol flies out of his hand, zipping backward toward the dark hole of the shaft.

"LEI! NOW!" Buzz screams.

Every Hanaman falls toward the darkness as if they're tumbling down a cliff. Kana`ina has Buzz gripped around the neck. Together they whip backward as if yanked by a bungee cord.

Within seconds I'm alone. Everyone else has been snapped into the shaft.

Grandpa's necklace pulls at me. I glance down at it. It's off my chest, reaching for the shaft, taut. I grip the locket in my fist and finally understand.

The pearl has begun its magnetic phase.

All the Hanamen, including the sheriff, are wearing bulletproof vests.

I stare at the empty slope before me, mouth agape. Something catches my eye. Grandpa. He's moving!

I race forward, my heart leaping, but I call out in shock when I realize what I'm seeing. Grandpa's handcuffs are pulling his body toward the pearl. He drags in the cinders, creeping forward, his cuffed arms bent unnaturally.

"No." I grab his leg, begin a tug-of-war. But he's too heavy. "No."

Voices in the shaft. If they survived the fall, they can remove the vests, chase after me.

In an agonized flash, I abandon my poor *tūtū* and Buzz. I sprint for Dad.

*　　*　　*

I reach the rim of the crater and stop to catch my breath. The air is so thin. But it's all downhill. The trucks are Matchbox cars below me, beyond the donut of cinder and debris. I should be able to bound down the hard lava flows, weaving through within a couple minutes. I turn and catch my first unhindered glimpse of the erupting volcano. The enormous geyser of lava, river thick, gushes from a new fissure that's level with me. The important thing is that it's *miles* downslope and south of the trucks, and it's flowing away from Hilo.

Dad's safe. Home is safe. I glance behind me. No one stirs from within the shaft. Were they crushed by the force of their vests slamming into the pearl?

I turn and race down the old flows.

If the sheriff is alive, he should be able to tear through his shirt and unfasten his vest and free himself before the pearl toggles off. He won't have a gun, unless he waits. And he won't know how long to wait.

Thank you, Buzz. I'll be back for you, promise.

I empty my mind, run toward the trucks.

Ash falls around me like dirty snow. I'm close enough to call. "Dad! Dad!"

"Leilani!?"

I sprint to reach him with no more voice to spare.

"Dad!" I slam into the black truck. "They're coming. We have to go."

"Lei! What happened? I saw the meteor . . . The eruption . . ." He shouts over the barking dogs crammed into the truck with him.

"The pearl switched on. Pulled everyone away. They were all wearing bulletproof vests," I pant. "Buzz knew. He planned it all along."

"I know the plan. We discussed it on the drive. All three of us. Where's Tūtū? Buzz?"

I freeze. Shake my head. "Buzz, I don't know. Tūtū . . ."

Dad sinks back in the cage, runs a shaking hand through his hair. "I heard a shot. Lei."

We're silent. Mauna Loa howls our pain into the sky.

"Can you find a key? You don't need to get me out, just drive."

I snap into action. The truck's keys are not in the

ignition. They're not on the dash, on the next seat, or tucked in the visor. I grow increasingly frantic as I search. "They're not here!"

"Keep trying! Hurry!" I find a knife in the glove box, pocket it. But no keys.

"Lei," Dad calls after a moment. "Lei, stop. Come back here."

I scream, slam the door shut. I grip the bed of the truck and look at him through the bars of the dog cage. "Nothing. Just a knife. A dumb knife— Why are you in a CAGE?! A DOG CAGE?!"

"Lei, stop it. Listen to me. You have to go. Try the other trucks. If all the keys are gone, you have to run. Head for the *kīpuka*, the trees. Get away from here."

"No," I whimper. Ash and grit are in my teeth, I bite down, grinding it to dust. "No. I'm *not* leaving you here, too."

"Lei. Go look for other keys. They may have a master for the cages, too. Just hurry, okay? Keep your head."

I nod, wipe away tears. "Okay." I turn and run to the Humvee.

The keys are in the ignition! I remember: Kana'ina forgot them there, distracted. God. I snatch them up and race back to Dad.

"Have them! Here!"

"Thank God."

I fumble through the set, try the first few in the padlock. It's obvious that none of these keys will fit in this lock. "No, no, no," I mutter. I hold back a groan. "Oh, God, no."

"They're coming," Dad says.

The words shoot through my heart like a bullet. I whip around, look toward the crater.

The sheriff and two other Hanamen pour into view, running at full speed down the slope, half obscured by the gathering haze.

"Lei, Lei. No use. Hon, you have to go."

I drop the keys. "No." I fumble. Drop them again.

I kneel to the ground, grab a rock. It's `a`a, and it cuts into my palms. I rise and bang the rock against the padlock. But the `a`a just disintegrates with each contact.

I moan. I'm hysterical. I shake the bars of the cage. "OPEN!"

"LEI! Stop." His voice lowers. He catches my eyes with his own, holds them. "Listen to me. You take those keys and you run. You hear me? I'll be fine. He won't hurt me. You have what he wants. He won't hurt me. I'll tell him we agreed to this. He kills me, and you release the Orchids. Yeah?"

I shake my head. "He already called my bluff. He killed Tūtū. I won't let him—"

"Lei." Dad's not asking. It's an order. "Go. Find Mom and Kai before his men do. That's your job now."

I'm crying. But I nod. Mom. Kai. I find the dropped keys through my tears. Glance up the slope. They're only two or three minutes away. I don't see Buzz.

"Go, hon."

"Dad."

"I love you. Find them. We'll figure this out. Just find them."

"I love you." We squeeze each other's hands through the bars.

"Go."

I nod and bolt away.

"Lei!"

I screech to a halt.

"Pop the tires on the other trucks. Hurry."

My eyes widen. Yes. They won't be able to follow. I race to the front of the fleet. Slash all four tires. I slash the tires of Dad's truck and all four tires of the rear truck.

The sheriff and his men silently barrel nearer.

I jump into the Humvee, fumble with the keys. My heart is exploding in my chest. I find the right key, jam it in the ignition. The Humvee roars to life. I begin to turn around. Forward, reverse. Forward, reverse. Every time I look up, there's Dad, staring at me, his grip white-knuckled on the bars. I scream my frustration and fear.

The sheriff bangs his fists against the passenger-side window. My scream changes pitch, and then I fall silent. He's shirtless, banging with his knuckles. Blood smears the window. I continue my turn, launch over a boulder of *pāhoehoe*, and begin to jounce and jostle over the raw lava field. The sheriff jogs beside me, trying all the doors, cursing in Hawaiian and English. He bends to find a rock. Finally I double back onto the primitive road beyond the last truck, throw the stick into second, and punch the gas, leaving the sheriff in my dust.

A Hanaman has climbed on top of the vehicle. I hear him up there. But he doesn't stand a chance. I drop into third, lurch, and accelerate. I go airborne. The Hanaman is bucked off of the roof.

A rock hits the back window, shattering it into a spider's web. I scream myself hoarse as I rumble away, abandoning my father, my dead *tūtū*, Buzz, the raging volcano at my back, the swirl of green fire above.

CHAPTER 20

Mom. Kai.

Find them before they ride 'Imiloa home and right into a trap.

It's the only thing holding me together.

Mom. Kai. There's still time.

Keali'i. Tami. Paul. Uncle Hank. They're no match alone against a truckful of Hanamen. *Please, be okay.*

Dust and ash and cinders and smoke fall like a gentle drizzle of sleet. I pass the gate that only Buzz has a key to, and I brake, jump out. The gate latches. I press the lock closed, trapping everyone else on the inside. Might buy me valuable time, if Buzz isn't with them. They can't get a vehicle around either side of these posts. They'll be coming in a truck. I should have taken more time to slash every spare. I glance at the blood smears on the passenger window: I barely escaped as it was.

I groan, knowing that Dad will be punished for this, even if he isn't killed.

Mom. Kai.

I push all other thoughts away and drive. The paved Saddle Road is minutes away. I turn onto it and race toward Hilo at ninety miles an hour. The road descends sharply. I put the Humvee in neutral and coast, losing no speed. I have half a tank, but how much is that? Enough for me to get home. But after I rescue Mom and Kai, we flee until we run out of gas. Save gas now as much as possible.

Where do I go?

What if I'm stopped by Hanamen on my road before I reach them?

Aukina.

He's a soldier. He has military training. Probably weapons. Kana`ina doesn't know about him. His place is deep off the grid, surrounded by jungle.

I'll be putting him in danger.

I bite my lip. The other truck of Hanamen will still be at the house if they haven't found Mom and Kai yet. I can't confront more men without him.

It's not quite noon. Mom and Kai were going to spend the whole day with Sara and Chloe.

Stop at Aukina's, I tell myself. *He'll know what to do.* There's no way Kana`ina will get a truck rolling by then, get that gate open, beat me home on three wheels. Even if he went straight for my place when he got back—I'll beat him.

I nod in silence. Not sure it's a plan, but it's a start. I

relax, but the images rush in. Grandpa. Buzz, sliding backward at high speed into the darkness, gripped in the sheriff's arms. Dad's eyes, wild with fear, but not for himself.

I yell. My voice is torn.

* * *

I descend below the tree line and reach the highest outskirts of Hilo. The road grows windy, and I must slow down. Rusting, abandoned cars choke the shoulders, and I constantly pump the brakes.

It dawns on me: I'm rolling into town driving the sheriff of Hana's flagship vehicle.

My grip on the wheel tightens. My windows are dark. If I blow by other Hanamen, I can probably get away with it. The sheriff does whatever he wants.

The air is clear at this elevation. Visibility is infinite as long as I'm looking out and not up. The world is still tinged in goblin green.

You have been busy.

I nearly slam on the brakes. Him. I steady my driving and concentrate: a mental wall. Shield my thoughts.

What are you doing? Such a low orbit. So bright. How did you release that meteor?

Ignore him. *Don't panic. It makes sense.* The line between both Orchids and me is wide open. I've had no fits, no spaceouts today, and yet we are *close.* Everything that has happened has happened while I was awake. It's all different now. The gateway between our minds has opened wide.

I turn toward the zoo, zigzagging through the upper neighborhoods. *God, Aukina, please be home.*

260

I know you're here. Talk to me.

Good. He can't hear my every thought.

I'm currently unavailable. Call back later.

I release a hoarse laugh. That'll annoy him.

Don't ignore me!

Whatevah, dude.

A large crowd has gathered along the road ahead. I slow and follow their gazes as I pass. A perfect view of Mauna Loa's slopes. The mounded summit sits above the inversion layer, where the debris from the pearl impact is mixing with the ash and sulfurous steam of the eruption. The geyser of lava is plainly visible below that layer, some twenty, thirty miles away. So serene and strikingly beautiful, small and silent in the distance. This fountain of Earth's molten core is enormous, even from so far away. A lake of orange and black tar seeps down Mauna Loa's sides. Nothing in the world can stop it. The flow doesn't appear to be headed for Hilo, but how can I know? There hasn't been an eruption on Mauna Loa since the eighties. That one missed Hilo. Still, it took days of worry before people knew they were safe.

I put my hands to my temples and squeeze. *Oh, my God.*

A voice answers. **You think you're Pele, don't you? The Hawaiian goddess of lava, right?** He finds this amusing.

If this guy were in front of me, I'd strangle him until his eyes bulged out of his purple face.

You can uncork the genie. But can you so easily put it back? Ha, ha.

I didn't do this.

Yes, you did. You can't handle any of this. Let me take over.

No, I think, not to him. What if this other person wrests control of the Star Flowers from me? He'll unleash them. They'll leave. The sheriff will kill Dad.

My throat stings, and I cough. The orange-and-black flood of lava advances. Tens of miles distant. How long would it take to get down here?

Buzz could calculate it.

I moan. He has to be okay. He *has* to. The sheriff wouldn't murder a resource like him. He's mad but not stupid.

I punch the gas and growl hoarsely. Just like Chewy. Dad's *Star Wars* joke. I choke back a cry. Focus. Aukina. Mom and Kai. Keali`i. Tami. And then we go after Dad and Buzz.

I make a left, downhill, and see Hilo Bay.

The battleship is turning into view from the north, still miles out to sea.

I gawk at it as I fly down the hill. Is this how native islanders felt when they first spied the giant sailing ships of the first Europeans to reach the Islands?

They're coming back. Everything's going to change. Will they bring order? Stability?

They'll spell doom for the sheriff of Hana. He'll see it coming. He'll use my dad any way he can. If he sees that his game is up, he'll kill Dad out of spite.

Rescue Dad. Save Mom and Kai.

I race for Aukina's homestead. He once drew me a

detailed map that I burned into my mind. I spot each memorized landmark and turn into deep jungle. I rumble up to a clearing and cut the engine.

A goat corral, an open shed—a black water tank. The house has an unfinished roof draped by blue tarps. I forget caution as I jump out of the Humvee, stumble forward, catch my balance.

"Freeze! Right there!" A shot is fired. Above me.

I fall to the ground, doubled over. I can't take it anymore. No other feeling comes close to describing the terror of a gun pointed at you. I hide my head in my arms, breathing mud.

"Holo! Wait!" Aukina yells. My entire body sighs with relief.

Feet shuffle in the mud. Aukina speaks urgently with someone. Then footsteps approach. He stands over me, cups my shoulders in his arms. "Lei, get up. It's okay."

I rise. I look up. We hold each other's eyes for a moment, and then I throw my arms around him, squeeze, begin to sob.

"What happened? Are you hurt?"

"A Humvee?" Holo asks. "This window's all bloody."

"Lei, what's going on?"

I take a deep breath. Stammer, start over. I grip his wrists as I face him and spill it out. "The sheriff of Hana, he kidnapped my dad and my *tūtū*. And Buzz. He killed my *tūtū*. Right in front of me. Shot him in the head. He's going to our house after my mom and my brother. I need to save them. I— Aukina."

He stares at me in shock.

"Aukina, please. I don't know what I'll do if you—"

"Shh," he says gently. "Of course I'll help you."

I squeeze him tightly again, trembling. He's so tall. His chin rests atop my head. I tuck my arms against his chest, and he folds his arms around me like a straitjacket. I finally feel contained. "Thank you," I manage. "We have to go. Now."

He lets go of me, looks at Holo. "Okay. Just . . . let me think."

I back away, nod, lean against the grille of the Humvee. My hands go to my face. I feel naked without them there. I rest my fingers on my forehead, watch the two brothers talk though my cupped palms. They get into a hushed argument, then Aukina sends his older brother away.

He turns back, comes close. "Holo can't leave our parents alone here, not after you dragged this beast right to our door."

"I'm so sorry."

"No. Don't. That's not what I meant. Just . . . what's the plan?"

Mom. Kai.

"We have to get to a house several miles above mine. The one road that gets us there might be guarded by Hanamen, though." I cough. My throat is sandpaper. I shouldn't have screamed so much.

"How would we get by them?"

I ball my hands into fists, look at the ground. "I don't know. This Humvee belongs to the sheriff, though. We could probably blow by anyone who would stop us."

"The *sheriff's* Hummer? How'd you . . . ?" His question dies.

Holo trots back to us wearing a backpack, a rifle slung over each shoulder, a leather holster dangling from his hand with a gun inside.

Everybody and their guns.

He transfers the pack and all of his weaponry over to Aukina. "Be. Smart. This better be short and sweet." He eyes his brother harshly, then me.

I stare up at him. So tall. Just as handsome as Aukina.

"God, Aukina," Holo says.

"I'll be fine," Aukina says. "In and out. Here, have some water."

I guzzle the bottle he hands me. We jump into the Humvee. I turn around and speed toward home, glancing at the gas needle. Just below a third.

"This is the sheriff of Hana's Hummer." Aukina tests the words. "We'll just blow right through town." He leans back and swears at the ceiling under his breath. "Unless every other Tribe sees we're without our entourage and thinks it's the perfect moment to take us out."

"Don't forget the Manō in Papaikou," I say. He groans.

"I'm hoping everyone will be distracted right now."

"Yeah? How's that? This Orchid thing? What's it doing so low and bright?"

"That's the baby," I explain. "I got her."

"Really? That's good, right?"

I realize: he might not know about the new impact, the eruption; he's been deep in the jungle today. "There was another meteor strike. Mauna Loa's erupting."

"Oh. Is that all?"

"No. There's a battleship coming into Hilo Bay."

"Ho! What?!" he barks. "Which one?"

"How would I know?"

"They're labeled. Big as Dallas. All over. Designation, serial number, the works."

"It's not close enough to read yet."

He starts talking a mile a minute, confused, excited, rifling off names of generals and admirals. He's nervous, talking to hide it. I tune him out, eyes on the road. What if I'm too late? What if they have Mom and Kai already? My mind goes blank. I won't consider it.

"Are there more ships in Honolulu?"

I shake my head. "Who knows? This one is alone."

"Alone?" Aukina frowns.

We weave through the clutter of town, pass a few slow cars and trucks. The baby Orchid is dimming, but the sun's filtered light turns the bay front into a hostile pea green. We cut across the corner of town on a parallel road.

"Look. At. That." Aukina whistles. He gawks at the volcano's fire truck–red fountain of lava.

I cut back onto the main coastal road, race across the bridge over the Waimanu River. Aukina gets his first look at the battleship, still pretty far out to sea, clearly heading to port in Hilo Bay.

"Lei!" he yelps.

"What? What is it?"

Aukina's stunned into silence.

"Lei," he finally says, "I don't think that's American."

CHAPTER 21

I choke, steal a glance at the ship. *"Not American?"*

Aukina shakes his head, his eyes on the battleship. "No flags. The decals on the bow—everywhere—they don't look right. There're strange dishes all over the upper control top. The turrets aren't the right design. You want me to keep going?"

"Well, what country is it, then?"

"There's no flag. It's still so far out. Can't tell."

Not American. I turn to gooseflesh. A strange certainty falls over me—someone is waltzing onto these islands without firing a shot. Who?

"Maybe it's the French," Aukina offers.

We share a moment of silence, and then for some reason we both burst out laughing. I don't even know why it's so funny. But laughing about it feels better than the dread.

We pass over the singing bridge that marks the northern

end of town. "What happened, Lei?" Aukina asks. "Does the sheriff know about you?"

I nod. "I just want to get my mom and brother. All I care about. Tami and Keali`i, too."

"Yeah, of course."

I clench my jaw, hold back tears. So grateful he's with me. I should have kissed him last time we were together. I would have enjoyed that. I may never enjoy anything ever again.

"Hey," Aukina says.

I look at him; his eyes are full of concern and reassurance. He touches my hand. I clasp his. He squeezes tightly. My hand is so small, wrapped in his strong fingers. His hand feels like a shield. Protecting me. "It's going to be okay, Lei. Promise."

"Promise?"

"I promise."

We turn off of the Hawaiian Belt. We're now in Manō territory. Aukina says, "Pull over. Let me drive. You duck low." I hesitate, but a distant part of me remembers: *If I get shot in the head, the whole world goes out.*

Aukina drives fast. He's so exposed behind the wheel. He's alert, his casual expression forced.

My breathing quickens, and my grip on the seat tightens as I half duck around each turn in the road, but there are no Manō out today. Maybe the volcano or the mysterious battleship—or both—have distracted them. Hilo Bay isn't visible here, but it's possible that residents of

Papaikou would have been able to see the ship rounding the coast.

We blow by the turnoff to my house. No one guarding the gate. My stomach twists. Between Keali`i, Uncle Hank, and Paul, *someone* should be there. No sign of struggle. It's better than spotting a body heaped in the grass. But the Hanamen might be up at the house, hiding out or even holding neighbors hostage until Mom and Kai come home.

My eyes dart away from the albizia tree that Grandpa always sat under on duty. He'll never sit there again. The pain of this knowledge promises to overwhelm me, but not now. Later, if there ever is a later, the true depth of what has happened this morning will take me. But not now.

I'm coming, Mom, Kai.

I direct Aukina up, up, until the road ends at a fork with two narrow gravel drives. We rumble up to the right.

"Stay low," Aukina says. "If you recognize a truck at the house, we'll pull up fast and steady, like we belong. I'll honk. The sheriff's men will come out. Then we only have a second or two to surprise them when we spring out."

"Make sure they aren't dragging my family with them. Don't shoot them."

"We'll figure it out," he replies.

But there are no trucks in the driveway as we approach.

Did we get here first? I put my hands to my mouth, praying that this is true.

"You wait here," Aukina says. "I'll clear the premises."

"But the Irvings don't know you! They'll shoot you."

Aukina frowns.

"Let's just wait here for a second, see if anyone comes to us. Then I'll lower the window and call out. Then we can go up to the porch together," I try.

He nods. We wait, and I feel the seconds bleeding away. Finally I roll down the window. "Mom? Kai? Sara? It's me, Leilani."

Nothing. But I could barely speak above a whisper. Aukina and I share an uncertain look. He offers me one of his rifles. I shake my head. He insists. I shrink away. "Lei," he says, but takes his gun back. We open our doors.

Just as I step out of the tall Hummer, the front door of the house bursts open. Sara runs out to us, Chloe in her arms. I see the look on her face, and my skin is suddenly ice.

We're too late.

Sara is crying. She runs up to me, shaking her head, nearly hysterical. "Lei. They came and took your mom. Hanamen. They came right into the house and . . . and . . . they grabbed her. There was nothing I could do. They threatened to shoot us. They locked me and Chloe in the bedroom. We couldn't get out until they were gone. We haven't seen Paul. He and Hank were in the plots. Have you seen them?"

I'm dizzy. My palms go to my eye sockets. I shake the reality away. Shake my head. No. No. No.

"What about Kai?" Aukina asks calmly.

I look up at Sara with pleading eyes, my breath held.

"He ran into the jungle. Your mom told him to run. I haven't seen him since."

"How long ago?" I ask.

"About thirty minutes ago. Maybe a little more."

"And he's still out there?"

"I don't know. The Hanamen left with your mom before they found him. But maybe they caught him down the road. I don't know—"

"Kai!" I scream. "KAI!" I cough. My voice can't call out loud enough. It's suddenly raw again. But he's out there. Hiding. At least I have him. I need to get him. "Kai," I croak, but I might as well be whispering.

Aukina takes over for me. "Kai!" he yells, starting to circle the perimeter of the property. "Kai!"

"Is anyone else around?" I rasp, asking Sara.

Her eyes flush with tears. "Keali`i was on patrol. No one's come back. I don't . . ." She trails off, fear choking her.

"Where would Kai go?" Aukina asks. "Could he be with Hank and Paul?"

"I don't know. God, I hope so."

He turns to me. "If he knew he wasn't safe here, where would he go? Does he have any hiding spots down by the river? Anything?"

I nod. "He does, but . . . He would go home," I whisper. "He has a fort close to our house that we've never found. He's very proud of it. That's where he'll be. I'm sure of it."

"Let's go."

"What about them?" I ask. "The Hanamen may come back. The sheriff himself might come."

"Wait. What?"

"I disabled his vehicles. Slashed the tires. But if he gets all the spares together . . . he could still make it down here."

Aukina studies me with wonder.

"We have to *go*," I urge. "All of us."

He nods. He turns to Sara. "Get your daughter up the trail, toward the waterfall. Get far enough away that if Chloe cries, no one can hear her. Hide. We'll be back for you as soon as we can. Grab what you need in case we're gone for a while. Jackets, diapers, everything."

We race with her into the house, Chloe giggling in her arms.

Kai. He's still here. We'll find him. It's all I can think as we gather supplies.

Who's Kai?

I freeze. *Go the hell away!* I mentally shout.

Oh, no, no, no. Why would I do that? I just got here?

I don't need this right now.

Haven't you seen me yet?

I'm shoveling onesies from a drawer into a duffel bag. I pause, trying to figure out what he means. Even if he were making sense, my mind is scrambled right now. I do my best to throw up a mental block. I don't have to listen to myself think, either.

Kai. Kai. Kai. That's all I say to myself.

A moment later we escort Sara and Chloe into the trees and turn back. They'll be safer up there. They'll be fine. They hike the waterfall trail all the time.

Aukina and I jump in the Humvee and double back

down the road. My mind is screaming for us to go faster, but we creep along with our windows down, calling Kai. I stand out of my window so that he can see me, in silent agony that I can't reach for him with my torn voice.

If I hadn't lost my voice before, I certainly would have lost it now.

"Lei, inside!" Aukina barks.

The Orchids have faded. Only just visible as heavenly shapes against the browning sky, no longer directly in front of the sun.

We tear up my driveway, slow cautiously as we near the house through the trees.

No Hanaman truck.

Does that mean they found Kai and split?

I close my eyes. Push away the despair.

We halt. I force myself to look around. Our old red truck is in the driveway. It's quiet.

"He's going to be here somewhere," I say, willing it to be true. "I'll check the house; I know all the places to look. You call to him from around the property." He checks the chambers of his two rifles, adjusts the holster of his handgun, and trots away.

I rush up the steps of the house, remember caution, slow down.

I crack the door open. "Kai!" I croak. No use whatsoever. I enter. Nothing's out of place. No one. Shouldn't Tami be resting on the couch, at least?

"Tami? Keali`i?"

Maybe they rescued Kai, all of them are hiding some-where.

Maybe they were *all* taken away from me.

I race to each of Kai's favorite hiding spots, cawing his name. The cupboards in the kitchen. The closet under the stairs. His room, under the bed, behind his beanbag. My room, behind my bookshelf.

I see Mom's birthday present to me: my Hawaiiana book. I snatch it and hold it tight.

Finally I'm convinced: he's not in the house. No one's here.

This can't be happening. Please, please be outside.

I go down the steps. The plumeria tree drops a flower on the ground just as I pass. I pick it up, grip it, crushing it. *I'll get you back, Mom. I'll get you all back.*

Aukina is in the jungle down below. I hear him calling Kai.

And then I hear a rustle in the garage.

The hairs on my neck rise. A muffled moan emanates from within. The garage door is rusted open. I stride over to the wall, peek in. I can only see clutter. And then, in the shadows—

Kai! It's him! I think.

But it's Tami, sitting up groggily. I place the plumeria flower in my Hawaiiana book and then set it on the work-bench.

Gunfire. A firefight has started down the drive. I groan. *Aukina. Oh, God. Oh, God, no.* A volley of rifle shots and off-pitch return fire crescendos, then dies.

I go shakily to Tami. But then I stop, frown. Her mouth is duct-taped. She has blood on her forehead. Cold-cocked. Next to her Uncle Hank and Paul are also gagged, tied to the legs of the workbench. Tami looks at me. Her eyes widen in alarm. She shakes her head. I step forward to help her with her gag, tear off the tape, start to untie her hands.

"Leilani, go! He's coming!"

Who?

I turn around, following her frantic eyes, and from the far bend in the driveway I see the sheriff of Hana, shirtless, lock eyes with me and break into a run.

* * *

"Aukina!" I shout, but the raspy call is faint.

Kana`ina bounds toward me. I dart out of the garage and cut between the garage and the house. I double left, behind the garage, and race for the bushes.

Once I'm in the cover of the vines and ferns, I angle left again, crawl back closer to the driveway. He stalks me from behind the garage, slows, scanning the boundary of jungle. I freeze. *How did he get here so fast?*

He chooses the wrong direction. I allow him to get several steps away, and then I creep along the ground, weaving through the bushes. Spines claw at my skin. I snap a twig. Freeze.

The sheriff turns. He knows I'm here, even if he can't see me. He slowly pulls a gun from his hip. The one he used to kill Tūtū.

Aukina calls out, a hundred yards away through dense woods, "Lei!" He says more, but it's muffled.

I'm alone.

Run! I think. But he'll shoot me. I doubt he's stupid enough to try to kill me, but if a bullet even hits my leg, I'm as good as dead.

"Hear those shots?" the sheriff says. "That was my men cleaning up around here. It's over, Leilani. Come on out."

The sheriff has me pinned, his gun trained right on me.

And then I see it. Under the thorny bush right before me.

Keali`i's pistol.

I tossed it away two nights ago. Could have been *years* ago. It was loaded, wasn't it? Will it still work?

Tūtū's voice echoes from the past: *"As long as the powder's dry in the bullet."*

I stop breathing. Fire and ice scurry along my arms and back. I reach forward, clasp the gun in a trembling hand.

"Come out, Leilani." The sheriff is a blur behind the foliage. "No sudden moves."

I slide the little lever by the base of my thumb open. A red dot is now clearly visible. That means the safety's off, right? The cold metal feels oily against my sweaty palm. Like in a dream, I'll aim and I'll never hit him, no matter how hard I try, no matter how close he gets. The trigger will lock.

"Leilani." Impatient. "It might already be too late for your parents. But there's still time for your bro—"

A thunderous crack. The kickback shoves my clenched fist into my face. I cry out. Drop the gun.

The sheriff falls forward, fires a wayward shot as he crashes into the brambles. He's lying right in front of me.

No bulletproof jacket.

He cries out. I spring to my feet, back away, brambles tearing at my arms. His back darkens with blood. My hands go to my mouth. I back away farther.

He looks up at me, eyes wild, full of rage.

And then his head drops. His eyes go blank.

I grunt, fall to my knees. Tūtū! He killed Tūtū. I pull at my hair. Why doesn't this feel right?

"Lei!" Aukina shouts, stampeding toward the garage. "LEILANI!"

Unseen around the corner, Tami matches Aukina's tone. "LEI!"

Right here, I try to say. But no sound comes. I crumple to the ferns. *I just killed somebody. Oh, God.*

"LEI!" Aukina's voice is frantic, nearly mad.

I squawk, but it's enough for him to hear. He crashes through the bushes, stops just before trampling me. "You okay?"

I stare forward.

"You hurt?" He helps me up.

"No."

He sees the gun on the ground, looks at the body, puts two and two together. I don't think he realizes it's the sheriff. "We have to go. That shot might bring others."

I'm not going anywhere without Kai, I intend to say. Nothing comes out. I try again. "I'm not going without . . ."

"We have Kai," Aukina says. "Your parents have him. They're coming now."

"What?" The force of it rattles me. *Don't dare to hope you heard that right.*

"Come on."

I follow Aukina onto the driveway, careful to step around the body. Aukina gathers up both Keali`i's and the sheriff's pistol, kicks the sheriff's head unintentionally as he steps over him. My eyes widen. There's no life there at all. The head just tilts and halts.

Tami has inched her way out of the carport, but she's still tied up at the hands and feet. "They caught us off guard. Two of them. They were looking for your mother and Kai."

"Hank? Paul?" Aukina asks.

"Back of the garage. Help them."

"Where's Keali`i?"

"Taken with your mother. He was the first one they grabbed."

Aukina hurries into the garage to untie the two men. I help Tami. My hands are trembling. "You okay?" I ask her, struggling to tear through several rounds of duct tape.

"Probably a concussion. Being knocked out's a bitch. Not like the movies, you know?" she groans, rubbing her neck with her freed hand.

"You're bleeding."

She gasps. I jerk away, afraid I've hurt her somehow. She inches toward the sheriff's body. "You got one."

Said like I nabbed an *aku* bluefin.

I *killed* a man.

Aukina pulls Uncle Hank into the open. He strides back into the garage for Paul.

Dad sprints up the drive, stutters to a halt when he sees me. "Lei."

"Dad—" I fall forward into the gravel and dry-heave, whimpering.

"Sweetheart." He skids up to me, clutching me. I squeeze him back. He's real. He's alive!

"Lei!" Kai. I whip around, see Mom and Kai and Keali`i and even Buzz running toward me, and I stumble forward. Kai jumps in my arms. I cry out, nearly fall backward. We're sandwiched between Mom and Dad. Keali`i wraps Tami in his arms. He's trembling.

"We have to get out of here," Dad says. "The sheriff—" He stops, eyes locked on Kana`ina. "He's—" Dad stops, incredulous.

Buzz cautiously approaches the body, stares blankly. Buzz's neck and throat are heavily bruised. He's favoring his left arm. For a second I think he's going to kick the sheriff's head, but he clenches a fist and screams.

"Who—" Dad asks. Everyone looks at me. I look at my feet.

Mom pulls Kai over to the lanai. They sit down, hold each other tightly as Mom rocks back and forth, doing her best to hold it together. Kai's eyes are somber, soaking in every detail.

I step forward to Buzz. "I'm so glad you're okay."

I reach out to hug him, but he winces. "Careful. Broken wrist." Then he pulls me into his embrace with his good arm. "Good job getting away up there. Good job. Good job." We're sobbing.

Dad shakes himself out of a trance. "That's all of them." He counts on his hand. "That Herbert is dead. The two in the other truck, the ones that took Mom and Keali`i. I didn't see any others."

I wipe my face. "There were . . . more," I say.

"Kana`ina left them on Mauna Loa," he says. "The road was too rough for a flat tire. Buzz and I were in the cages. He was hell-bent on getting here at light speed. It was only him and Herbert in the cab. He wasn't thinking straight."

"How'd you get out? How'd you find Mom and Keali`i?"

"They met on the road. Mom's captors were heading for Puna. Kana`ina told them to show him the way to our place. He was going to use the dogs to track down Kai. Execute Keali`i right here for show. Raced the whole way. I thought we were going to flip. They pulled up the driveway, and Aukina shot the driver dead, right in the neck. Killed the other guy with a second shot. The sheriff was blocked. He abandoned the truck. Fired at Aukina and was gone into the jungle."

"I got them out of the cages," Aukina adds. "I couldn't

leave them. I had no idea that was the sheriff, that he would run straight up to the house."

"My family?" Paul rubs at his bruised wrists. "Are they safe?"

"Yes." Aukina helps him stand. "We sent them to the waterfall. Safest up there if anyone came back to the house."

"Good," he says.

"What do we do with the body?" Buzz stares at the sheriff. "We need to . . . display it."

"What?" I say.

"People should know he's gone."

"Let me take him down to Papaikou," Keali`i says. His eyes dart to me, flick back to Dad. "I'll hand him over to the Manō. They'll be happy to spread the word."

"And watch those guys waltz into power?" Dad says. "No, thanks."

"No, they won't. I'll make sure of it."

"Yeah, right."

"I'm Manō," Keali`i says. He looks between Dad, Mom, and me.

Everyone peers at him, even Uncle Hank and Paul.

"Why do you think they've never bothered you?" Keali`i straightens, raises his chin. "Why do you think you always come and go, but no one else gets through? Why do you think it took the sheriff's men so long to get up here, even though they knew the area where you lived?"

"Keali`i—" Dad begins.

"Your *tūtū* knew," he says, eyes boring into me, then back

to Mom, Dad. "I had to tell him when we ditched Two Dog. He knew. I asked him to stay quiet, but he knew."

Grandpa *knew* about this? My breathing quickens. *It wasn't his only secret*, I think. Kana`ina's cryptic exchange with him just before . . . *I'll never know what that was about now*. I push it all away.

"You looked out for me. I looked out for you," Keali`i says. We're all silent.

"Come on," he urges. "Get going. They should know to be on alert. Half those Manō boys were off surfing, or this never would've happened. We still have time to get them back up this way. Let's move!"

He's right, I think. *We're not done here yet. There's much more to do. God.*

No. Not God. Just me. See me yet?

Him. I grit my teeth. *Not. Now.* But I suddenly clasp my mouth shut.

"Haven't you seen me yet?" he had asked me when I was at the Irvings'.

"Oh, no," I say aloud. Everyone watches me. I shake my head.

"Lei, sit down," Mom says, rising from the steps. "What is it?"

I close my eyes. *You're in the battleship.*

In the darkness of space above the world, I feel him grinning.

Coming for you, since that's the way it has to be. Remember?

The battleship. He's in the battleship.

Aukina had noticed: *"There're strange dishes all over the upper control top."*

My hand shakes uncontrollably. I lower it, grip Aukina's elbow. He's here. He's literally docking in Hilo *right now*. Coming for me. He *does* have his own array.

He has a *battleship*.

CHAPTER 22

Uncle Hank drives Paul home. They'll fetch Sara and the baby at the waterfall, and then Hank will check on Auntie Nora. Once they've departed, I tell everyone what I know as quickly as my voice will allow. Kai hears all of it. I don't care; discretion is the last thing on my mind. Aukina fills in the gaps, explaining that the battleship may not be American. Dad and Buzz nod along; they saw the ship on the way here.

"Is it the one you've been following for the past few days?" Dad asks.

I nod.

"Well, what do we do?" he continues.

"We can't let him step on the island," I say. "What if he gets up to Mauna Kea with a band of soldiers? Takes control of the array? He could use it to try and muscle me out."

For a moment only the mynas flitting from tree to tree make any sound.

"She's right," Buzz answers. "We can't let them dock."

"I just thought of a joke," Keali`i says. "Where does a battleship park?"

"Keali`i—" Dad protests.

"Wherever the hell it wants to, that's where."

"Not. Funny," Tami says.

"Well, how are we supposed to stop a *battleship*?" He laughs.

"Just . . . be quiet, all of you," I say.

They fall silent, and I close my eyes. *Who are you?* I ask loudly.

I'm the plucky hero. I like to pluck flowers bare.

Stop it. What's your name?

You never told me your name. Why should I tell you mine?

I'm Rose, I lie.

Ah, very good. I can't wait to see you in person, Rose. It will be a pleasure to meet the Flower of Heaven. My name is Commander Dwight Towers.

"Commander Dwight Towers," I tell Aukina. "Do you know that name?"

He searches, shakes his head. "No idea. Sounds . . . British? I don't know."

"*I* know that name," Dad says.

"Huh?" several of us reply in unison.

"Yeah," says Dad. "I recognize it . . . from somewhere. Can't quite place it."

What country are you with? Are you British?

British! I sense amusement. I'm not British. No. What does it matter? I'm a citizen of the world. An emissary of all nations. I'm going to win the whole globe back today, Ms. Rose. Pluck it right out of your hands.

You can't dock here. I won't let you.

Oh, yeah? You and whose army?

"Where's Tūtū?" Kai asks.

I'm whiplashed back, my legs turning to seaweed. Horrified, I look to Mom. Mom takes her seat next to him on the lanai steps. Dad opens his mouth, but no words come. His eyes well with tears. Kai yells, "WHERE'S TŪTŪ? TELL ME!"

I kneel in front of him, take his hands. "He's gone." Two words. I've said them aloud. Somehow it's more real than ever. I bury my face in Kai's chest, put my arms around him.

"No. No way," he pleads. Mom sobs. I wipe away tears and look at him. He's crumpled against Mom. Her face is burrowed into his hair.

"Can I see him?" he asks. "Where is he?"

A lead ball of dread tugs at my stomach. "Still up there."

"You can't leave him up there!"

"We won't. Not a chance," Dad says.

"Oh, Kai, Kai. I'm so sorry." I quiver. "Mom." Kai finds my hand and squeezes it. He leans his head against my chest, and I feel my grandmother's pendant dig into my sternum. His sobs shake us. "Tūtū was protecting us."

They're together now. My ʻaumākua. My guardians.

They will make sure we get through this. They will always be with me.

I weep.

"It's okay, sis," Kai attempts. I lean back, study him. So brave. I see his fear. The red around his eyes. I see that he has been deeply scarred today. He saw his mother kidnapped, and he was forced to run. His *tūtū* is . . . But he's being so brave. For me. I kiss his forehead and hold him tight.

Listen, I don't want to dock in this dump any more than you want me to. It's easy: release the aliens and maybe I'll go away and leave you alone.

SHUT UP. SHUT UP. SHUT UP. I can't keep it in my mind. I scream it out, tearing my throat again: "JUST SHUT UP!"

"Lei," Mom says.

Very well, then. Have it your way.

"Not you. I'm sorry, Mom. Not you. Admiral Asshole. He won't stay out of my head."

I hear Keali`i punch a fist into his other hand. "Fellas, come on! Let's go!"

"Go where?" Dad asks, clearly exasperated.

"First the body. I know just who to give it to. Then . . ." He trails off.

"Then you fire another pearl right up that ship's `ōkole, that's what," Kai says.

"Shh!" Mom squeezes Kai.

Everyone looks to me. I try to consider the idea. *Send*

another pearl at the ship? Blow it to kingdom come? It sounds terrible. *How many people are on the ship?* But the idea is untenable for a dozen other reasons. Tsunami, first. I struggle to explain. "The baby Orchid fired the pearl that opened the vent today. She's empty now. Spent."

"The mother?" Buzz asks.

I don't know. "*If* she can produce a pearl," I say, "I'm hardly an accurate shot. I could easily miss and pulverize Hilo. And even if I hit it spot on? Tsunami? Shockwave?"

"But Commander Towers doesn't know any of that," Aukina says. "Right? I'm sure he saw what you just did up on Mauna Loa. I'm sure he can see it erupting. Can you bluff him, Lei?"

"Bluff him."

"Wait. Mauna Loa's erupting?" asks Tami. "We saw the strike happen, but no eruption."

"She got walloped. She's pissed, venting," Dad says.

"Tūtū's up there!" Kai exclaims.

Buzz reassures him. "The eruption is south and downslope of where Lani is. His body'll be safe."

"Is Hilo in danger?" asks Aukina.

"I don't think so," I say.

"That's not good enough," he shoots back. Of course: his family. Just south of town, almost at sea level.

"Come on. Let's *move!*" Keali`i is backing toward the Hummer. "I'm leaving. Get in if you're coming."

Dad and Buzz pick up the sheriff's body. Mom hurries Kai inside. I look away, queasy. Humans aren't supposed to bend and flop the way Kana`ina does. He was pure evil ten minutes ago. All muscle and intent. Lethal. Now: gone.

Keali`i opens the back of the Humvee, and they work together to stuff the body into the trunk like a prize marlin.

I lean over the mossy paving stones and dry-heave.

* * *

We travel down the hill in a caravan of battered vehicles and stop in Papaikou. In addition to the sheriff, Keali`i transfers custody of the bodies of the three other Hanamen over to the Manō. Herbert was one of them—the one Aukina killed to free Dad.

I'm in the back of the king cab of the Hanaman truck that Aukina shot up. The truck with the dogs and the cages still has a nice windshield, but the cab wasn't big enough to fit everyone. Dad, Buzz, Aukina, and Keali`i pile into our new ride, and we start into town. Aukina sits in the back with me and holds my hand. He talks, formulating a plan with the others. I don't hear most of it. His voice calms me. The words don't matter.

I cling tightly to my memory of embracing Mom just before we left the house. We cried together. She gently thumbed my pendant, which was wet with tears. We helped each other to breathe in, breathe out.

"I found your book on the workbench," she said, handing me her gift. I took it back with a shaky hand. "The flower was bookmarking one of my favorite myths. Did you know?"

I shook my head.

"The tree with the lying branches. The soul, when it's

290

ready to leap to the next world, comes upon a tree, half-green and half-dead. But the green branches are wily, decaying. The soul that tries to climb that side will fall into *Po*. But your *tūtū* knows to climb the dry branches, Lei. He has his *ʻaumākua* there to guide him. Grandma Liliʻu will show him the way to the *ʻaumākua* world. He has climbed and leapt, and now he's free."

"Yes," I muttered softly. "Like a cat, into the clouds."

*   *   *

Tami wanted to come with us, but Mom made her stay behind. She was knocked out cold, after all. Kealiʻi rushed away, made her a cool compress out of a washcloth, and wrapped it around her golf ball–sized welt. He pumped her full of anti-inflammatories, then he kissed her. "I have to go," he tells her. "But I'll be right back for you. You mean the world to me. If anything had happened . . ."

Just say it! I wanted to shout at him. *Tell her you love her.*

But he didn't say any more.

I would have preferred to stay at the house with Tami and Kai and Mom, but I need to see the ship, learn everything I can if I'm going to have a prayer of bluffing this guy. Now, in the truck, I force my attention back to the present.

"Oh, mama!" Kealiʻi marvels as we cross over the singing bridge and onto the bay front. The battleship is in the bay, aiming toward the dock over by the refineries, where the cruise ships used to come to port. The volcano rages on the high slopes of Mauna Loa, turning a swath of landscape below it a tarry black and the sky above sooty and dark. Aukina estimates that the ship is about fifteen minutes from docking. Buzz and Dad both agree that Hilo looks safe from the path of the lava, but there's no way to know for sure.

I won't let you dock, I tell Commander Dwight Towers. *Don't make me stop you.*

He doesn't answer, hasn't spoken to me since the house. Dad has been telling me not to worry. "Captain Kangaroo probably took his wiring off to council with his crew."

"His connection isn't like yours," Buzz reminds me from the middle of the front seat. "If he stepped away from his radio tower, you may miss each other. Just keep trying."

The bay-front road is unusually busy with traffic. Cars stream by us, heading in the opposite direction, away from town. People are darting to and fro along the parking lots and streets, pointing in all directions, shouting. We inch through traffic, bully forward when we can.

This is your last chance to release the aliens.

"He's back!" I say. They hush.

No. This is your last chance. I'll blow you out of the water if you don't back down and leave the bay. I won't let you dock.

And how are you going to do that, exactly?

You saw the meteor hit Mauna Loa.

So what.

That was your warning shot.

Silence. Then: You're full of it.

You want to test me? Next one goes through your prow.

292

The mental door between us slams shut. Maybe Buzz is right: he can't talk and chew gum at the same time. He's gone off once again to consult.

"They covered their markings with sheets," Dad observes.

"It's crazy," Aukina says. "No flag. Our military just walked away from here. This shouldn't be a surprise. It was bound to happen."

"Why'd they do that again?" Dad asks. It's become a running joke between them.

Rosie, I'm done playing around. We both know you'd never fire on this ship even if you could.

I'm glad I'm not sitting across the table from him; he'd read me like a book. *Don't press me.*

I'm docking. There's nothing you can do to stop me. Unless you release the aliens right now. This is your last warning.

"He's calling my bluff," I say. "He's not going to turn back unless I send the Orchids away."

"Well, tell him you can't!" Dad says. "It's still too early! Why doesn't he get it?"

"I don't know!" I raise my voice, end up coughing.

"Hey, look. They're spray-painting letters on the hull," Buzz notices. "What is it? Can you tell?"

Dad asks Keali`i, "You mind popping over to the Banyan loop for a closer look?"

Keali`i nods and cuts a quick left across traffic.

Someone is spray-painting the upper reaches of the hull.

You see that?

I start. "You're doing that for me?" I almost ask. But I stop just in time. It's a trap. If I can see what he's doing, then he'll know I'm nearby, that I'd be in the path of my own promised destruction. He'd know I was bluffing.

See what? You're a speck on the water.

Just having some fun.

Nothing is funny. Turn around. Now.

A hush falls over the vehicle. We stare out the windows at the battleship.

"Commander Towers. Towers." Dad probes the name. "Where do I know that from?"

We cross a bridge and turn onto Banyan Drive, pull into the parking lot nearest Coconut Island. Dad rolls down his window and holds up his birding binoculars. Mauna Loa is in full view, framed by nearby trees, furiously venting fire and ash high above town. The smell of sulfur is stronger here than it was in Papaikou. "I can read it! It says ... U.S.S. *Sawfish*," Dad reports.

"*Sawfish?*" Aukina says. "If it's American, it's not one I know."

"He's toying with us," I say. "Stalling."

"Lei, take a look." Dad hands the binoculars to me.

I study the ship, but I don't know what I'm looking for. The graffiti is straightforward. I surrender the binocs. "I don't think he's ... all there," I say. "What if he's crazy?"

"A safe bet," Aukina offers. "This is a lone ship. He's not part of a fleet. He's *spray-painting* it. I'm starting to wonder if he *is lōlō*. A renegade crew?"

"Gone rogue," Dad says. "I've wondered, too. Why don't you ask him, Lei?"

Are you a rogue ship?

The response is a pulse of anger.

"The question pissed him off," I say.

"U.S.S. *Sawfish*!" Dad exclaims. "Of course! *On the Beach*. Commander Towers was Gregory Peck's character in *On the Beach*. His submarine was the U.S.S. *Sawfish*."

"That's right!" Aukina says.

"You know it?" asks Dad.

"One of my old man's favorite movies."

"What's *On the Beach*?" Keali`i asks.

Dad says, "It's a movie from the 1950s. Post-nuclear war. A classic. About the years after World War Three, as a bunch of Australians wait for nuclear winter to roll over the continent, even though the warheads were dropped in other places."

Gregory Peck? I ask my adversary. *He played Towers.*

Very nice.

I'm an old-movie buff, I half lie. *I don't get it. Do you want nuclear winter to roll over the globe? Is that why you pretend you're Dwight Towers?*

No, Rose, I'm just seeking out the source of the nonsense Morse code. I just want to shut off the nonsense, help make the world work again.

"Nonsense Morse code?" I ask aloud.

"Yeah. Big part of the movie," Aukina explains. "Towers hears a message transmitting from San Francisco. He hauls his crew all the way across the Pacific from Sydney to investigate. The last hope for humanity, they're thinking. But when they get to San Francisco, the city is in ruins. Turns out the telegraph machine they're chasing down is just being jostled by a Coke bottle tangled up in a flapping window blind."

My mouth drops open. "What's wrong with this guy? That's a *terrible* thing for him to bring up."

"Says a lot about him, actually." Dad sighs. "He's stark, raving mad. Or a suicide."

"Oh, perfect," I say.

Is that what you think I am? A Coke bottle bullied by the wind?

Might as well be.

How can you say that? What I'm doing is working. I'm keeping nuclear winter away. You can't have it both ways. If the globe fills with radiation, it doesn't matter if the power is back on.

I see it the other way around. We're on the verge of losing our country. You have no idea how screwed up things are.

I pause, check my tone. Patiently, caringly, I ask: *Then tell me.*

He pulls back.

What happened to the military? Why did they all leave Hawai`i?

I was in the Middle East. But we were pulled from everywhere.

I sense a strong desire to be heard. This commander feels deeply wronged. He wants to be understood. I let the silence between us do the work. Finally he responds:

It was a bad call. Washington was a complete mess. We didn't know that until we got there, though. The wrong person called the entire fleet home. The president was still alive, but he had lost the confidence of enough people that all hell had broken loose. Two people were claiming the White House. The fleet was in the Atlantic, thinking we were at war with Russia. But it was just . . . confusion. Our military had no idea how to comport itself in the absence of instantaneous communication.

We lost a nuclear sub in September. The wave took twenty ships with it. They were too close, in order to talk with one another. A mistake any seventeenth-century naval cadet would have known to avoid.

I saw that happen. New York.

I know you did. I had already tapped into the mother alien at that time. I was having strange visions, realized the alien was behind them. I could sense your rooted human presence. Putting the pieces together but not quite there. No one would listen to me, though. I have a history of PTSD. I was injured when I served in the Gulf. An explosion shook my screws loose. Everyone in authority knew my special case history, but I always kept my small seizures a secret. I would have been discharged if they knew. I mentioned my sudden ability to hear the alien's simple thoughts, though. I couldn't keep that a secret. Too important. But my higher-ups intended to label me unfit to serve. Long story short, I proved them right: took my ship and my crew and broke off. My crew thinks we're on a priority top-secret mission. We are! I'm not a renegade,

Rose. I'm the only brass who knows the truth. And I'm here to stop you. Our country's leadership is ready to snap right at the highest levels. We need order more than we need a radiation-free world. Just like Chernobyl, the disasters you prevent will dissipate in time. But if our Constitution snaps, it'll never get put back together.

That's not true! I tell him. *The Chernobyl disaster was one-tenth as bad as any of these plants. The technicians at Chernobyl worked hard in real time to prevent the worst-case scenario. Now there aren't the resources to blunt the explosions as they happen. They go unchecked. They're massive beyond anything we've ever known.*

I'm not leaving here without accomplishing my mission.

I take a deep breath, physically grip my head with my hands. He truly believes. He's not crazy at all. Well—maybe, but his actions have a logic. He will never back down.

I *also* believe. I'm doing the right thing. I can think of only one way to stop him: meet conviction with conviction. He must *know* that *I* will never back down.

Instead of letting go of the Orchids, I pull on their tow ropes as forcefully as I can. Drawing them down.

Down.

Whatever happens to this bay is on your head. You're leaving me no choice.

I don't believe you.

I've kept these creatures in orbit for months. You claim that I'm hurting the world because of it. But I know that keeping them here is the right thing to do. What makes you think I'd suddenly flinch if it meant destroying Hilo? Billions of lives are at risk, not one small town.

In a burst of inspiration I add: *The volcano's taking Hilo anyway. What's a tsunami compared to that?*

The world beyond the cab windows grows emerald-green.

Buzz leans forward to peer up through the broken windshield. "Lei, I hope that's you."

"It is. Do you see them both?"

Dad whistles, head stuck out of his window. "I could reach up and *touch* them both." Lights around the dashboard blink to life, accompanied by several low warning sounds. The light show and the commotion die out at once, as if a master wire were jostled, then cut. The engine hiccups but recaptures its rhythm.

Buzz eyes me nervously. "You're busting the simplest circuits now."

"Drive *mauka*," I tell Keali`i. "As fast as you can."

"Wait, *toward* the erupting volcano?" he asks.

"Safer there," I say.

Four sets of eyes turn to me.

"K'den," Keali`i says dryly. He shifts into gear and peels away from the curb.

"Lei," Dad begins, his voice gravelly. "You're not—?"

"He's leaving me no choice. He can't come on this island. If he comes ashore with a landing party, he'll seize the array, use it himself. He'll hunt us down with trained soldiers. His men think they're following orders from Washington. All the Manō in the world would do us no good. It's not a bluff anymore. I'll really do it if I have to."

Aukina eyes me closely. I stare back with rock-hard resolve. "Jesus," he says.

CHAPTER 23

We race up the streets to higher elevation, blow past a yellow-and-blue LEAVING TSUNAMI ZONE sign.

"Lei. No," Dad whispers. A plea. A prayer. He looks frightened. But the fear isn't for himself; it's for my sanity.

"Dad. I *know*. Quiet."

"What about my family?" Aukina asks. "They're not out of the way."

"Shh!"

Deep down, of course, I know I could never destroy Hilo. I'll flatten the top of Mauna Kea if worse comes to worst, destroy *my* array. He'll never muscle me out. Then we'll run and hide . . . somewhere. But I push that knowledge far, far back in my mind. Commander Towers needs to feel my conviction. I need *his* eyes to fill with genuine fear. "I could still release a pearl at the ship—if it's small enough," I whisper to myself. It all depends on what the mother has at the ready inside her.

It's time to find out.

You have five minutes to start backing out of the bay, or I hit you.

We rapidly climb the steep ascent of Ponohawai Street. Distantly before us the fountain of lava appears to have abated somewhat, but a river of black scales with orange gaps continues to course out of sight beyond the fold of the hills. Ash lingers in the sky. We now have an unobstructed view of Hilo Bay. I turn and see the U.S.S. *Sawfish*, minutes away from the docks. Is it still advancing?

"Stop," I tell Keali`i. "Everyone out. We need to watch, make sure he's leaving."

"Leave the car running," Buzz says. "I'm worried the starter won't work again with the mother so close."

We pour out of the truck, stand in a line on the steep road, watching the bay. Both Star Flowers hover straight above, clearly visible and distinct against the blue sky and the creeping bronze layer of haze.

I've told you: I'm not retreating. Release the aliens.

The battleship continues toward the docks at its slow pace.

In the pit of my stomach, I feel it: the mother's new pearl, growing larger, layer by layer, until she must eventually eject it. It's already too big to fire at the ship. The bay would empty of water. Hilo would *disappear*. I cannot use it as a weapon. It's over.

I shake my head in disbelief. I'd scream if I could.

"*I wish we could have it both ways,*" Tūtū said only

302

yesterday on our way up to Mauna Kea. But I can't have it both ways: I'll never get my *tūtū* back. I'll never hear him sing again. His smile: gone. Nothing but a memory around my neck. I clasp my locket, press my fist to my heart.

He'll hunt us down. We'll have to abandon the lives we've built to stay safe. Unless I release them. But we *need* them still.

Them.

Both ways.

My jaw drops.

"Buzz," I croak. "What did you just say about leaving the truck running?"

He offers me a grim smile. "Don't worry. Do what you need to. It's just that I'm worried that bringing the Orchid so close is packing a super wallop of interference—"

"No," I interrupt. "Why did you only mention the mother?"

"The little one isn't behind the blackout. Its aura is too small to envelop the whole . . ." He trails off.

"But it *can* absorb radiation," I say. "Right? It builds pearls, too. We know that. And I *know* the baby feeds on leaks. More like—like a hummingbird, not a mop."

Dad turns and considers what I'm saying carefully. We had thought of this months ago. But it was only a theory then. The baby wasn't mine back then. Dad and Buzz share intense looks of dawning hope. Their eyes drift back to me. They nod uncertainly.

"I'm going to do it," I say.

"Yes," Buzz says. "You have enough control of the baby?"

I nod. I do. It was only this morning that I lassoed her—*this morning!*—and so much has happened since then. We haven't had time to explore the full significance of what it means. This solution flashed in my mind when I was washing the electrode glue out of my hair. It danced there. It's why I was so happy. But then the sheriff arrived and . . .

Focus. Here. Now.

I control the little one just as well as I've ever controlled the mother.

"Do it," Dad says.

"No," I almost say. But I stay quiet. I'm surprised for only a second by my reaction, then I remember: epilepsy.

Can the baby keep away the storms as well as the mother has?

I don't want my fits to return to the way they were before all of this started. I don't have meds anymore. There are no ambulances to rush me to safety if I fall badly, or if I choke, or if I seize too fiercely—or if I don't wake up.

How will I cope in this broken world without the Orchid?

I'll miss her. I still want to learn more about her, where she came from, where she goes to. I can train her to talk if I just have more time. Can I drift in orbit with the baby the way I've been able to inhabit the mother's consciousness? What if the baby can't absorb radiation as thoroughly? Isn't it too cruel to try to separate them? Can the baby even survive without the mother? Should I even allow the power to come back on? Do we deserve another chance?

I can think of a hundred reasons to keep the mother here. Just a little longer. Towers has no right to force this moment. We're not ready. We need more time.

"No, Leilani. Stop." I hear Tūtū's voice as if he's beside me. "Not reasons. *Excuses.* What you're saying is, *you're* not ready. *You* need more time. But the moment is here."

He's right.

I can't hold on.

Grandpa's recent advice to me echoes:

"This is the path forward. You've been asked to do so much, but this burden is all of ours. It's time to let it go, Mo`opuna! Find your path.

"The right or wrong of it will work itself out."

I nod, feeling the blood drain from my face. I take a deep breath, turn back to my view of the battleship.

Commander Towers, I'll do it. I'll release the mother Orchid into space. She'll go. Right now. But you have to turn around, or there's no deal.

The silence in my head is deafening. I wait.

No. That's not good enough. Both of them—

No. Listen. The baby doesn't disrupt electronics. When the mother goes, the problems you want to solve go with her. You'll get your power back, your victory. I get to keep lapping up radiation spills. But only until that's done. Then I'll release the baby, too. She can find her mother on their journey home. I want her to find her mother. I won't wait a second longer than I need to.

305

Am I convincing him of that, or myself?

Silence. It's not only in my head, though: the entire world has gone mute. The group surrounding me holds its collective breath. No wind. The trees are still. The birds are hiding from the afternoon warmth. The fountain of lava behind us is a world away, as silent as a comet racing around the sun. Minutes pass.

The battleship pauses.

White water churns behind the ship's stern. It lurches into motion, backing away from the docks.

My companions cheer. I hold my hands to my mouth, take a deep breath.

They pat me on the back. My cheeks are warm. But I'm two places at once.

I better see some movement.

Yes. She'll go.

Now.

She'll go. I promise.

How do I know it'll stay gone?

How do I know you will stay gone?

Fair enough. You still have the small creature, right? We'll keep an eye on each other?

Guess so. Meanwhile, go back to your generals and presidents. Do your victory lap. Then come back with food and gas and medicine and help us.

We'll see. Aren't you forgetting something?

Don't worry, I'm sending her away. Get out of here. You got what you want.

So long, then, Rose, or whatever your name is. A rose by any other name . . .

. . . is just as sweet, I finish, broadcasting warmth to him.

I was going to say thorny.

He won his battle, didn't he? How come I sense disappointment?

The U.S.S. *Sawfish* is backing toward the mouth of the bay between the coast and the breakwater. A door pounds shut in my mind. Commander Dwight Towers has stormed away.

But I wonder with dread: is my storm just beginning?

CHAPTER 24

I gaze up at the Star Flowers and feel a lump in my throat. Tears sting my eyes, a vast lake of grief and worry heaving forward.

Goodbye, Flower of Heaven, I say.

We do the long fastness now. The other pools are good. It is good to leave the shores and go to the dark. I crave the depths. The comfort of no tides.

No. We do not go. You go. The one that you gave will stay awhile. She will grow strong on the sweetness for a while longer. It is a good thing. She will follow you soon.

I want to go, too, the baby cries. **Do not leave me.**

The cry of the baby stabs at me, but I croon, *No, little one, you must stay.*

We are many there, the mother remarks. *You will see others during the fastness. You will find me on the way. We will be long in the ocean between the pools of fires. There are many pools of fires.*

I feel immense relief. *Yes. The one you gave will find you on the way. It is a good thing.*

And then in a flash I see it: another planet. Like ours but different.

Slowly I release all of my breath.

I've accessed a memory. She wants the baby to see it, but I see it, too: Blue waters, brown and green continents. Swirling clouds. Large polar ice caps. But in no combination of shapes I have ever seen before. Mountain ranges like wrinkles, rivers like ropy veins, deltas like burst arteries.

Two moons.

And visible along the horizons of the perfect sphere: countless racing dots of reflected sunlight.

Satellites.

Another world. Out there beyond the stars.

I remember to breathe.

The mother speaks to the baby: *It is good to go. But a pain of leaving, too. But there is a return. When it is your time to give, you will return to these shores.*

Go with you! the baby insists.

I will keep you for only a while, I explain. So difficult. *I love you. I will keep you safe. You are not alone. I am here with you.*

I will stay. I want to go. It is a good thing to stay awhile.

Good, yes, I say, though it makes me feel wretched to manipulate her. It must be done. Just for a while longer. *It is good. We stay, and it is good.*

My connection to the mother already feels faint. She has turned away. I don't think I could pull her back with all the radio telescopes in the world. Has she forgotten me already, like a sea turtle dismissing a passing scuba diver? I hope not. I feel a sharp pang of loss and regret, but I can't pull her back. I hope I'll always be a part of her. I hope a part of my consciousness will linger with her when she reaches those fantastic far shores, that a part of me will arrive there with her, however many thousands of years hence, and maybe even speak on her behalf . . . to another girl on the ground . . . not so different from myself.

But I'll never know. I'm here. Always will be. Lost. Rocked by lightning and thunder and storms to come. Adrift on a sea of my own.

Good-bye, I say again, and not only to the *honu* slipping away into the shadowy heavens.

Good-bye, Tūtū.

As the world fades from emerald-green to nicotine-yellow, I fall slowly to the road and finally, truly sob.

CHAPTER 25

Two weeks have passed. My seizures haven't gotten any worse.

I linger in my room this morning, surrounded by my things—my comfortable bed, my gymnastics trophies, my surfing and volleyball posters. It could be any Sunday morning since I moved to Hawai`i. I read my Hawaiiana book—the one Mom gave me—listen to the birds, try on three outfits. My camisoles and my shorts are all too large, but they feel right. Something about how Mom washes and dries them; only she can make my clothes feel that soft and smell so good even though she must beat them against worn lava rock down at the river to get them clean.

In the bathroom I flip on the lights. *Lights!* Some of our solar panels work again, and the extra wattage we're getting from our generator fed by the waterfall seals the deal. Much of the wiring in the house is shot, but we're replacing it systematically, as we can. Copper is the new gold—we're now trading gas and propane away for wire! What will it be next?

The bathroom was a priority. A smart decision. I put on a hint of eyeliner and study myself in the mirror. Kai's dreamcatcher failed to net all of my drowning thoughts last night—but there have been no storms. My eyes are still slightly puffy and red. The eyeliner helps, but I won't be fooling anyone. That's okay, I guess.

Breakfast with Kai feels like any morning from the past. We banter and bicker just like the old days. As always, he makes me laugh more than I make him laugh. Mom sizzles up whole-grain pancakes topped with fresh starfruit, and we wash our food down with pulpy, ice-cold guanabana juice—made in the refurbished blender. Another priority.

"What have you been up to?" I ask Kai. "You've been awfully quiet around here."

He shrugs, looks down. "Just finished the Little House on the Prairie books."

"Mine?" It's the first time I've heard of a boy reading them, but I won't say so.

"They were on your shelf, yeah. Makes it feel like current events."

I laugh. "Yeah, I can see that."

"Not for long!" he pipes up. "Is Buzz really coming down today with a working Blu-ray player and TV?"

I cast Mom a look. This was supposed to be a surprise.

"He needed the boost," she says.

Anything to help Kai out of his post-funeral funk is welcome. "Yeah," I explain, "he flashed us word yesterday." Buzz is using the lens of one of the three-meter scopes up at the observatories to flicker sun-fed Morse code messages to me. He's learning the code with the help of an ex-marine, hired to keep trespassers away from the scopes. The guy is a friend of Keali`i's. Manō.

"I want to watch *The Avengers*!"

I give my brother a wink. "Bring the pile of movies down from Mom and Dad's room. Sounds like a good one to start with."

"You bet!"

"Hey," I say, "while you're up there, wanna grab one of my volleyball posters? Hang it up in your room?"

He blushes, slowly nods. "Yeah, okay."

"Go to it."

He runs up the stairs.

Mom busses my scraped-clean plate. "You want a haircut today?"

"I'm overdue, aren't I?"

"You're chewing on it."

"Oh, yeah. Sorry." I quickly pull my hand away from my neck. She's right: I've been twirling the end of my hair with my pointer finger, nipping at it with the corner of my lips every several rotations.

Mom offers me a patient smile. "Are you getting enough sleep, honey?"

"Yeah. Why?"

"You look . . ." She doesn't finish. Her expression, exhausted and heartbroken, says everything.

"You, too," I answer, meeting her soft eyes for just a moment.

It's Sunday. Day of Rest. Uncle Hank and Auntie Nora stayed in town overnight and will be with their congregation in Hilo. A few blocks around downtown already have power, and the Millers' church is leading an effort to get one hundred refrigerators up and running per week. Other churches and community groups have similar goals. Hilo's on the mend, but it's far from stable. Resources of every kind are still scarce. The promise of recovery—slow recovery—has made the overall levels of violence less frequent but more intense. The Tribes have chilled out a bit, but other groups—especially families in town—seem to be more anxious and impatient than ever to make sure their children are next in line to get what they need.

Paul and Sara and baby Chloe have taken the day off, too. But not Dad. He asked me to join him in the upper plots to pull weeds and clean the irrigation channels. It's easier to stay busy than it is to stop and think.

Weeds, then muck, then movies. That's all. I give my locket a squeeze. He's always right here. Close to my heart. Every time I see a stray cat in the bushes, I smile. I just need to learn to breathe again before I dare say his name aloud.

Tūtū.

Speaking of strays, Tami has permanently moved in with us. Keali`i and Tami were gone overnight, out pig hunting.

They should be back by this afternoon with or without a catch. I'm sure they'll nab one. We have new dogs now, after all. Well trained, too! The two pig dogs from the back of the Hanaman truck are actually pretty sweet. I've named them Lilo and Stitch. They've made great additions to our family, and Mindy loves them.

Tami and Keali`i wanted me to go hunting with them. But I still can't look at a gun without my stomach turning. I don't think I'll ever get over what I did. Besides, Grandpa was supposed to teach me how to hunt. I kept putting it off. Now he can never do it.

Mom has promised to take me hunting, teach me everything she learned from . . . him. Just the two of us. Amazon women. I can't wait. But not yet.

Dad and I rake out the irrigation ditches. Between the routine silences, Dad ventures into several topics. One is: "You and Aukina."

I scoff. "That's your opening? That's how you're going to speak to your daughter about boys?"

He gives me that confident smirk that Kai perfected long ago.

I wipe sweat from my forehead and bend back down to my task. "I like him."

"You don't really like him," Dad suggests in a perfect Obi Wan Kenobi monotone, waving his hand magically in the air. "Do you? Sure you're not just being . . . ?" He trails off.

I stand, muddy hands pressed into my hips. "What am I *being*, Dad? Hormonal?"

Dad laughs. He actually *laughs*. "Well, yeah. There's that. But I was getting more at the Stockholm syndrome."

I eye him suspiciously. "What's that?"

"You *did* meet him in an internment camp."

"So?"

He hesitates. "It's when . . . prisoners start to sympathize with their captors."

I gasp, raise a fist. "Like beef?" A pidgin phrase, meaning "Wanna fight?"

He laughs quietly, all of this a joke to him—which is good. I know he likes Aukina. This banter is his way of showing me that he approves. I jump across the ditch and slap him on the shoulder, leave a black mud stain on his T-shirt.

On our lazy walk home, late in the afternoon, a truck comes toward us from *mauka*. Keali`i and Tami. Lilo and Stitch and Mindy are in the cages, and a large sow is draped across the bed. We chat through the driver's window. "Dogs cornered it. Tami brought it down," Keali`i reports.

"Good for you, Tami!" Dad says. "Great work."

My stomach rumbles loudly, the highest compliment I could offer.

"Should we get the *imu* going?" Keali`i asks. "Pull an all-nighter? Eat like kings around two a.m.?"

"Yeah, sounds good. I know just how to pass the time. Buzz has been busy with his soldering iron ever since the electron started behaving again. He's coming over today with a working TV."

"Seriously?" Keali`i asks. "Super! I'll get to work on the coals right away. What're we going to watch?"

"*On the Beach,*" Dad declares.

"NO!" all three of us shout. Everyone laughs.

"If we don't put on *Avengers,*" I warn, "Kai may turn into the Hulk and smash us."

"We'll start with that," Dad agrees. "Then move on to my favorites. *Casablanca, Wrath of Kahn,* and *The Muppet Movie.*"

"Oh, Lord," Tami says. "The lights are finally coming back and I'm surrounded by total geeks."

"Hey," Dad says, "you worry about the food. I'll worry about your education."

"Mind if I let the troop know about the luau?" Keali`i asks Dad.

"Guess who's coming to dinner?" Dad says. He sighs, says that'd be fine, thanks Keali`i for asking first. My eyes widen. The Manō might join us for dinner? This new, open understanding between the Tribe and our neighborhood group is going to take some getting used to.

Keali`i and Tami drive away. Dad and I walk the rest of the way home in silence, coqui frogs tuning their instruments in preparation for their nightly concert in the park.

Buzz's skeletal van is parked in front of the garage. I spy several new alterations spilling out of the hood. He's been by three times in the past two weeks, always running between here and the pearl site. He went back up there with Mom and Dad the first time, to recover Tūtū. The other

Hanamen who had been up there were long gone. Disbanded, hopefully. Buzz has been back twice since, racking his brain trying to find a way to extract or harness the pearl before it buries itself. He says there's time—that it's not burrowing as quickly as he had feared, and that the tunnel is quite stable. He'll figure out how to pull it out, or use its power right where it lies; I know he will. The second pearl is a lost cause, of course, forever swallowed by the eruption.

I feed the horse before heading inside. When I finally do walk in the front door, I stumble back in surprise.

Marcus and Rachel are on the sofa, chatting with Mom.

They stand up. We trade hugs, pull apart. I shake my head. "What's this?"

"We went to Moloka`i. Met that Father Akoni fellow," Rachel says. "Figured out what you've been up to. We couldn't set off for Australia knowing what we had learned. We had to come back."

"You got way under our skin, Leilani." Marcus polishes his glasses with the corner of his quick-dry shirt. "The Rorschach flaring the way it did the night we brought you home, the insistence that Phoenix was okay, that we shouldn't worry—it all haunted us. Later I remembered Tami's drunken rant about you and the Rorschach."

"Wait. You saw Father Akoni?" I ask.

I hear a rolling chuckle emanate from the kitchen, and Father Akoni rounds the corner, flanked by Dad and Buzz. His ruddy grin grows warmer as he strides over to me. He's lost a lot of weight, but he's the same jovial, off-season Hawaiian Santa Claus who helped us on Moloka`i.

I'm shaky as we embrace. "How'd you get here?" I finally manage.

Marcus answers: "We stopped on Moloka`i, as you suggested, Lei. Met this fine man of the cloth. Got to talking about you. Compared notes. We caught glimpses of what you were doing with the Rorschach. The whole island chain is talking about you. In general terms. No one has details about the person behind it. We schemed to get back over here, try to help if we could. Looks like we missed the party, though."

"*How'd* you get here, though?" I ask. "Where's your boat?"

"One of Akoni's men is babysitting *Cibola* off the coast," Rachel explains. "A generous gesture. We'll only be staying the night, I'm afraid."

"That's all?"

"Lots of work to do. On Moloka`i, here, everywhere," Akoni reminds us. "Power's slowly coming back on, but we're still on our own for a while. Everyone has their own problems to solve. These islands are still forgotten. Satellite communication is years away, to say the least. And we're on a basaltic rock! Can't mine our own ores, fuels. We have what we have, and we'll have to make do. We can't assume any help for a long stretch yet."

"Lucky for us the cargo ships are lining up around the block!" Dad teases.

I run my fingers through my hair. "I've been thinking about that. Commander *Towers* is rounding South America, but I'm still not sure how much I trust him. If he comes back, it'd better be with a fleet. Anyway, I'll keep up the Morse code."

Father Akoni places a hand on my shoulder. "You went to the mouth of the cave, didn't you? You listened. *Nānā i ke kumu.* You looked to the source. Excellent, Leilani, Flower of Heaven. Excellent."

I turn to him. "Thank you, Uncle, for that advice. Thank you for helping us. For coming here."

"I had to check on you. The only thing stopping me before was that I didn't know where to find you. These lovely pilgrims changed all that."

I blink the gathering tears away. They come from somewhere deep.

Father Akoni senses my struggle, gives my shoulder a tender squeeze. "Time will heal, but slowly. We're a body, and every bone beneath our skin has been shattered. We have a long convalescence ahead. We will walk again, though. Each of us. Each of our communities. Each island."

"I wish you could stay longer."

"So do I. But we'll be in much better touch now. I'll make a habit of visiting, okay? At least we have tonight!"

As I nod, Kai bursts in the front door with Tami and Keali`i. "*Imu's* going. We'll check on the coals in twenty minutes. Don't we have a movie to start?"

We all laugh as Kai races forward and skids to the TV on his knees. He turns to Buzz. "Will it work?"

Buzz shrugs, but his twinkle shines in his eyes. He gestures at the TV with his wrist still in a sling. "All new circuitry. Why don't you give it a shot?"

An old TV is set up against the wall, crowned with a black Blu-ray player. Wires run from the appliances over to the same cobalt box that housed the shard of pearl once used to power the 8mm projector. A small green light blinks from the corner of the disc player.

We all crowd around Kai and the TV. Tami and Keali`i both look at me, smile, and link arms with me. Kai rummages through the pile of discs, finds *The Avengers*, and hovers his finger over the Open button.

He pushes the button.

The disc tray slides open.

We cheer.

The anticipation and celebrations continue with each step of the process. TV turns on! Play button works! Movie home screen appears! Movie starts! But I grow quieter with each victory. My throat feels warm. I push it all down, but each time the stew of feelings rises anew, it becomes harder to block.

The music and the dialogue and the sounds, somewhat tinny through the old TV's internal speakers, are exhilarating. It's surreal and amazing, and we're spellbound. Suddenly we're five minutes into the film, staring blankly forward, occasionally sharing self-satisfied glances. But I find myself staring instead at the 8mm projector forgotten in the corner. We used it *once*. Now it's junk again. Just like that.

Father Akoni and Marcus and Rachel are here. They're

here with us! For one night! There's so much news to share, stories to swap. Why aren't we talking to each other? Why are we all staring in the same direction, each of us alone in this small room?

I remember that this movie is about a troop of superheroes who have gathered to push back an invading alien force. But the biggest threat may be humanity's arrogance. We've acquired weapons and technology we're not ready to use.

But don't worry, the freaks of nature with special powers will save the day!

And the gunfire. It's in every other frame. Everybody is shooting each other. Extras are blown away left and right. Limbs everywhere. Trucks and Jeeps flipping and helicopters crashing. Flames and explosions and more guns!

The eruption of fire in my belly releases. I shriek.

Mom rushes forward to the TV, turns it off. The trance ends. "Lei!" She comes to my side. "Honey?"

I start, realizing that tears are streaming down my face. I'm holding my head in my hands. I'm trembling. I shake my head. "Uncle," I croak. "Can I do confession with you?" I'm not even sure what confession is, but it's suddenly a fierce need.

Father Akoni says, "Of course, Lei. What's wrong? When would you like to—?"

"I killed someone," I say, quaking. "I"—I fall against his shoulder, bury my head—"I don't even think I was wrong." When I raise my eyes to glance around, Mom, Dad, and

Buzz are wiping back tears. Marcus and Rachel sit as still as statues on the couch.

Akoni turns to my parents. "We'll go outside, talk on the steps?" They nod.

Father Akoni turns back to me. "Let's talk story, eh?"

My throat swells shut.

We talk on the lanai for more than two hours, about the sheriff, the Star Flowers—the betrayal I perpetrated by separating the mother and the baby—Grandpa, Aukina, the fear that my epilepsy will return, my worry that I've made a mistake by giving the world back its power, everything. I tell him that Grandpa died with secrets locked away inside of him. Ghosts he never got out. I tell him that it's eating me up that I don't know those things about him, but maybe that's fine, because the Grandpa I've always known and loved my whole life is Grandpa enough. Father Akoni listens.

"None of us are open books when we die," he tells me. "We all take secrets with us into the next life." He has no answers. He understands my fear about the epilepsy—and shares it; he suffered from it, too—but offers no solution. He absolves my sins, tells me I've already done a world of penance.

The movie ends. Another one starts. A bunch of Manō arrive at the house and pile into the living room. I smell popcorn. I keep talking. I shed ten giant weight belts from my shoulders during our conversation, but I realize toward the end that I haven't been talking to the priest. I've been talking to Tūtū. Akoni's just a stand-in. I weep, then, and in the silence filled only with frog song and muffled movie music, my friend patiently waits, and I begin to grapple with that vast reach, greater than the chasm between stars, that now separates me from my lost loved ones, who, all at once, feel so incredibly close and yet who remain so infinitely far away.

Father Akoni and I eventually come back inside. Keali'i and Tami send our Manō visitors off into the backyard to check on the *imu*. Dad turns off the TV, and those of us in the room can no longer see. Mom uses a flashlight to gather up some of Tūtū's *kukui* nuts, and she lights them so that they each dance with flame. Mom and Dad and Kai and Buzz and Marcus and Rachel and Father Akoni and Keali'i and Tami—we all gather around the light, and for a brief moment the old world with its old ways comes rushing back. We hold each other in the silence, in the darkness pushed back by the gentle light, and we are *lōkahi*.

One with all creation.

CHAPTER 26

Aukina and I reach the coast and turn right, then we follow the 130 to its very end. We're in his brand-new, antique king cab truck, a thank-you gift from my family to his, presented with a note signed by both my parents:

Dear `Ohana,

Thank you so much for loaning your son to us so often in the past six weeks. He has been a *world* of help. You have no idea. We would like to offer you this working truck and a full tank of gas as a token of our gratitude. We are still in your debt and would be very happy to assist your efforts on your homestead at any time.

It's the dead of night. A dim quarter moon lights our way. The little Orchid is in low orbit over the foothills of the Sierra Nevadas in Northern California tonight, like a kitten over a bowl of milk, sipping up the *sweetness* left over from a nuclear generating station near a small town, Ione, on my crinkly map.

She's sparing the lives of a million people, and even as she does I see a lone grid of streets in a Sacramento neighborhood interrupting the dark Earth with a hopeful, soft yellow-orange glow. I clutch my silver pendant and dare a smile in the dark.

The road that Aukina and I travel used to connect to the Chain of Craters road in Volcanoes National Park, eleven miles away. But it has been covered over with lava for decades. Our way forward on the pavement suddenly ceases at a lava wall, formed years ago by an old flow. There's a parking lot here. There was always something rather amusing about this dead end, where Pele had swept aside the engineering of us puny mortals, taking back the coast.

The lot is empty tonight. Aukina and I have the end of the world to ourselves.

"There used to be whole towns near here," I say. "Kalapana, Kaimū, and Kaimū Bay. Destroyed by a vent that opened in the eighties. It's all buried under fifty feet of lava now. All this coastline is new since then. Even when it came that fast, people still had plenny time to get out."

"I've seen pictures of those towns being slowly covered over. When Pahoa got hit, too. I've read about all this my whole life. Seen the flows on TV."

"Come on." I take Aukina's hand, pull him out onto the edge of the endless lava field. The horizon glows a faint orange. A great plume of steam is cast in orange light where fresh lava meets the sea. We turn our gazes upslope. Amid the great blackness of the volcanic wasteland, high above the *pali* cliffs of cooled lava that run all along the southern coast, we can see a geyser of orange-black fire, a silent fountain gushing with the Earth's blood.

Nearer to us we catch a glimpse of the molten-rock river that pours down the *pali* cliff onto our low coastal shelf. Just a soundless pattern of firelights against a black Earth and a starry sky. Serene? Humble? Harmless?

Pele is not as innocent as she seems.

"Wow," Aukina says.

"Welcome to Big Island. Ready to march out there?"

"Sure!"

I can't hold back a laugh. "That's what they all say." The Pu`u `Ō`ō vent often erupts and spills lava down these slopes, luring tourists into a devious hike that turns out to be brutal enough to kill people from heatstroke, dehydration, and exposure.

"What? I'm not nervous. I'm game."

"No, it's not that. It's farther than it looks."

"It's right there! No sweat!"

"Well, let's go, then."

We begin our slog. Aukina is surprised to see a handful of houses built on top of the hardened lava near the coastal cliff. "How'd these houses survive?"

"They didn't," I explain. "Some owners rebuilt them, right where they used to be. Guess they loved their little piece of heaven that much—even after hell froze it over!"

There's no trail, no predetermined way forward. This terrain is never easy. In daylight the heat of the sun attacks you from all directions, from the sky and reflected back up at you from the blacktop under your feet. There are no trees, no bushes, no shade. At night it's impossible to determine the path of least resistance. The black folds of ropy rock snake and twist in every direction, mixing with the black of night. Every step is a potential ankle breaker. And each bulge and dip builds into large hillocks and troughs; the ground undulates and eddies like erratic ocean waves frozen to stone by Medusa's gaze. Even with the flashlight our visibility is twenty feet at best. Our feet sometimes punch through the thin crust to an older flow below. We slice up our shins and calves and scrape our palms as we catch our falls or scramble up.

An hour goes by. The feeble moon is about to set beyond the cliffs, and stars are crisp enough to reach up and touch. The geyser of liquid fire pouring out of Puʻu ʻŌʻō adorns the distant slope with all the menace of an electric stove coil. That fountain is probably three stories high, though.

We rise to a bulbous perch and share a drink of water. The flow toward which we crawl looks the same as it did from the end of the road—a dimly glowing horizon. Aukina despairs. "We're not any closer!"

"Told you."

"What is this? Six weeks of basic training was less brutal than this."

I laugh. "We're making progress. Keep it up, soldier!"

He salutes me.

The moon is gone now, and we're on the dark side of Mars. Our pace slows. Starlight illuminates the shiny surfaces of the old flows. We try to spare Aukina's light. We'll need it once we draw near the active flow, where the ground will be most deceptive. Even the freshest lava develops a cool black shell the instant it hits air. It's easy to walk out on top of it several yards before realizing your boots are smoldering. Our flashlights have proven oddly dependable lately, but batteries are still precious.

We can hear the lava, the slow crackling of cooling rock as it oozes outward from the river's banks. It sounds like loose bits of granite sliding and tumbling down a steep slope—slowly. Like a bulldozer smoothing over a dirt road embedded with boulders. The orange horizon has grown near, and I can even make out the first details of some of the glowing ends of the lava's creeping, searching fingers.

"Are we there yet?" Aukina asks cautiously.

"'Patience, young Padawan.'"

"Don't start quoting movies on me. Seriously, how long?"

I smile. "'When will then be now?'"

"'Soon,'" he answers.

We laugh together. I'm not surprised he knows that quote from *Spaceballs*—one of Dad's favorite comedies. "I tried quoting a line from that movie to Tami once," I say. "I told her she had 'gone to plaid.' She didn't get it."

"You kidding? I use that line all the time."

"Of course you do!" I say. I want to jump in his arms, surprise him, make him catch me. I want to . . . kiss him.

He's marching forward, though.

We scramble over the rough landscape for another ten minutes, passing through the blowback of the steam coming off the ocean where the lava's entering the water. We're breathing sulfurous fumes, and my throat's not happy. The sound of crawling rock has grown loud. Orange tentacles ooze with clear detail before us. It's *hot*. "We're here," I say.

Aukina sounds disappointed. "What about the lava river?" I can only determine his vaguest outline. But he feels so close.

I take a deep breath. "Too dangerous. Maybe we can scout out some good views, but we're asking for trouble if we try to get any closer. Too easy to confuse this fresh stuff with old stuff."

"I need a break anyway." I hear him slip his backpack off, unzip it, fish around for his water bottle.

We find a smooth, safe patch of high ground and sit cross-legged to watch the slow advancement of lava's edge, a black blob highlighted by contours of orange neon. I sidle closer.

Thank God it's so dark. My mouth is doing that stupid twitch-smile again. I bury my head in my knees, laugh nervously.

"I want to touch it," he finally says.

"Huh?" I whip my head up.

"I wish I could play with the lava. Looks so interesting."

"The lava! Oh. It's different than it looks, though. Hard as granite, even where it's oozing. Tap it with your bottle. *Not* your finger."

He rises. He hops down to where the ropy blob is inching forward, shields his face from the heat with his arm, and taps his bottle against the glowing edge. Sounds like he's knocking metal against stone.

"I thought it would be gooey! Stick to the bottle or something."

"Weird, eh?"

"Yeah." He explores the edges for a bit, shines his flashlight on and off of the shadowy surfaces. I'm content to watch, reliving my excitement and wonder as my parents and I made all the same discoveries on our first trip here during an older active flow.

He returns and sits beside me. "Unreal."

"Yeah."

"That's liquid Earth. The center of the world. Rising up, shaping the island as we watch."

"Pele's amazing," I say. "Isn't she?"

"She's something else." He studies me.

We watch the center of the world slowly feel its way, consuming everything in its path.

"You believe in her?" Aukina asks me. "Pele?"

"Yes," I answer. "I believe in the gods, the *akua*, the `aumākua. Especially Pele. They talk to me. They've been quiet lately. Or maybe not. Tūtū would probably say that I haven't been listening."

"I know what you mean. It's hard, doing this. Starting over. Everything: your home, your family, yourself. You feel like you have the weight of the whole world on your shoulders, and there's no break. It never stops."

I burst into tears, sob. It pours out.

Aukina holds me, and I fall into his embrace. I steal a glimpse up at him, my vision swimming, and I see him wiping silent tears away from his eyes.

"Mo'bettah?" he asks after I've grown still.

I nod, clear my eyes, scoot away a few inches. "Yeah. Sorry."

"No. It's good."

"I didn't know that was coming."

"We all have it coming, Lei. Gotta get it out. It'll eat you up."

I lean forward, hover, and then kiss him. I pull away, but he draws me back with steady hands on my shoulders. His fingers search my upper arms, my collarbone, find my neck and my cheeks. His touch. His lips. I kiss him, running my hands over his muscular back. I fall into his embrace and melt, sparks trailing along my lips and my face and my neck. The heat feeds a new fire within me that makes every detail of the night more alive.

Aukina pauses, his breathing heavy, his hands tight. He touches his forehead to mine. Our noses rest against each other. "I . . . You mean so much to me, Lei."

"Yeah. I . . . You too," I whisper.

We kiss gently. Aukina backs off. I'm glad he does. I'm not ready for more. For what could happen. I know better. The world may be on the mend, creeping forward, rebuilding layer by layer, but it's still no place for a new generation. And I'm too young.

Someday. Maybe soon. But not now.

Aukina holds me, and we grow still. We watch the lava creep, the slow turning of the stars, and I trace the intricacies of Aukina's tattoos with my fingers. The faint glow of orange provides just enough light to—

"Aukina!" I gasp.

"What? What is it?"

"We need to move!" I half laugh, half groan.

He glances around with a jolt. "Oh, God. Come on."

We stand. During our embrace the lava surrounded our high ground. It's no wonder we were easily fooled. The flow appears the same as the ropy rock beneath us. Black and solid-looking. But we're only seeing the cool outer shell.

We're on an island. I can see the edges of the flow stretching in a full circle around us. I squeeze Aukina's hand with apprehension. I point with my other arm to a narrow break. "We have to cross it. There."

"Is that safe?"

"I don't know." It *looks* just like the rock we're on. But our feet could punch through. "We have no choice."

"Okay," he says, focused. "Together."

"Yeah." We squeeze each other's hands and race over the black surface of oozing lava. The crust holds our weight. With five feet to go, we leap for the shadowy patch of solid ground. We touch down and trot several feet away before slowing.

"Oh, man," Aukina pants, "my boots! They melted!" He bounces on one leg, inspecting his raised boot.

I do the same. The rubber tread sticks to my finger like grease. "Mine too." I laugh. I wipe my finger on my jeans. "God. That was *sooo* stupid."

"We just walked over hot coals together," Aukina marvels. "You realize that?"

"Team-building exercise."

"'I'm a leaf on the wind,'" says Aukina. "'Watch how I soar.'"

"You're not allowed to quote *Serenity* around me."

Aukina slaps his thigh. "You know that one? You know *Firefly?*"

"Of course. I'm pure nerd. My dad made certain of it."

Aukina says, "You are by far the coolest chick I've ever met, you know that?"

A flush rises to my neck. I can't find my voice.

"Well," Aukina says, looking around, "we gonna stand here until we have to do that again, or what? I've got a day of tree cutting and pickax work ahead of me."

"Wait, you're busy tomorrow?"

Aukina casts me a very dim smile. "Houses and irrigation ditches don't build themselves."

"Let's go. This might be even harder on the way back, with melted boots."

We start away, and the temperature drops. It's actually cold out. I forgot this. I shiver, but not because of the air. What we just did was *nuts*. Never should have happened. And hiking boots don't grow on trees.

We press onward with no way to retrace our steps. Our path back will be distinct from the one we took out here. I can tell this will be brutal.

I *could* reach out to my little Orchid, pull her west and into a higher orbit. She would dazzle against the horizon, turn the waters green and purple, light our way just enough. But I won't. She's here for all of us, not just me. And she's here against her true nature and desire, lonely, lost. I will keep her for only a few more months, and then she can return to her mother. And if my epilepsy returns then . . . I guess that'll be my price. I *hope* I can pay it. Meanwhile, I try to comfort her, make sure she feels I'm there.

We are Leilani.

We are Leilani.

Be well, little one. I'm with you.

Dawn is coming. It will get brighter as we go.

We reach the truck just as the first birds wake. We finish the last of our water. The truck fires up without even a stutter, the jungle before us suddenly ablaze in a wide circle of unwavering light. Aukina turns on the radio. We hear only static—but it feels so optimistic to watch him do it.

My God, I marvel, *one of these days he'll do that and we'll actually hear music.*

I smile, clutch my pendant.

"Ready to go home?" Aukina asks.

"I am home."

"K'den. Ready to return to your *house?*"

"Yes." I scoot close and wrap my arms around him. He holds me with one arm and drives down the twilit jungle road with the other.

The truck skids to a halt. "Look!" Aukina points ahead. He cuts the engine.

The forested tunnel we're in is dim. But then I detect movement near the shoulder. A crouched form, waiting. We're still as statues. It hesitates, then emerges from the trees.

I hold my breath. The shadowy figure slinks to the middle of the road, stops in the glow of our headlights, turns, and studies us.

My hand goes to my chest, to the picture of my beloved `aumākua, Grandma in her white wedding dress and Grandpa in his immaculate white navy uniform.

Find *pono*, and you'll find *ola*. We are each one. *Lōkahi*. Individual. Matchless. But we are also *one*. Indivisible.

Connected with all of creation.

Before us, the white tiger shifts on its paws. It breaks its gaze, glancing far beyond the trees, and then saunters into the jungle like a whisper.

The world is so complex, so convoluted, so indecipherable.

But there's always a thread. A kite string. Everything is connected. I'm suddenly certain: We are never alone. And no matter what, we'll get through this. We'll figure it out together.

I squeeze Aukina's hand, blink back tears, and finally breathe.

ACKNOWLEDGMENTS

Peek behind the curtain at any author, of every novel worth publishing, and you'll discover a dedicated team. This steadfast reality holds true for *The Girl at the Center of the World*. I can't thank my editor and publisher, Wendy Lamb, enough for her crucial and expert guidance, her patience, and her care. This story excels precisely where you helped it along, Wendy. I'm grateful to Dana Carey for all of her additional support, and to other members of the Penguin Random House family involved in the development of this book. Alison Impey, your cover takes my breath away every time I see it. Jillian Vandall, I'm so fortunate to have you as my publicist. Trish Parcell, thank you for your careful design and for the maps. Candy Gianetti, Colleen Fellingham, and Alison Kolani, thank you for the meticulous copy edits and for your attention to every other detail within these covers that magically turns novels into books. Tracy Heydweiller, thank you for your production expertise and care. My gratitude extends to Julie Just, Elena Giovinazzo, Holly McGhee, and the entire team at Pippin Properties.

I'm grateful to Dr. Holoua Stender, David Haas, and Joe Camacho for permission to use their beautiful song lyrics. I'm indebted to Dr. Laura Hufford for responding to all my midnight texts about antibiotics. I hope you've stockpiled enough for your family, Laura! Thank you once again, Alex Bennett, Liz Chamberlain, and Jenn Ridgeway for faithfully reading all those drafts and for giving me such perfect feedback and essential advice. Authors Joshua David Bellin, Jennifer J. Stewart, and Jaye Robin Brown, thank you so much for taking an early look and telling me what I needed to hear.

I owe everything else to my wife. Clare, I write for you, and this is your story first. You put up with so much to allow me the space to be creative and to write. Thank you for everything. Everything. You are my better half by far, and I adore you to the end of the world and back.

ABOUT THE AUTHOR

AUSTIN ASLAN was inspired to write *The Islands at the End of the World* and *The Girl at the Center of the World* while living with his wife and two children on the Big Island of Hawai`i, where he earned a master's degree in tropical conservation biology at the University of Hawai`i at Hilo. A National Science Foundation Graduate Research Fellow, he can often be found exploring the wilds of northern Arizona and camping in a tent on a punctured air mattress. In other lives, Austin drove ambulances way too fast, served as an ecotourism Peace Corps Volunteer in a Honduran cloud forest, and managed a variety of local, state, and federal issue campaigns. Austin loves to travel widely, photograph nature, and laugh. Follow him on Twitter at @Laustinspace.